China hand

'A swarm of bluebottles buzzed around his head . . . He saw now where that smell, that post-mortem smell, the world's worst smell, came from. Blood in the bath.'

Dr Death, the press had called the double killer, so surgically had he carried out his dismemberments. Dishevelled, deranged Simon Meakin, an abattoir assistant with raging religious mania, gives himself up. There is overwhelming evidence against him for the murder of a vice girl, not least her head on a plate in the freezer of his bedsit.

His rambling confession makes no mention of the second victim – an unidentified oriental girl, a virgin. What possible connection could she have with a convicted local prostitute? Detective Inspector 'Jacko' Jackson wants to know.

Who would Meakin have turned to for help as he wandered in the wilderness while he was on the run? Someone, Jacko suspects, with an exotic but troublesome bit on the side who asked him to get rid of another body.

In Frank Palmer's latest police thriller in the 'Jacko' series, the hunt for clues to the Bad Samaritan goes from the Peaks of Derbyshire to the waterfront of Shanghai.

And, when a lonely, terrified Jacko is held by security police as a spy, will he refind faith in religion abandoned years ago? More to the point, will his prayers be answered?

What critics say:
'One of the best delineators of the criminal landscape.' Philip Oakes, *Literary Review*
'An outstanding series.' Mat Coward, *Morning Star*

CHINA HAND

Frank Palmer

Constable · London

First published in Great Britain 1994
by Constable & Company Ltd
3 The Lanchesters, 162 Fulham Palace Road
London W6 9ER
Copyright © 1994 by Frank Palmer
The right of Frank Palmer to be
identified as the author of this work has been
asserted by him in accordance with the
Copyright, Designs and Patents Act 1988
ISBN 0 09 473620 0
Set in 10 on 11 pt Palatino by
Pure Tech Corporation, Pondicherry, India
Printed and bound in Great Britain by
Hartnolls Limited, Bodmin, Cornwall.

A CIP catalogue record for this book
is available from the British Library

Excerpts from 'Rock O' My Soul' (Lonnie Donegan – © 1958 Tyler Music Ltd, of Suite 2.07, Plaza 535 King's Road, London SW10 OSZ) and 'Lonesome Traveller' (Lee Hays – © 1951 Cromwell Music Ltd, of the same address) are used by arrangement with the Essex Music Group.

The words from 'This little light of mine' and 'Hand me down my silver trumpet' are taken from the record 'Gospel songs and spirituals for little children' – © 1969 Salvationist Publishing and Supplies Ltd.

The extract from *Nice work* by David Lodge is published by arrangement with Martin Secker and Warburg.

Special thanks to Sue Williams, Mark Shardlow and Andy Heading for refreshing recollections of China and Hong Kong and the Rev. David Hilborn for reviving memories of Sunday school.

The East Midlands Combined Constabulary and its cases are fictional. So, too, are all characters, institutions and events in this story.

For Lisa

1

Sex, the avoidance of, preoccupied him.

He flicked through the Bible he always carried in his mind, seeking and finding a cautionary text. 'And the sexually immoral . . . their place will be in the fiery lake of burning sulphur.' Revelation, he knew for certain; chapter 2, verse 8, he seemed to recall with less certainty.

For a moment, just an intestine-tightening second, he wondered if he'd been wise to pack away his clerical collar. At home, a collar was a mark of ministry carrying with it the obligation of honourable behaviour.

Was what he was doing honourable? Questionable, for sure. Risky, without question. But honourable? He sought and found a justifying text. 'I have become all things to all men so that by all possible means I might save some' – First Corinthians, chapter 9, verse 22.

The humidity, the hot mass of humanity around them, reminded him he was 7,000 miles from home in a heathen land; a country where some men of the cloth, soldiers of the cross, rotted in jail.

He'd been right, he decided, not to wear it, not to draw attention to himself.

Displays of affection there would have to be, to avoid attracting the interest of security on the train, having her false papers re-examined.

He glanced along his shoulder. Just a slip of a girl, really. Yet she was on the run with a price on her head.

So small her steps she seemed to be trotting at his side, measuring the length of the long, teeming platform in feet; or rather half-feet, so tiny her black flat slippers.

She was dressed like a peasant, baggy black suit accentuating the unhealthy paleness of her face, more the colour of sun-bleached wheat than yellow.

It was a long train, seemingly never-ending, with sturdy, bottle green carriages and gold lettering.

The soft seats behind lace-curtained windows were still empty – awaiting the tourists, businessmen and privileged party officials in sober suits who would arrive at the last minute.

The hard seats were packed already by people who'd been herded into cavernous waiting-rooms, squatting alongside their bundles of belongings until they were released in a desperate scramble to match places with tickets for which they had been marshalled in queues for three hours.

The engine came into view – huge, green, red-wheeled, diesel; a mighty sight.

A sharp elbow dug into his powder blue safari suit at the small of his back below his heavy rucksack. She half raised a hand which carried a basket of food to last them through the first leg of the week-long journey ahead.

He nodded and followed her through the thinning scrum, taking the basket. Hand on her elbow, he helped her up the two steps. He shuffled, side-on, by a copper vat of boiling water into the crowded coach.

Tip-up seats ran the length of the aisle, occupied already by non-sleeper ticket holders, rounded backs against the side of the carriage, facing rows of uncurtained bunks in metal-framed triple tiers. He couldn't make up his mind whether it reminded him of a refugee camp or the spartan headquarters of the mission where he trained.

He clambered clumsily over the battered cases and tied-up bundles and round the feet of the sitting passengers.

She stopped half-way up the aisle. Four men were stretched out on thin green mattresses on the bottom and middle bunks. All stared fixedly at him, dark eyes locking like lasers on to his blue ones, travelling upwards to inspect his long, blond hair. All ignored her as she pointed with her chin towards the top two. They were on opposite sides of an already cluttered gap just enough room beneath the carriage roof to slide in.

They would not be sleeping together. No need for First Corinthians, chapter 6, verse 8 – 'Flee from sexual temptation' – which he had on subconscious standby.

His prayer had been answered.

2

A year later

Dr Death, they'd dubbed him, so surgically had he carried out his dismemberments.

In the morgue they had almost pieced together his white victim. Only her head was missing. Didn't matter that much now.

They had a face – early twenties going on late forties. They had her face because they had her hands. Through her fingerprints, they had her name from Records.

'Fancy her, Jacko?'

The sergeant in the passenger seat was looking down on a photo of Debby Dawson pinned to a sheet which summarized her life: married, divorced, a kid in care, six convictions for prostitution. Not yet twenty-three.

The notion was so gruesome that Jacko didn't answer. Flash bastard, he grumbled to himself. Hasn't seen her on the slab. Half a dozen bits. No head.

At a crawl he circled a flower-filled roundabout with a sign which pointed left to the Royal Infirmary where the pathologist had put the bits together like a jigsaw puzzle with one piece missing.

The sergeant nodded him straight on.

His mind turned left towards the infirmary mortuary and stayed with Dr Death's second victim – the oriental girl. They had her head. For what it was worth. Her face had been stoved in beyond recognition. But no feet and only one hand. No prints from Records matched the four fingers and one thumb.

A virgin, the pathologist had said.

What possible connection could an oriental virgin have with a convicted local prostitute? he'd asked himself over and over again.

And why cut off her feet? An identifiable deformity of some sort? And her right hand? To recover a recognizable ring?

No other answers came.

Next question.

A sighing silence. Then, angry with himself: Does any of this speculation matter?

Debby Dawson's murderer was a double killer. Had to be. The doctors had been conducting experiments for a fortnight since that fisherman hooked and landed the first arm and the frogmen recovered most of the rest of the two of them.

Adamant, they were. Same anatomical knowledge. Same professional deftness at dissecting. So there had to be a connection. So catch their killer and ask him. Right? Right, he told himself emphatically.

'Turn at the old chapel with the grey lead dome,' said the sergeant, looking ahead down a narrow, busy road fronted by shops with more eastern than western names above the windows.

'Right?' asked Jacko, mind still in the morgue.

'Left,' said the sergeant with an irritated jerk of his thumb towards the pavement.

Beyond the grey lead dome on top of the old chapel was a bright green dome above a new mosque.

Lots of religion around here, Jacko mused moodily. A long-lapsed congregationalist, he'd disavowed religion in his grammar school days, blamed it for most of the conflict in the world. Or rather the men who had misinterpreted it for their own ends, their lust for personal power. He didn't trust men of the cloth, any cloth. Rich pickings for 'em here, though; plenty of souls to be saved in this rundown neighbourhood.

The sharp-suited sergeant was jerking his thumb left again towards a park behind green iron railings. 'That's where we nicked her once, giving head. Maybe some customer's still got it.' He let out a heartless laugh.

Pity she didn't bite yours off, Jacko thought, just as harshly.

He didn't like his passenger, Sergeant Dan Payne, who everyone called Window because, Jacko assumed, they could see right through him.

He was much muscled, around thirty, already coarsened by the job. In the police service, Jacko believed, there's a thin line between coarseness and corruption. Or maybe he saw something of his former self in Payne, twenty years ago, before family and fatherhood and that small handful of special friends had smoothed the rougher of his edges and taught him to think, to care. Maybe, he conceded with a private honesty that had

12

come with age, he didn't like being reminded of the way he once was.

'A kerb-crawler?' he asked.

Window Payne nodded.

'Maybe that explains it.'

'Explains what?'

Dumbo, thought Jacko. It was blindingly obvious. But he ran his theory through his mind again, double-checking.

Maybe the killer's a cruiser. He picks up Debby Dawson who was happy to hop in his car when the price was fixed. Next trip he wrongly thinks the oriental girl walking home minding her own business is on the game, too. With the language barrier, she could have thought he was offering her a lift or asking directions. By the time she realized what he was after, it was too late.

All he said was: 'The connection between the two victims.'

Payne looked at him blankly, then indicated left again into a maze of shabby side streets with more satellite TV dishes than he'd ever seen on any middle-class estate.

Bollocks for brains, Jacko decided, following his directions.

'Sorry to drag you out of bed, Lou.' Window Payne used great sarcasm accompanied by a malicious smile.

In neighbouring counties they say, rather cruelly, of Derbyshire men that they are strong in the arm, weak in the head.

Jacko wondered who they had uppermost in mind – Payne or Lou, who was stripped to what remained of his waist and had flabby arms and an unshaven face too empty to be described as confused. 'What's up?'

Payne looked theatrically at his watch. 'Still, it's nearly opening time.' His broad shoulder barged the door open wider. He cocked a thumb over the other. 'Detective Inspector Jackson from headquarters crime squad.'

Lou hopped back to save the long, grubby nails of his bare, dirty toes being trapped beneath the stiff door. A ginger cat shot into the hot terraced street past Jacko's black shoes as he followed Payne inside.

Naked back to the wall, Lou pulled at the zip of his stained jeans but gave up a couple of inches short of the deep button in his huge, hairy belly.

He was forty-plus, probably fifty, with unkempt hair streaked with grey, big and heavy all over, including his fumbling fingers.

Nothing like surgeon's hands, Jacko noted.

A bright August sun was shut out as the door closed. A boarded-up ground-floor window kept it out.

The room was so dark it took a second or two for his bespectacled eyes to take it in. His nose didn't need that long. Congealed plates and silver foil containers from a Chinese takeaway were in an untidy pile on a filthy carpet beside a lumpy once pink, now mottled couch. All had been licked clean. Explains the cat's quick getaway, Jacko deduced. To him the second worst smell of all was cat dirt. This was sweet and sour cat dirt.

He reached into a pocket of his plain grey suit for his Bensons, lit one before offering them round. He took a long draw. Bottom lip protruding, he directed the smoke directly up his nostrils.

Payne declined. 'Nice place you've got here.'

Lou took one. 'What's up then?' A flat, elongated, back of the throat accent.

'We're looking for your Debby.'

'Not here.'

'Why not?'

'Done a runner.'

'When?'

'Why?'

'I asked first.' A sadistic smile.

'A couple of weeks back.' A second's thought. 'Three weeks come tomorrow.'

'Why?'

'Search me.' A phlegmy cough. 'Why? Is it non-payment of fines again?'

'Why did she leave?' Payne's handsome face had lost all trace of feigned amusement.

'Just walked out. Said nothing.' A sad sigh. 'New chap expect.'

'Left you before?'

A headshake, sadder still.

'Take her things?'

'Hasn't got many.'

'Did she go out to work?'

'Search me. She leads her life. I lead mine.'

14

'Bullshit. She kept you.'

'Bollocks. She don't even cook for me.' He nodded down at the dirty plates.

'She's kept you in cigs and booze for the last couple of years.'

'Don't pimp for her, though.' Lou was blustering now, finally provoked. 'Never.' A short, angry silence. 'What's this about?'

Jacko answered. 'You know about the two women we recovered from the Derwent.'

'Read about it in the *Evening Bellylaugh*.'

Jacko put on his sorrowful face. 'I'm very sorry to have to tell you that one of them is Debby.'

Lou sucked in his bare belly. 'Oh, fuck me, no.' His tattooed shoulders hunched. 'Not one of 'em that were cut up.' Chink of his backside showing, he lowered himself like a robot on to the mottled settee. 'Oh, Christ.'

His elbows went to his knees, his mouth to his hands. He finished his cigarette like that, took another, and chain-smoked through the next hour . . .

They had met at a pub off the market place three years earlier. 'Knew she was on the game. Everyone knows.'

Her pimp had kicked her out, to make room for a blonde teenager, a better commercial proposition. She'd been sleeping around, in abandoned cars when business was bad. Lou took her home, back to this place. A bed for a screw. She stayed. 'It was just a roof. That's all. Some nights we did it. Mostly we didn't. Too tired.'

She went out early most evenings working a street off Normanton Road, picking up kerb-crawlers. Businessmen, some of them, on their way home to supper with their suburban wives. 'Never brought them here. Always in the backs of their cars. Waste ground on summer evenings, side streets when it was dark.'

'How much?' Payne asked.

'A pony for full sex, but never with her clothes off. Fifteen for a blow, ten for a hand-job.' He reeled them off as though he was reading a menu. 'Half a dozen tricks on a good night. Enough to pay her rent.'

'How much?' Payne repeated.

'A ton.'

15

A hundred quid to share this hovel, thought Jacko, and he let go a snort.

'Just to supplement the social,' said Lou, cigarette dangling. 'Can't work.' He thumped his bare chest. 'Bronchitis. Chronic.'

'So what happened to the rest of what she earned?'

'She supported her kid.'

'The kid's in care.'

'But presents and outings now and then and pocket money, like.'

'And?'

'Food, fags.'

'And the rest?'

A defeated sigh. 'She was on crack, wasn't she? That's twenty a deal.'

He said he didn't know the name of her suppliers or regular clients, except for a few of the cars they drove.

'Any trouble with clients?'

A matter-of-fact shrug. 'The usual. You know, "You didn't give me time to come so I'm not paying." '

'Violence?'

'The odd black eye and split lip.' He started to weep. 'Not from me. Never laid a finger on her.'

Genuine grief there, Jacko acknowledged. Not just for a lost meal ticket. For companionship, a love of a sort. Anything to some people, even a relationship like that in a place like this, was better than despairing loneliness.

There are no Julia Roberts in inner-city red-light districts; no Richard Geres to clothe them and install them in penthouse suites.

'Any bother recently?'

'Only that.' Lou nodded to the roughly cut hardboard that covered the curtainless window.

'A dissatisfied client?'

'A Bible thumper.'

A puzzled pause. Then Jacko asked, 'What happened?'

'Followed her, threatening hellfire and damnation. Put a brick through it.' A surprised look. 'It was in the *Evening Bellylaugh*.' He stood wearily, still in a daze. 'Got it somewhere.'

A jumble of papers, some stained vivid orange by cat pee, spilled on to the holed carpet when he yanked open the tight door of a cheap, chipped sideboard.

'Been saving it to claim on insurance,' he explained, muttering, as he sorted through them. 'What about criminal compensation? What's the rules? Do you think I'll get . . . Here it is.'

The month-old tabloid *Evening Telegraph* was folded at an inside page with the headline: CLEAN-UP CRUSADER LANDS IN LAW'S ARMS. Beneath it:

A one-man campaign against kerb-crawlers in the red-light district landed a church-goer in court yesterday. Simon Meakin, 29, admitted throwing stones through the windows of a car and a near neighbour's house because he suspected them of haggling over a price for sex.

He was brought down in a flying tackle by WPC Helen Rogers as he fled the scene, the Derby Stipendiary Magistrate was told.

Miss Martha Chan, prosecuting, told the court: 'He confronted a motorist and a woman talking through an opened car window, accusing them in rambling biblical terms of engaging in prostitution. The windscreen was smashed as the car was driven away. The woman was chased to her home where the front window was also smashed.'

After his arrest, Meakin, of Raymonds Avenue, Derby, told WPC Rogers he had used cobblestones from nearby road works, adding: 'It was the will of God.'

The motorist, Miss Chan added, claimed to have been lost and had been seeking directions but the prosecution accepted the woman concerned was a convicted prostitute.

Mr Percival Manners, defending, said Meakin lived in an area plagued by prostitution which the authorities had failed to control. 'He decided to take unilateral action which may well have its roots in a recently discovered interest in religion.'

Stipendiary John Barrington, referring to social inquiry reports, said: 'I see his conversion follows the break-up of his marriage and the loss of his job as an abattoir chargehand.'

So deeply did Jacko frown that his eyebrows dropped below the top rim of his spectacles and his forehead displayed more vertical than horizontal creases.

He could hardly believe what he was seeing. He read it again to himself to make sure: 'Abattoir chargehand.'

His eyes went back up the story to 'Martha Chan'. It was just about the only oriental-sounding surname he knew. Excitement surged through him. Jesus, he thought, you could have the name of the killer and his other victim here before your very eyes in this one short story. Good Lord.

He took a deep breath and read on to the final paragraph, too hyped to take much interest: 'Sentence was postponed, pending medical reports. Bail was granted, despite prosecution objections.'

Jacko's eyes went back to the penultimate paragraph. He read out loud, 'Abattoir chargehand.' Pause. 'Mmmmm. Where's Raymonds Avenue?'

That smell. Worse, much, much worse, than cat mess, even sweet and sour flavoured crap.

It invaded his nose, mouth, lungs when he opened the door to the attic bedsit with the landlord's key.

He just stood there, for several seconds, gagging, sagging, unable to walk in.

Not the smell from the unmade single bed with twisted, soiled sheets. Or the pile of yellow-and brown-stained underwear and sweat-stiffened socks beside it.

Not the smell from moulding bread on a plate on a white-ringed coffee table. Or the mouse droppings beside it.

Not the smell from a milk bottle with contents that had set in a yellow cheese. Not hard cheese; melting, on the move with maggots.

His face felt as though it had been hit by a fireball when he opened the door to a room that hadn't been ventilated for days. Its suffocating heat was magnified by a closed window through which the sun shone with unremitting equatorial cruelty, glass panes shimmering silver. Not the smell from the flies that had died and fried on its ledge.

Oh, for a cigarette. He felt his pockets. No, he ordered himself firmly, be professional. Scenes of crime won't want this room contaminated with your ash.

He walked in as if treading on thin ice, unnerved eyes on a wall poster, stark lettering on a Dali-style background: 'Without the shedding of blood there is no forgiveness – Hebrews 9: 22'.

All he did was follow his nose across the flowered crusting carpet to a brown door beside a curtained-off mini-kitchen.

18

A swarm of bluebottles buzzed around his head, drinking in the sweat on his face, when he pushed it back with his foot. Head down, eyes shut, he frantically wafted them away with demented hands.

Eyes open, he saw now where that smell, that postmortem smell, the world's worst smell, came from.

Blood in the bath. Set hard like matt paint, all blacks and browns, but blood all right. A ring of it round the sides. Streaks of it on the bottom, like mud left by the tide.

A bloodbath.

Among the light brown scum, butcher's knives, a chopper and a saw.

A slaughterhouse; an abattoir.

Don't be sick, he told himself. Don't contaminate the scene with your spew. Be professional.

He turned away, head down.

His sense of sound took over.

Not the clamouring of the flies head-butting the window.

A low, monotonous hum from a small fridge-freezer in the curtained alcove with a cracked sink and greasy cooker.

He wrapped his handkerchief round his little finger and hooked the top door open.

The head of Debby Dawson looked out at him, ice blue eyes frozen over.

Thin threads of whiteness in the frost, delicate as cobwebs, had aged her still further, but with great dignity.

3

'Warning,' said black letters on gold. 'Smoking can cause lung cancer, bronchitis and other chest diseases.'

Mood morose, Jacko read the warning words again, for something to do, fed up with waiting, wanting to get on with it, to do anything but stand here and think. He pulled another cigarette out of the packet by its tip and lit up. Overnight his consumption had risen from thirty to forty.

He'd been late home, went into the spare bedroom so as not to disturb his sleeping wife, hadn't slept much anyway and was up early carrying downstairs an ashtray with half a dozen screwed tips in it.

Bad for you, no doubt about it, he chided himself, taking a deep drag. As damaging as this job. 'Police work can cause stress, split personality and other mental diseases,' it should say on warrant cards. He could give it up easily; easier than cigarettes. In twenty months or so he would do when he'd got his thirty years in; not a day too soon.

He'd been attacked by a killer dog, been shot at, snatched from the mouth of a weir, stranded on sandbanks, seen most things in his years on the Major Crime Squad of the East Midlands Combined Constabulary. Never before had he come face-to-face with a severed head.

He loved crime novels, wanted to write them when he quit; wanted to be half as good as Wambaugh. He was recalling one of his now. About a patrolman in *The Choirboys* who found a decapitated head in a road crash and, for sheer devilment, showed it to rubber-necking passers-by. He'd laughed when he read it, wasn't laughing now.

A real downer, this; a bad dose of the police blues.

He turned his back on the fast-filling incident room, not wanting to talk. Face grim, he looked out of a first-floor window, not wanting to see.

He didn't want to think either, but think he did, no other option.

It wasn't, he realized, just the discovery of Debby Dawson's head on a plate. It was the shock of not being all that shocked. He'd taken it in his stride, had done all the right things, called out the right people, supervised the scenes search, initiated the hunt for the missing Simon Meakin, checked discreetly on Martha Chan and found she was alive and well and had been in court that day. Ah, well, he'd ID-ed the killer, if not his second victim; win some, lose some.

He'd worked till gone midnight. Throughout he'd been on auto-pilot. Professional, true, but where were his feelings, his humanity?

Lost, he feared, in a career that had seen lots of cops change from midnight door-triers to pen-pushers and form-fillers, from amiable amblers on the beat to stormtroopers wading into soccer crowds and picket-lines.

Lost, he lamented, along with much of the respect of the public they served and morale within the service.

Lost like the innocence of his childhood when everyone knew the difference between right and wrong and good and bad and heaven and hell.

Lost like a soul incapable of shock or grief at the sight of the head of a woman, a child's mother, somebody's daughter, in a fridge-freezer in an attic bedsit in the back streets of Derby.

Dear God, he sighed to himself, what's become of me?

He drew in more damaging smoke and breathed it out, looking down on the waters of a river, olive green in the shade of the police station and courthouse.

Across the road was the town hall with imposing pillared entrance and concrete steps which ran down to the water's edge where that angler had hooked on to the first bit of Debby Dawson.

Last night, in the infirmary morgue, he had watched the pathologist put her back together again, the missing piece in place. Holy Humpty-Dumpty. Jesus Christ. He shook his head, just a flick, like his mum used to flick a duster out of an opened bedroom window. Oddly, it seemed to scatter away the cobwebs that clogged his depressed mind.

He began to wonder how far upriver Simon Meakin had dumped the bits and pieces. Not in the Peaks where the waters came down from high hills, sparkling and clear. They'd have been snagged up in a weir or a tree's roots or something long before they reached here.

Why did Meakin keep Debby's head and not the oriental girl's right hand and feet? Where were they, if not in the fridge-freezer?

Ah, well . . . another headshake, dismissive this time . . . they'd ask him when they found him. If they found him alive. He rather suspected they'd drag him out of the river, all in one piece.

'Sorry for the delay.' A woman's voice, southern, crisp, no signs of weariness in it.

He turned from the window. Detective Chief Superintendent Carole Malloy led three other women into the incident room. One of them looked oriental. For no good reason, he assumed she might be an interpreter.

New Man Jacko wasn't. Sometimes he kidded himself he'd rather like to be. Sometimes he regarded them as wimpish.

His trouble was that he'd been brought up by a doting mother who dusted his untidy bedroom while he lay beneath the blankets. His first wife always ironed his shirts before going off for secret sex with a sergeant. His second wife, ten years younger than him, mother of his son, certainly expected him to shop, operate the microwave and Hoover now and then, but only because she did most of the gardening.

He liked women, right enough; loved working with them. They talked about things other than the collars they'd felt, the exes they'd charged, the screws they'd had. Sure he outranked his women partners, but he tried – at least he tried – to treat them as equals.

To have had Carole Malloy, a woman eight years younger than him, foisted on him, not as an equal but as his superior, had been hard to handle at first. She had been imported from Scotland Yard as the CID chief in the shake-out that followed a wrongful arrest scandal in which Jacko had been heavily involved.

She'd been seen by everyone, Jacko included, as a political appointment, a sop from a trendy new chief constable to the feminist lobby on the left-wing police committee.

Even when she rescued him from crime prevention, the salt mines of the police service, where he'd been serving his sentence in the wake of the scandal, he'd dubbed Chief Superintendent Malloy Little Velma after the mystery woman in his favourite Chandler book – a nickname which, to his horror, had stuck.

They had only worked one job together – a deeply disturbing war crimes inquiry earlier that year. The truth, he privately admitted, was that he hadn't handled her. She'd handled him with that rare combination of encouragement, ideas and criticism.

Now he was trying to treat her as a boss who just happened to be a woman, was calling her 'Guv', wishing he could have been this open-minded twenty years ago, wondering what the younger generation, the likes of Window Payne – working under her for the first time – would make of her.

Just the sight of her seemed to lift his gloom.

As usual, she was soberly dressed in a dark suit. Her short, ginger hair was trim and neat. Her blue eyes, normally alert and sparkling, were dull and tired from working through the night.

They rested on him. Astonishingly, the left lid closed in a wink, saucy, like Anne Robinson signs off *Points of View* on TV.

Fuck that, Jacko thought, shocked. He wasn't going to wink back to a boss who just happened to be a woman. He'd never be that much of a New Man. He let his head drop and he sat down.

Most of the dozen or so who had waited in the incident room, all but one of them men, all sergeants and above, were sitting at desks and didn't attempt to get up, which, Jacko appreciated, would suit her. Not a CID boss to stand on ceremony was Little Velma Malloy.

Jacko had stubbed out his cigarette and was sitting in the nearest seat, an executive chair, padded arms, adjustable. It squeaked when he rocked back to study the women who'd followed her in. He recognized only one – a civvie from HQ public relations office. Behind her came a uniformed WPC with a farm-hand's heftiness and a small, dark woman with a smiling oriental face. Both hands and feet intact, he noted.

'Right.' Little Velma nodded at a divisional DCI, an over-weight veteran.

'Not a trace,' he said with an exhausted sigh. 'We've hit all the night shelters, stations, squats. Not a sighting.'

'What do we know about him?' she asked.

Window Payne answered. 'Born and educated locally. Apprenticed at the abattoir at sixteen. No previous arrests. Married childhood sweetheart at twenty-two. She's a year older than him. A kid within a year. Happy as a pig in the proverbial until seven, eight months ago.'

'And then?'

'She got preggers again and started on about needing a bigger place. He began acting differently, strange. Just withdrawn at first, staring into space. Then he banged on about the Chinese getting it right. Families should only have one child.'

'Did he want her to have an abortion?'

'At first. Then he got religion. The whole hog, Catholicism. Kept going on about the slaughter of infants. He became dead against. His wife couldn't make head nor tail of him. She wanted to take him for counselling. He said his priest was the only counsellor he needed.'

'Have we checked him?' Velma looked back at the DCI.

23

A curt nod. 'Hasn't seen him since some unholy row months ago. Meakin became a Baptist after that. He fell out with them, too. Sally Army then, and a Free Church.'

More clubs than Peter Shilton, thought Jacko.

Window Payne resumed. 'Wifey...' Little Velma's mouth pursed and Jacko smiled. '... talked about a trial separation and going back to mum's for a break. He walked out. Claimed the TV was transmitting ungodly messages to him. He's been in that bedsit since.'

'What about his job at the abattoir?'

'Decent wage with overtime,' Payne replied. 'No money problems. Doesn't smoke or drink.'

No wonder he's gone potty, thought Jacko, beginning to cheer up.

'Then he started taking days off to parade with "Jesus Saves" placards in the market square,' Payne continued. 'Got himself sacked.'

The hefty policewoman sitting on a straight chair with knees wide apart made her first contribution, rather timidly. 'I 'eard him giving a sermon one Saturday to shoppers. Disjointed rubbish.'

A smile from Velma encouraged her to go on. She outlined her rugger tackle arrest of Meakin on the double charge of criminal damage.

Jacko had her pegged now – WPC Helen Rogers.

She was mid-twenties with a country girl's face and voice. She was Jacko's height and not far short of his eleven-and-a-half stone weight. Being thumped by her would knock the holy spirit out of any Bible thumper, he guessed.

'A whiff at close quarters; worse than a crew yard,' she said expertly. 'Can't have bathed or changed for days.'

Velma summed it up with a sad expression. 'Obviously a very sick fella.' She looked at the oriental woman, perched on a desk, black eyes watchful; like a Chinese songbird's; as urbane and petite as the WPC was rural and rugged.

'That's why I opposed bail.' A classy, very English voice and Jacko had her pegged, too. She was not an interpreter, but Martha Chan from the Crown Prosecution Service, not only all in one piece, but looking good on it. He would have laid a week's wages there and then that all the boys would soon be calling her Charley. 'The beak didn't see it my way,' she added.

Can't blame old Barrington, the Stipendiary Magistrate, too

24

much for that, thought Jacko. JPs, lay and professional, were under orders these days not to remand petty offenders to prisons so overcrowded that some inmates had taken to sitting on rooftops, either in protest or to find a bit of spare space.

'What's the diagnosis?' asked Velma.

'Almost certainly schizophrenia.' Martha Chan seemed as expert on mental disorders as the WPC had been on farmyard smells. 'But we haven't got the medical report in yet.'

'Who's preparing it?'

'Dr David Saul up at Matlock Bath.'

Velma looked from her to the DCI, who said, 'Under the terms of his bail, Meakin went into his clinic for examination for three days three weeks ago. They haven't seen him since.'

'Maybe his solicitor got something out of him,' Martha Chan suggested.

Velma nodded absently, more important things on her mind. 'So what do we do?'

'Go public,' said the DCI, immediately.

'Wifey has given us his last photo,' said Window Payne. He handed round copies. Meakin, fair-haired and freckled, had a healthy, happy face.

Velma looked at Jacko. 'The lab says there were two different types of blood in the bath.' He nodded. 'So he's killed twice and dismembered both victims and we have to assume he could do it again.' Another nod, automatic. 'No alternative is there?' Jacko shook his head.

'OK then.' Velma paused for thought. 'Police are anxious to trace this man . . .' The woman civvie from public relations started taking notes. '. . . for elimination purposes . . . may now be unshaven and of unkempt appearance . . .'

She named Debby Dawson as one confirmed victim but made no mention of the recovery of her head or from where.

She asked for the public's help in identifying the second victim, widening the ethnic net slightly. 'Of South-east Asian or oriental extraction . . .' She directed her appeal at hotels who'd had women guests connected with a huge new Japanese car firm outside the city, or colleges with overseas students.

She looked round, democratically inviting contributions.

Jacko made his first suggestion of the conference. 'Or Chinese restaurants with staff who have left in sudden, unexplained circumstances.'

25

Velma nodded it into the press officer's note which was read back and unanimously agreed.

'Right.' Velma was finally satisfied. 'Crown Prosecution say we can use Ms Chan as our legal consultant.'

She smiled across at her. 'Perhaps you'll smooth the way in for us to start with Percy Manners, Meakin's solicitor. Take Inspector Jackson.'

She transferred her smile to him. 'Jacko, meet Charley.'

'What's this Percy Manners like?' asked Jacko.

'A shyster,' said Charley.

Unhurried, they were walking along a hot, glass-enclosed corridor, twenty feet or so above street level, through a boxy building that linked the police station to the courthouse.

'A one-man band,' she went on. 'Poky little office. A dicey ex-cop as his clerk. A fire-engine chaser, really, Survives on legal aid cases.'

Jacko knew the type: the sort of shady solicitor who fiddles bail with penniless sureties, arranges false alibis and rehearses witnesses in them.

Inside, the courthouse was much cooler but much noisier and dirtier. On the fawn-tiled first-floor balcony, the scruffy children of scruffy parents, waiting for their cases to be called, ran through cigarette ends and crisp crumbs scattered about the marble floor; the flotsam of any sizeable city's courthouse.

They studied the lists. John Barrington, the Stipendiary Magistrate who had bailed Meakin, was not sitting that day.

'Where's the Stipe?' Charley asked a black-gowned usher.

'Off ill.'

'Seen Mr Manners about?'

A nod towards an interview room down a corridor.

They stood around. A boy, not yet ten, ran up to them, looked cheekily at Charley and squeaked, 'You Chinky then?'

'Piss off, you snotty-nosed little bastard,' hissed Jacko.

Soon a woman came out of the room, weeping, a man's voice following. 'Worry not. We will lodge an immediate appeal.'

Manners was approaching fifty. He was wearing a slate grey suit, clearly off the peg, black shoes, not dirty but not shining either, white shirt with soft collar already beginning to curl, dark blue tie. He had a pale, worried face, watery eyes behind bifocals, dark brown hair beginning to recede.

26

Not much of a man, thought Jacko. Could be my twin brother. A smile, but only for himself.

'A word, please,' said Charley quite sternly.

'What is it?' An alarmed look as though he'd been caught out on some dodgy legal deal.

'In private, please.'

He turned back into the fuggy, sparse room with just a table and three wooden chairs. Jacko shut the door. No one sat.

Charley introduced him. There was no offer of a handshake from either. She looked at Jacko, to let him lead.

'We need to talk to a client of yours – Simon Meakin.'

'Why?' Manners' relief appeared visible.

'When did you last speak to him?'

'Why?'

'Please,' pleaded Charley.

'A month ago when he last appeared here on criminal damage. You were against us.' He looked at Charley, who nodded. Then he repeated, 'Why?'

'Not seen him since?' asked Jacko. A headshake. 'No phone calls, letters?' Another headshake. 'Any appointment due with him?'

'No point.' Manners looked at Charley again. 'We can't fix a date for sentencing until we get the medical report.'

'So you've heard nothing from Dr Saul either?' she said, frowning.

'No. Why?'

Jacko flicked his head in the general direction of the river. 'We want to talk to him in connection with the two severed bodies we recovered.'

Another grating 'Why?' with Manners beginning to look impatient.

'One of them was Debby Dawson.' The name appeared to mean nothing.

'The prostitute whose window he smashed,' Charley explained.

It meant something now. 'What have you got on him?' He spoke eagerly.

Jacko replied cautiously. 'There's a public appeal going out for info on him. Just to eliminate him. We're wording it carefully.'

'Better had.'

Jacko imagined pound signs about to flash in Manners' eyes. If the police had got it right there was a long criminal trial in it for

27

him. If they'd got it wrong, a long libel action. Either way, lots of lolly.

They sparred for a while, telling each other no more than they had to. Meakin, Manners explained, was his case only because he'd been duty lawyer on the evening WPC Rogers arrested him for window-smashing. He'd arranged a short stay for him at Dr Saul's clinic at Matlock Bath to get him examined – 'on the Stipe's say-so,' he added. He said he still hadn't yet got the doctor's findings. 'What do you want the results for?'

'So we know who we may be dealing with.' Jacko emphasized 'may'. 'If he makes contact, you'll tell us?'

'If he asks.'

'It's in his interests.'

'I act only in the interests and on the instructions of my clients.' Manners spoke huffily, puffing out his chest. Jacko nodded mutely. 'If you get to him first, you'll notify me before you interview him?' Manners added.

'If he asks,' said Jacko with a dull smile.

4

The A6 was busy with sightseers heading towards the Peak District, mile upon majestic mile of hills and dales with streams of clear waters and woods and moorlands, a beautiful bit of Britain.

Charley had directed him over the inner and outer ring roads and away from a town whose topography was being changed by dumper trucks and pneumatic drills before the ink on his new street map had dried.

He drove slowly, no option, on a road with dry stone walls which wound its way through rolling countryside studded with villages and copses.

They told each other about themselves. He talked of his wife, kid and dog and his twenty-two months left in the force. His fluctuating mood about the job was upbeat now. A nice trip always lifted any depression. Privately he was hoping his months wouldn't pass too quickly. Suddenly he realized he'd miss all of this – being tested on the big ones, puzzling things through, the camaraderie of the boys and girls in the squad, meeting new people.

Charley was almost thirty, born in the next county. Her folks were Hong Kong Cantonese. Dad, a widower, ran a restaurant. She'd studied law at Birmingham University, wanted her own practice one day.

'Changing sides,' said Jacko, accusingly.

She laughed, unoffended.

'Been briefed?' he asked.

'Dan Payne ran it by me over a drink last night,' she said with a contented little smile that told him she had enjoyed the date.

Don't think much to your choice of drinking chums, Jacko thought. 'What do you think?'

A simple little shrug that said: Open and shut. 'It's just a question of finding Meakin.'

'There's also the question of ID-ing the . . .' Jacko just managed to save himself from saying oriental. '. . . second girl.' She said nothing. 'Know what I can't work out?' No response again. 'The connection between a pro and a virgin.'

Charley gave this some thought. 'Maybe the second girl was into games; dressed up for him or something.'

Jacko knew what she meant – gym slips, nurses' uniforms, leathers, a bit of bondage maybe, not the full act. He gave his head an uncertain shake. 'If Meakin's got religion that bad, would he be playing around at all?'

She gave this longer thought, then appeared to give up. Instead, 'Beautiful around here, isn't it?'

The hills rose sharply now, trees elbowing each other all the way down to the roadside walls. Jacko had the impression of heading for the mountains. Like Switzerland, he supposed. Not that he'd ever been. With a young son and a dog that couldn't bear to be left behind, he and his wife always holidayed in the British Isles. His only foreign assignments in more than twenty-eight years' service had been an overnight in Amsterdam and a day trip to Paris.

Beyond a red-brick mill, closed and for sale, another casualty of cheap imports from the east, high, grey cliffs appeared among the trees and Jacko had the feeling now of entering a coastal town.

Matlock Bath lay in a gorge where the River Derwent bends. Terraced houses, pubs, shops and cafés, on one side only, as though standing on a seaside prom, looked out across the road on to a river, a domed pavilion, gardens and unlit fairy lights.

The Alpine impression returned with a sight of white cable cars in clusters of three running over a single-line railway track, the river and the road to a sheer cliff six hundred feet up, maybe more.

At a corner stood a Victorian building with a façade of local grit stone. 'Primitive Methodist Chapel – 1901' said an inscription at the apex of a newly tiled roof. The black board outside said: 'Mission of Adam' in fading white paint. The pastor's name – the Rev. Dillon Blades – was in new white paint, signifying a recent change of minister.

By the chapel was a road sign: 'Tor View Clinic'. Jacko turned left up a pot-holed corkscrewing track, a dizzy, dangerous drive.

Near the top, just below the brow of the hill, the clinic came into view behind a copse of larch trees – single-storey, red-brick, more 1939–45 than 1901, like an old army building. The entrance had a cantilevered roof over twin glass doors. He guessed it had been some sort of observation post in a war he'd been born in but couldn't remember.

He parked his grey Cavalier on rough ground next to a grassy plateau with picnic tables and benches and a big, stone-built barbecue. The sound of water running over stones, the smell of pines from the conifer plantations all around greeted him when he climbed out.

It was a steep walk on a grit path to the main entrance where a woman receptionist directed them up a long corridor with a grey, highly polished tiled floor, troughs of flowers on every windowsill and a low corrugated ceiling painted white. The place seemed to have been built into the hillside, following its contours, and it was another steepish walk.

Just before closed fire doors with a notice: 'Secure Unit – Staff Only' they reached Dr Saul's office.

'Hallo,' said a burly, bespectacled man behind a small desk in a gloomy, windowless waiting-room with a couch, a glass table full of National Geographics and grey filing cabinets along one wall.

Charley merely said who they were and that they wanted to see Dr Saul.

'What about?'

'Simon Meakin.'

He made a phone call. 'A couple of minutes,' he said. 'Time for a cigarette.' Charley shook her head. He offered a packet of Rothmans towards Jacko who took one and then a light from a yellow throwaway. 'Meakin, eh?'

'Know him?' Jacko lowered himself into a long brown seat with hard arms, more of a domestic settee than a therapeutic couch.

'Quite a case.' The man behind the desk introduced himself. 'O' Brien. Chief Nurse.' With his hair cut short, no sideburns, he looked more like a prison warder than a Flo, or even a Joe, Nightingale.

'Was he trouble?' asked Jacko, conversationally.

'More of a nuisance, I'd say.' A smile. 'He kept giving us extracts from the Sermon on the Mount. You know, blessed are the poor . . . turn the other cheek . . . love your neighbours . . . do unto others. You know.'

If Jacko did know, he'd almost forgotten who'd said what where in the Bible.

Dr Saul came in, earlier than expected, jerking his head towards an inner door. Jacko stood and screwed out his just-started cigarette in a metal tray on O'Brien's desk.

They followed him into a long narrow study with a big desk and ill-matching chairs, but no couch. On the carpet were untidy piles of papers and a dozen or so briefcases – black and modern, leather and old, all filled to overflowing. On the walls were pictures that seemed to have no theme – bright fruit in a bowl, a couple of landscapes.

The doctor sat behind the desk with his back to the window and his own, private landscape – a view across the gorge to a castle on the skyline above forests of fir trees; to cliffs, lined and worn yellow, like an old thick book on its side – a Bible, perhaps. He nodded them into hard chairs.

He was between fifty and sixty. An unaged face beneath white hair made it hard to be more precise. His dark, pin-striped suit was double-breasted.

'Simon Meakin, you say?' He looked at Charley with intent blue eyes. 'Is there a problem?'

'We haven't got your report.'

'It's not completed yet.' He spoke very brusquely.

'Can we have your interim findings?'

'What's the rush?'

Jacko came in, a bit brutally, but he didn't like dilatory doctors.

31

'We are seeking him in connection with the murders of the two women fished out of the Derwent in Derby.'

Now, if someone had hit Jacko with the news that a man he'd questioned had been released to commit double murder, he'd have been filled with grief and guilt.

Saul showed absolutely no emotion. 'My instruction from the court was to make recommendations as to his disposal on two relatively minor matters of criminal damage. He was here voluntarily.'

'Did you consider sectioning him?' Jacko had in mind a section of the Mental Health Act under which a patient could be detained, whether he volunteered to undergo treatment or not.

Saul said nothing, blue eyes burning; a man, Jacko guessed, used to asking all the questions, not being questioned.

'You saw him three weeks ago,' Jacko continued evenly. 'Is there a problem, some reason for the delay?'

'There are no blood tests or X-rays that can tell us if someone has schizophrenia.'

'Has he?'

'Even if he has,' Saul answered evasively, 'the right combinations of anti-psychotic medication and how it should be given have to be decided.'

'Has he?' Jacko repeated.

Saul's pale face flushed, but he stayed silent.

'Your findings, even preliminary ones, would help us build up a profile, help the police know where to look,' said Charley politely.

A dismissive headshake, teeth clenched, sighing. 'My obligation is to the court . . .'

'But . . .'

'Sorry. The Stipendiary ordered the report. He will get it.' Jacko suspected it was all he could do not to add: 'When I'm good and ready.' Instead: 'What Mr Barrington does with it then is a matter for him. I've no authority to release it to you or anybody without the court's consent.'

'But . . .'

'I think I've made my situation clear. Now, if you'll excuse me, I am expecting patients.'

Jacko saw no point in arguing. He knew when he'd run into a medical brick wall, was wasting his time. He'd tackle it a different way. He stood and turned his back on Saul, not saying thanks or goodbye.

No one was waiting in the dark, depressing waiting-room when they walked back through it.

'Bloody bastard.' Mild expletives when Jacko was in this mood, stepping out quickly towards his parked car.

'Oh, I don't know.' Charley was trailing slightly. 'Technically he's right, I suppose.' Her accepting attitude calmed and slowed him. She caught up. 'Strange, though, isn't it, all this biblical background?'

Jacko frowned, unsure. 'The Sermon on the Mount, you mean? If he's got religious mania . . .'

Charley cut in. 'Not just that. The names. Meak-in.' She broke it up, emphasizing the 'meek', and went on, 'David Saul.'

'David who did for Goliath?'

'And beheaded him with his own sword,' she added, darkly.

Jacko didn't remember that bit, just the stone in the sling. A clever smile was playing on Charley's face. He decided not to display his ignorance. 'You got religion, too?'

'Mum had. She brought me up on it. Church school and all that.'

Oh, Christ, Jacko groaned inwardly. This means blasphemy is out. In a bad mood he was inclined towards obscenities and blasphemy. 'As a what?'

'Anglican, of course. One more success for your church.'

My church? Jacko asked himself. He'd been christened a congregationalist on his mother's insistence but she never insisted he went to their Sunday school. He'd sung in the choir at the parish C of E church because his mates did, but only for a short while. Those long-winded sermons were a drag; only put up with them because the rates of pay were good and they had a youth club. He'd never been to church since, apart from duty occasions – the usual matches, hatches and dispatches.

He veered off towards his car but Charley carried on towards the top of the corkscrew hill. 'Old Barrington lives just down here.' She didn't look behind.

Jacko followed, surprised. He hadn't noticed any houses driving up. Must have been concentrating on not running over the edge, he decided.

His surprise went when she turned off the track. The low stone house was camouflaged by a high wall covered with creeping ivy which melted into the tangled undergrowth of brambles and pale ferns shaded by tall, knobbly trees.

Inside the wall was a small slabbed courtyard on which stood a three-litre Rover with C after the number, which made it very old – a quarter of a century at least, Jacko reckoned rapidly. It was the same colour green as the ferns, highly polished and looked in showroom condition.

Charley rang the bell on a pine door with bottle-end glass. A wizened little oriental man in a white jacket opened it. He showed them into a room with a picture window view of the hills on the other side of the gorge.

The furniture was heavy, dark wood, carved legs with thick arms. The table lamps and fruit bowls matched it. One wall was covered with dusty books, mostly military and legal. Oppressive anywhere else; airy here because of the outlook.

'Ex-army,' Charley explained. She waited until the servant had closed the door, leaving them alone. 'His houseboy.'

'Was he out east?'

'KL-based for a long time.'

Jacko knew from his own army days that meant Kuala Lumpur. 'But he's Chinese, surely, not Malayan?'

'Oh, we're all over the place.' She laughed lightly.

'A general or something?'

'Judge Advocate in the legal department, taking courts martial. A trained barrister. Became Stipe when he retired. An official of the diocesan consistory court, too. Very high church. A strange old stick.' She didn't explain why.

Soon Barrington came in, wearing a wine-coloured silk dressing-gown, dark suit trousers and white shirt, no tie; a tall, erect man, about sixty. Not old, in Jacko's view, but then the older he got, the more allowances he made for age.

'Sorry to trouble you when you're ill,' Charley said with an apologetic face.

'Just the tail-end of a mild bout.'

Of malaria, Jacko diagnosed from his eyes, their whites yellowy. They gave him the quick once-over when the introduction was made, settled back on Charley and stayed there, inviting her to do the talking.

'The Simon Meakin case,' she said. His case load was so heavy she had to explain. He vaguely remembered granting him bail for medical examination.

34

She motioned to Jacko. 'They're looking for him again. They want to question him about the two dismembered women in the Derwent.'

'Oh, my God.' He shivered, a painful judder running through him. Jacko knew it wasn't a recurrence of the malaria. 'I had no idea he was dangerous. None whatsoever. Otherwise I'd have remanded him.'

'No one could have foreseen this outcome, sir,' said Jacko, sympathetically. He briefed him.

'Oh dear.' The shivers had stopped but the pain on his jaundiced face still showed.

'You see,' Charley spoke hesitantly, 'it would help if they could get hold of the report you ordered.'

She explained the delay and difficulties they had experienced with his near neighbour Dr Saul.

'Very cautious is dear Dr Saul,' said Barrington with a tiny smile of approval. 'And rightly so.' The smile was switched off. 'But, in the circumstances, you shall have it, my dear.' He spoke beautifully, like an old-time BBC announcer. 'Tomorrow. If not sooner. Promise.'

The ageing houseboy brought tea in a steaming pot on a wooden tray. They drank it out of flowered china cups. Not Co-op tea this. Green-coloured and tasting minty, refreshing on a hot day.

Jacko told him all he knew, which didn't take long. To break the awkward silence that followed, Charley said, 'Beautiful view.'

'High Tor.'

'What's this peak called?' Jacko asked.

'The Heights of Abraham.'

'Very biblical.' Jacko shot a quick grin at Charley.

'Eh?' Barrington frowned, then smiled gently. 'Ah. Not quite. So called after that famous battle near Quebec. Remember?'

Jacko didn't, held his breath and was relieved when Barrington went straight on. 'When General Wolfe crossed the river, reciting Gray's "Elegy in a Country Churchyard".'

He looked towards the hills. ' "The curfew tolls the knell of parting day." ' A deep but quiet voice, face at peace now. ' "The lowing herds wind slowly o'er the lea." '

It all came flooding back to Jacko now. 'The ploughman homeward plods his weary way,' he wanted to say. 'And leaves the

35

world to darkness and to me.' Wanted to say, but didn't; not wanting to make a fool of himself if he hadn't got it quite right. Today he felt like a boy back at school, relearning his Bible and poetry.

'They scaled the Heights and caught the French napping,' Barrington went on. '1750 something, wasn't it?'

'About then,' said Jacko, playing safe.

'A great victory.'

When they had finished their tea, he waved them off in the courtyard.

'Nice old bod,' said Jacko walking uphill towards the car.

Charley said nothing.

'A bachelor?'

A nod.

'A confirmed bachelor?' Code for gay.

A saucy laugh. 'Not according to the legal grapevine.'

'Which is?'

'He orders take-outs.'

A new one to Jacko, so he frowned.

'From the Halcyon Health Club.'

New, too. His frown remained.

'A knocking shop masquerading as a massage parlour,' said Charley with a straight face. 'He can't go there, not in his position, can he? So they come to him. Always non-whites, they say. Blacks, Asians . . .' and then, with that clever little smile, '. . . orientals.'

Jacko strolled in silence. Am I shocked? he was asking himself. Well, I would be if he was kerb-crawling and then sitting in judgement. He'd have been shocked by the hypocrisy. But house calls were discreet and legal.

None of his business, he decided. Or was it? Could be if an oriental masseuse turned out to be the second victim. He made a mental note to check out the Halcyon Health Club unless they got an ID soon.

His mind strolled on. He'd slept with only white women and only a handful of those. He sometimes idly wondered about oriental girls – if it was true what they said in the army, that their tram lines ran the other way.

He looked down at Charley walking at his side. He'd never

36

find out from her, not with a girl who knew her Bible backwards. He smiled to himself. 'Fancy lunch on the way back?'

'Got a date with Dan Payne in the Dolphin,' said Charley. She didn't even say 'Some other time' and Jacko felt spurned and very old.

Little Velma Malloy showed scant interest when they told her they'd soon be getting the medical low-down on Meakin.

'He's walked in and given himself up.'

Charley looked stunned, said nothing.

Jacko felt relief. 'Where?'

'Matlock Town nick.'

'We could have given him a lift back,' he said with a mirthless laugh.

Charley didn't join him. Velma did. 'They're bringing him here with some parson who turned him in.' She looked down at her notes. 'The Rev. Dillon Blades from the Mission to Adam.'

Good God, Jacko thought. All this must have been happening at the bottom of the hill while he was at the top of it with Dr Saul and Barrington, the Stipe, getting nowhere fast. It would have been a coup to have spotted Meakin on the road and nicked him; worth a commendation. He liked the occasional commendation to balance the bollockings he regularly received.

The truth is, of course, that detectives seldom catch killers. Uniformed patrolmen often do, like those who got the Black Panther and the Yorkshire Ripper. This time, a parson, for christsake, while he, the ace detective, had been in the same small town, as clueless as Inspector Clouseau.

Velma put on a regretful face as she told him that she had assigned the divisional DCI and Window Payne to interview Meakin.

Jacko guessed she thought he'd have wanted the job himself. He didn't. The interviewing officers usually became the case officers and that meant weeks of boring dossier-building. Now it was over he fancied a few days with his family, then off on the next big one.

Velma looked at Charley. 'So thanks for your help.' She paused. 'We can call on you for the evidence review conference, I hope?'

'Please do.' A wan smile, disappointed, Jacko suspected, to be off the case.

Velma was looking at him. 'You and Helen Rogers can talk to this preacher man.'

She made him sound like a consolation prize.

5

In his bleached, crumpled denims, handcuffed to two brown-suited detectives, Simon Meakin looked and smelt like a blue cheese sandwich on Hovis; bewhiskered, overripe, rapidly going off.

Window Payne went ahead of the chained trio out of the station car-park, swaggering slightly, like the captain of the winning team leaving the field of play with his trophy.

Jacko opened the rear door of the car behind. Out stepped the Rev. Dillon Blades, a dog collar above a mid-blue shirt front under an oatmeal-coloured cotton suit. Thirty, no more; longish hair, very fair, eyes very blue, face very tanned but terror-stricken; like a missionary in the tropics about to be stuffed and cooked.

No jokes about cannibals and cooking pots today, Jacko vowed, leading the way upstairs. Blades gabbled softly, almost non-stop, a spring uncoiling. 'You'll see he eats . . . He's only had a bowl of cornflakes . . . You'll get him a change of clothes . . . He's been sleeping rough . . . He needs a doctor.'

Jacko said Yes to everything.

In the interview room waited Helen Rogers, already sitting, stout backside filling a small chair seat to overflowing.

'You'll treat him gently.' Blades paced in tight circles, eyes darting. Three times he was asked to sit. 'You've no idea of the agony this has caused me.'

Too hyped to grill yet, Jacko decided. 'Take a . . .' He just stopped himself from saying 'pew'. 'Please sit down, Mr . . . Reverend . . .' He was never sure how to address them.

Blades solved the problem for him. 'Call me Dill.' Pause. 'Please.'

'I'm Jacko. This is Helen. Drove by your church this morning. Methodist, are you?'

Finally he sat down. 'No.' Puzzlement. 'Oh no.' Enlightenment. 'No. My church bought the building from them years ago.'

The Mission to Adam, he explained, was non-denominational but broadly Pentecostal-based. Its main purpose was to save souls in eastern fleshpots like Bangkok, Manila and Hong Kong, from where he had returned just over a month ago after a three-year spell with his wife.

'Over here, in the west, the real task is to raise money to fund our work in warmer climes.' He'd fully unwound now.

'And the chap in denims who came in with you, is he a member of your congregation?'

'Oh, no.'

'Ever seen him at any services?'

A heavy headshake. 'Never before today.'

'So how did you two meet up?'

Dill Blades had gone to his church at 10 a.m. that morning to make final preparations for a big service taking place that night to give thanks for the raising of the new roof.

The man in the blue denim suit was sitting with bowed head, long, matted hair hanging down, in the front pew, praying loudly, groaning, 'Forgive me, Father, for I have sinned.'

Blades pottered about, not sure what to do. The man in prayer ignored him. Often he raised his face towards the retiled roof. Tears had washed clean lines down his dirty cheeks.

Eventually Blades sat beside him. 'Can I be of help?'

No response.

'What's your name?'

'Simon.'

'A good name. A fisherman's name.'

Tears. 'I have taken life, Father.'

'Call me Dill.'

'I have taken life, Father. I have committed bodies to the water.'

'Do you wish to unburden yourself?'

More tears as he sobbed out, 'Mark 6, verse 16. He is risen from the dead.'

Blades knew this to be a reference to the beheading of John the Baptist by Herod, who had unlawfully married his sister-in-law.

More biblical quotes followed, all ranted, some virtually howled. For a while Meakin claimed not to be Simon but Elijah. 'Moses commanded such persons to be stoned. John 8.'

'What persons?' asked Blades, an arm over his shoulder now.
'The woman.'
'What woman? Do you wish to tell me about her?'
'The one I stoned; the one whose head is on a platter.'

Holy Christ, thought Jacko, sitting back, not at all startled, contented, in fact. A clear confession to murder. No one outside the police station, apart from the killer, could know that Debby Dawson's head was on a plate in his fridge-freezer. He lit up a cigarette.

Blades took it as a signal for a break. 'Would you mind if I phoned home?'

Jacko nodded to a fawn phone between them. Blades dialled. A light voice, a woman's, came on. In a still tense voice he told her briefly where he was and why, with lots of Yeses and Noes, Dears, Awfuls and Don't Worries.

Then he looked at Jacko. 'Will I be long?'

A nod. 'Sorry.'

Blades talked back into the mouthpiece. 'Tell him to find a replacement.'

The conversation ended with another Don't worry.

He looked back at Jacko. 'I've had to cancel a cricket coaching session at the youth club.'

'Sorry.'

An understanding shrug.

'Play much?'

'Never on Sundays.' A serious smile.

Jacko laughed lightly.

'Only second team.' Modest, but not falsely so.

'Bowler or batsman?'

Blades propelled left arm over shoulder. 'Spin.'

'The chinaman?'

'Not in the evening league. Too expensive.'

Jacko laughed again, quite liking him, for a man of the cloth, anyway.

Blades was relaxed now, smiling slightly. Jacko deftly steered him back to Meakin.

Blades told them he knew only what he'd read in the *Evening Telegraph* about the two murders. He knew nothing of the hunt for Meakin because all this was taking place before that day's edition came out.

He'd asked the man in prayer, 'Do you wish me to call your family?'

'They have disowned me.'

'Or your own minister?'

'They have cast me out.'

'A doctor, perhaps?' No reply. 'Or a solicitor?'

Meakin flew into a frightening fury, condemning lawyers as sinners. 'They make demands, worse than tax collectors.'

'What sort of demands?'

'Unholy acts of worship.' He sobbed for a long time.

'Is there anything else you wish to share with me?' asked Blades when the weeping ceased.

'The other was an act of worship.'

'What other?'

'The other woman. A wrong act.' Meakin was mumbling. 'I have sinned.'

Jacko broke in. 'Is that all he said about the second victim?'

'Yes.'

'You see, we know who the first woman was. We have her name. We know nothing at all about this other woman. Anything at all would help.'

'That's all he said.'

Jacko nodded.

Meakin seemed to settle down – or so it had seemed to Blades, who gave him a bowl of cornflakes with milk and sugar. 'I don't think he'd eaten for days. He'd been sleeping rough. In a wilderness, he said, of brooks and water, of fountains and valleys. Deuteronomy, you know.'

Jacko didn't.

'We keep things like that, packets of soup, hot drinks, I mean, in a small kitchen next to my den.' A small, sad shrug. 'For wayfarers.'

Buttered toast was refused. 'Man does not live by bread alone,' Meakin had said solemnly.

Blades felt himself in a deep dilemma. 'All these things were

41

being said under seal of confession,' he explained urgently. 'As sacred to a man in my position as a doctor's oath. But I knew I just couldn't let him go. Not just because he's dangerous. He's in desperate need of help. But it had to be his decision to come to you, not mine. Do you follow?'

Jacko nodded.

Gradually Blades had turned to the subject of what to do now. 'Shall we seek help?'

'Who can help me?'

'The Lord can.'

'How?'

'With Deuteronomy, perhaps.'

'The Second Book of Law!' Another rage, almost a frenzy, in which Meakin accused Blades of being a Judas. 'It went on and on, much of it incomprehensible, much of it in tongues I didn't recognize.'

Jacko raised a questioning eyebrow.

'As a Pentecostalist I practise glossolalia . . .'

Jacko cocked his head, still not following.

'Tongues and their interpretation. Fills your spirit, it does. "They began to speak with other tongues, as the Spirit gave them utterance." Acts 2:4.'

Jacko kept his own tongue still, hoped he didn't look too much of a doubting Thomas.

'I see you have misgivings.'

'I'm a detective.'

'Some of us find great peace in communicating with the Lord in a language that passes all understanding.' Blades was speaking now with great enthusiasm, his face radiant. 'It really does free the spirit. I have read of missionaries about to be killed by natives suddenly speaking their language and being saved and the tribe turning to Christianity.'

Jacko tightened his lips to kill a cynical smile. 'But you couldn't understand the prayers Simon was sending up?'

' 'Fraid not.'

Meakin's rage blew out. They knelt in prayer together. Blades quoted out loud from Moses' last words to his people. 'Beware that you forget not the Lord, your God; that you keep His commandments, his judgements and his laws which I have given you.'

He whispered to Meakin, kneeling beside him. 'And what law did Moses give us in Exodus?'

'You shall not kill.'

'What is the right thing to do, Simon?'

'Face my judgement.'

'How? Where?'

'Will you bear witness for me and speak as I have spoken to you?'

'Of course.'

'Take me to the law.'

He drove him to Matlock Town nick.

Simon wept as they parted.

Blades wept as he signed, left-handed, his long statement.

Jacko sat alone and in silence after Helen had taken Blades at the DCI's request to see Meakin in the recording interview room.

He sighed deeply. Oh, Jesus. No blasphemy intended. I may not believe but thank Christ some do. I've been wrong about them. They're worth their place in their heaven, some of these ministers, these preachers, if only for doing no more than holding the hand of the sick and troubled in their hour of need. The world would be a poorer place without them.

Helen lumbered in, breaking into his revised thoughts. 'How they doing?' he asked.

'Not at all well.' She shook her head heavily. 'He keeps rambling and breaking down. Percy Manners is there. Dr Saul's on his way, too. The chief super wants me to collect Mrs Meakin to see if she can make any sense out of him.'

She picked up her notebook from the desk. At the door, she turned back, looking at him, accusingly. 'You and the Rev. didn't make much sense either at one stage. What, in God's name, is a chinaman?'

He laughed. 'Left arm spin. Lovely to watch.' She frowned. 'They can turn the ball both ways.' She still frowned. 'With the wrist. He makes the ball spin the way the batsman isn't expecting.'

'How's he do that?'

'Sleight of hand,' said Jacko, smiling slyly.

' 'Ey up, me duck.' A local accent, badly mimicked. Jacko looked up from Yellow Pages to find Charley Chan at his shoulder.

43

He was pleased to see her, glad of a break from phoning Chinese restaurants seeking AWOL waitresses. 'Your idea,' Little Velma Malloy had told him. 'Get on with it.' In a trade with massive mobility of labour, several hard to say and harder to spell names were cropping up. He was wishing he'd kept his mouth shut.

'Got this.' Charley dropped a single sheet on his desk. 'Hand-delivered.'

He lit up a cigarette and read. Tor View Clinic, the photo-copied page was headed. It was dated that day, so Barrington, the Stipe, had kept his promise and wasted no time in leaning on Dr Saul.

'Private and Confidential,' it went on. 'Authorized eyes only. Summarized note for court and file. Subject: Simon Meakin. Current age: 29. Referred by: magistrates' court.'

It was a scruffy document, mistakes typed over or Tippexed out. Each short paragraph began with one word in capitals. What followed weren't sentences but punchy phrases.

HISTORY: Local-born, educated, married with young family. A potted version of the window-smashing charges followed.

COMPLAINT: Hallucinates religious powers, hears and talks to voices etc.

DIAGNOSIS: Schizophrenia.

TREATMENT: Medication to be decided.

RECOMMENDATION had been hurriedly completed in scrawled handwriting. 'Treatable.'

NEGATIVE INFLUENCE: A Nonconformist minister of charis-matic quality. Was to suggest probation on condition of non-association with same. Assume now overtaken by later events.

Saul had signed above 'Medical Superintendent'.

At least he's right about that, thought Jacko, moodily rereading the last phrase. 'This doctor doesn't waste words.'

Charley looked over his shoulder. 'Always types his own stuff. Always uses lay language.' Her own seemed to have been in-fected by Dr Saul's pithiness. 'Should see some of the long rig-maroles we have to plough through.' She nodded downwards. 'Maybe the Nonconformist minister is worth the once-over for background.'

Jacko slashed two words with a yellow highlighter. 'What's charismatic?'

'A bit like you.' She laughed warmly and patted his shoulder.

'That's sexual charisma.' A deadpan face hid the delight that he was feeling. 'What's it mean in a religious context?'

'An ability to convince and motivate, I think.' She thought. 'For good or evil. Take Charlie Manson or – what was his name? – the Rev. Jones, that cult leader in the Guyana mass slaughter thing. Late seventies. They overpower their followers mentally, take life-or-death decisions for them.'

'Brainwashing, you mean?'

'In a religious context, it means, I think, those who openly practise the gifts of the spirit. Supernatural gifts like speaking in tongues.' Doubt flickered across Charley's face. 'Doesn't it?'

Jacko put on his search-me face.

She nodded down at the report. 'It certainly proves religious mania. How are they getting on with him?'

Jacko wasn't really sure and wasn't really bothered. All would be revealed at the evening conference in half an hour's time. 'Trouble, I hear.'

'What sort?'

'He keeps relaying messages from God to them.'

'A symptom of schizophrenia.'

'Yep. Do you think Joan of Arc suffered from it, too?'

It was incredible how much of what he had learned at school was returning, for the first time in years. Now he wished he hadn't remembered the story of Joan's divine guidance when she took on the English.

Charley looked at him as if he had slandered a schoolgirl heroine. With her churchy upbringing, he understood. His look would have been much the same if someone maligned Humphrey Bogart.

'Mind if I . . .?' She fingered the papers in his out-tray with Dillon Blades' statement on top.

'Help yourself.'

She picked it up and sat beside him.

He slipped the doctor's report in his pending tray and got back to Yellow Pages.

'Sorry for the delay.' Little Velma Malloy bustled in. She was always late, so great the pressure on CID chiefs these crime-ridden days with murders so plentiful that a one-off case involving a non-news name – like a pensioner or a black – didn't rate a line in any national newspaper.

She held her briefings in the incident room, not conference or lecture halls so, Jacko suspected, her subordinates could get on with their work instead of hanging around, waiting for her.

A shrewd boss was Velma; a slave-driver whose slaves didn't realize they were being driven.

'Right.' She looked at the DCI who had a big silver tape-recorder on his desk. He forwarded it, checking a fast-revolving counter, stopped it. 'This is just an example of what we've been getting all afternoon.' He flicked a different switch.

A man's voice gabbled such gibberish that Jacko thought he had recorded a foreign radio programme by mistake. Not a single word was recognizable as English. He was switched off.

'What is it?' asked Velma, perplexed.

'Sounded like Hebrew to me,' said Window Payne.

On again. The torrent of jumbled words continued. Off.

'It's mumbo-jumbo,' said the collator, a dark, taciturn man, late forties, Jacko's age.

'It's all like that.' The DCI wore an exasperated face.

'He could be speaking in tongues,' Jacko ventured, knowledge-ably.

'What's that?' asked Payne.

'A Pentecostalist means of prayer.' Charley stole Jacko's thunder. 'Not practised in most established churches.' Now she had the floor she kept it. 'Any taped confessions under caution?'

The DCI shook his head vigorously.

'Still, we've got what he said to the Rev. Dillon Blades.' Charley waved the statement she had taken from Jacko's in-tray.

'What's your recommendation?' asked Little Velma, tiredly.

'Charge him. Murder. Two counts.' Charley looked and sounded very positive.

'We've no ID on the second woman. That still right, Jacko?' Velma looked at Jacko who pulled a fed-up face, answer enough.

'We can charge him with a female unknown,' Charley persisted.

'I don't like it,' said Velma, flatly.

Jacko came in. 'Me neither.'

Charley looked at him, definitely a glare. 'You've got to charge him with something or apply to the magistrates tomorrow for an extension to hold him,' she said, accurately enough.

'And we won't get it.' The DCI spoke firmly. 'Dr Saul wants

him back at Tor View Clinic. He says he's unfit for further questioning. What's more, our quack agrees.'

'Is there a secure unit up there?' Velma asked.

The DCI and Jacko nodded.

'We're not going to get anything out of him in his present state,' the DCI went on. 'He's almost catatonic. His wife, that preacher, Percy Manners. They've all had a go. Nothing but gobbledygook.'

'We're going to have to charge him,' said Velma.

'Just charge him with Debby Dawson for the time being,' Jacko suggested.

'Why?' Charley again, protesting slightly. 'We've got his admission to Dillon Blades that he put both bodies in the river. We've got scientific evidence that both were dismembered with the same cutting technique.'

Jacko knew why. A long-ago case that haunted him still. He wasn't about to explain; not here. Instead: 'We can get a remand on one count. It will give us a week to work on the other girl's ID.'

'Messy,' said Charley, dismissively.

'He could be right though.' Velma, quietly, head down, thinking. 'Once we get her ID we can talk to him about her. If we charge him, we can't without Manners' approval.'

Good tactics, Jacko acknowledged. One of the reasons why he liked working for Little Velma. Once you have laid a charge you can't interview an accused again without his lawyer's consent. With a shyster like Manners as his brief, he doubted that they'd get it. They had enough on the Debby Dawson case without a confession. No charge on the second woman would mean they could question Meakin about her when he was fit again.

He decided to back her. 'Which we won't get.'

'Won't it seem odd to the public?' Charley was beginning to back down. 'I mean, you've linked the two cases in news releases all through.'

'You can say in court that we want a remand in custody, pending further inquiries into a similar serious matter.' Velma's code to tell the public a second murder charge is coming, Jacko realized. 'When he's next up you can ask for a twenty-four-hour remand to our custody so we can talk to him about the second case. We should have her name by then.' She looked mischievously at Jacko.

'Right-o.' Charley accepted the decision, smiling.

There was unanimous agreement not to oppose Meakin's transfer from his police station cell to Tor View Clinic after he'd been formally charged with the Dawson murder.

'Court tomorrow then,' said Velma.

The DCI put down the phone after talking to the magistrates' clerk. 'All fixed. A bedside court at the clinic. Ten thirty.'

Rare, but not unique, thought Jacko, privately agreeing. Humane, really. That's it then. There'd be a couple of celebratory pints in the Dolphin for a difficult job almost done, then early home.

Velma was looking at him. 'Take that tape up to your parson pal and let him have a listen. Run it past Dr Saul, too.'

Jacko resisted. 'Saul will be seeing Meakin soon.'

'But he hasn't heard the tape.'

'And Blades was with him all morning and couldn't make much sense out of him.'

'He still got more out of him than they did.' She flicked her head towards the DCI and Window Payne.

'But . . .'

'Jacko.' Sharp. 'You raised the question of talking in tongues. You follow it up.'

Cow, he thought angrily. Slave-driving bitch.

When, oh when, will I ever learn to keep my mouth shut?

6

The back of his white jacket half turned, Chief Nurse O'Brien was standing at a stout grey filing cabinet in the dismal waiting-room at Tor View Clinic. 'Brought him back, have you?'

'He's following on in a paddy wagon when we've charged him,' said Jacko. 'I've come ahead in the hope of getting five minutes with the doctor.'

'Engaged. Take a seat. Won't be long.' O'Brien turned back fully to the task of filing papers in green folders with name tags on metal rims. A chain ran like a silver umbilical cord from the buckle of his belt to the lock at chest height.

Jacko slid the strap of a brown leather case which contained a battery-operated tape machine from his shoulder and lowered it on to a table.

He picked up an ancient *National Geographic* and flipped through a few pages. Outside was a bright, blustery August evening. Inside, in a room without windows, he could barely see to read. He put it down again.

O'Brien pushed in the cabinet's lock, took out the key, palmed the chain into a ball which he slipped into a pocket of his dark trousers. His hand came out with a packet of Bensons, Jacko's brand.

He approached, rattling the packet. Jacko took one. O'Brien lit it with a green throwaway he'd taken from a glass tray full of them on top of the cabinet.

'Thanks.' Jacko sat back in his chair. 'Your secure unit's escape-proof, I hope.' He grinned through the smoke.

'Better be,' said O'Brien, darkly but smiling. 'We've got an arsonist under observation in the other room. His turn-on is haystack fires. Can't have him wandering around the country-side at harvest time, can we?' A laugh, cut off quickly. 'A hundred per cent proof,' he added with a serious face.

They chatted for a while about Meakin's illness. Not a Jekyll and Hyde condition like the media sometimes paint it, said O'Brien, who was talkative and, therefore, to Jacko anyway, likeable. 'Most sufferers are quiet and shy and live in a dream state. Once we get the cocktail of drugs right, the majority improve rapidly. We probably won't have to keep him here long.'

They'd get him better in good time to start the life sentence that was bound to come, Jacko was thinking. Pity they didn't treat him before he'd killed two young women.

The inner door to Dr Saul's office opened, brightening the waiting-room. Out walked John Barrington, the Stipendiary Magistrate, dressed in a dark suit and silver tie.

Odd place to find a man off duty with malaria, Jacko thought. He rose from his chair, hiding his surprise. 'Hallo, sir.'

'Ah, Inspector.' Barrington sounded pleased to see him. 'Caught him, I hear.'

'Yes, sir.'

'Had my clerk on. He's fixed a special court here for tomorrow for me to take. Just been checking the arrangements.'

'Feeling better?'

'Much.' A healthy smile. 'Living on the doorstep; convenient, wouldn't you say?' Jacko said Yes. 'Day room 10.30 a.m. then.' He strode out, erect but leisurely.

49

O'Brien flicked his head towards the open door. Jacko picked up the tape machine case by its strap, walked in and up to the doctor's desk where he put it down again.

'He's arrived then?' said Dr Saul, sitting, not taking much notice.

'*En route.*' Jacko hovered until he'd got Saul's attention. 'We'd like you to listen to bits of this, if you will.' He undid the case, switched on a pre-set section from Meakin's recorded interview. 'We can't understand it.'

Saul switched off interest as he listened to a couple of minutes of Meakin talking in a local accent but in a foreign-sounding language. Eventually, and above it, he said, 'Well, you wouldn't, would you?'

Jacko turned off. 'What's it mean?'

'Nothing that anyone will ever make any sense of.'

'Is it glossolalia?' Jacko had looked this up. 'An ecstatic utterance of unintelligible, speechlike sounds,' the dictionary told him, 'regarded as caused by religious ecstasy.'

'You can hardly call it that. It's a word salad, very mixed. A symptom of his world being pulled apart. Part and parcel of his illness. When he recovers he won't know himself what any of it means.' A thin smile. 'You're wasting your time, Inspector.'

'Ah, well,' said Jacko with a sigh.

Saul sat back. 'Look.' He looked away. 'Sorry if I was uncooperative earlier. But, er . . .' looking up now, nodding towards the closed door, '. . . the Stipe's hot on procedure. The military man in him, I suppose. He's given me a dressing-down before for releasing reports he's commissioned without his clearance.'

It was an apology of sorts, Jacko decided, even if he was passing the buck. He believed in accepting apologies, mending fences. Not that he had much of a forgiving nature; more that he never knew when he might want to use him again.

'No harm done, doc,' he said pleasantly.

If you excluded Debby Dawson and an unknown oriental girl, he added privately and bitterly.

So many cars were parked around the bottom of the corkscrew hill that Jacko had to walk some distance from his, which he'd left in front of a row of shops on the prom.

The breeze was scattering grey smoke in no particular

direction from a back-garden barbecue. The sweet, appetizing smell reminded him that he hadn't eaten since breakfast twelve hours earlier and then not much after his disturbed night.

A stream of people was heading his way, blacks and browns among them, all too well dressed to be tourists.

Oh, Christ. Jacko stopped so suddenly that the encased tape machine swung forward on his shoulder. That thanksgiving service at the Mission to Adam is tonight. Now. He started to turn, to seek out the nearest pub and wait there.

'You look like a radio journalist.' John Barrington's quiet, cultured voice at his shoulder.

Jacko twisted his head. 'I was hoping to get the pastor to listen to something on this.' A steadying hand had rested on the leather case.

'He'll be busy for an hour or so.'

'So I see. I think . . .'

'Come, too.' An inviting smile.

Jacko stood still.

'It will do you no harm.' A light laugh. 'I'm on my own.' His hand gripped Jacko's elbow.

They started walking again, Jacko being almost propelled. 'You a regular here, then?' he asked, just to strike up a conversation, already knowing he wasn't.

A headshake. 'C of E. It's just that they've asked everyone locally who contributed to their appeal fund. Neighbourly, really. It should be quite interesting.' He smiled. 'Fun.'

A couple of pints in the Dolphin would have been more fun, thought Jacko.

They followed the crowd down a flagstoned path and through an open arched door. The church seemed the wrong way round. The seats, most of them filled, faced sideways in long rows. Not pews, really; lines of identical chairs, soft blue fabric on black steel frames.

The place seemed much too light, too airy with a high sloping roof of polished timber in herringbone pattern. All but one of the walls were white.

The cosmopolitan congregation faced a wall of pale, worn bricks, recovered from old buildings, Jacko guessed, and tastefully reconstituted. At its centre was a cross in blue tiles with a white dove above.

51

Part of the brick wall was covered by a curtain, deep maroon, hanging from a brass rail. In front of it was a square sort of stage, three reconstituted bricks high. On it was a semicircular platform on another three bricks. On that sat a four-piece band; drums, two guitars and a piano. The whole place had a buzz, the expectant air of a miners' welfare on concert night, waiting for the curtain to go up.

Barrington sat on an end chair in the back row, apparently planning a quick getaway. Jacko side-stepped beyond him and took the next seat, putting the tape machine between his feet on a rust-coloured wall-to-wall carpet with very thick pile.

Barrington lowered his head. Jacko raised his, looking curiously about him. There were many children in the congregation, some babes in the arms of straw-hatted women. There was much chatter and laughter.

The young man in front of him had gelled, spiked hair and five rings in pierced ears – three in the right, two in the left. That was one more than the girl next to him who wore a short, tight red dress and a black skull-cap. When she knelt to pray, Jacko noticed she had heavenly legs.

Suddenly, he looked away. Should I really be doing this – lusting in church? he asked himself sharply. Think of all those Old Testament plagues. The locusts could get your French beans.

His eyes travelled forward and rested on three men sitting on the semicircular platform, not a dog collar among them. All were immaculately dressed, Dillon Blades in a slate grey doubled-breasted suit, brilliant white shirt and a dark, paisley tie.

He stood and walked forward to a pine lectern from which hung a red velvet cloth, four words embroidered on it in gold: 'New Life in Jesus'. He picked up a hand microphone. He raised both arms. 'Welcome. Welcome.' Everyone settled into a smiling silence.

He called for a hymn. Everyone stood and launched themselves into a jolly tune Jacko didn't recognize.

His eyes ranged on. They stopped with a start on the front row to his right. At an oriental girl.

He studied a side-on view of a small, compact body. White silk blouse, a black buttoned-up waistcoat with gold braiding. Black glossy hair in a sort of kiss curl over her ear. Shiny skin, more brown than yellow, stretched tight over high cheekbones. Bee-stung lips protruded as she sang with gusto.

Beautiful, he acknowledged without a trace of lust. Once, he thought sadly, the girl in bits on the slab in the infirmary morgue, three pieces still missing, must have looked like her.

The singing stopped. Jacko sat. 'Before you sit . . .' Jacko stood. '. . . say hallo to your neighbours. Introduce yourself. Make them welcome.'

Jacko and Barrington gave each other embarrassed glances. 'I'm Dennis.' Jacko turned. A man, early forties, prematurely bald, was offering his hand, smiling warmly. He took it. 'Jacko.' He sat hurriedly, realized no one else had, jumped up again.

Into another hymn, another new one, with a vague rumba beat. Dillon led the singing in a deep melodious voice aided by his mike amplified from two black loudspeakers each side of the maroon wall curtain.

Everyone finally sat. Blades gripped the edges of the lectern tightly, eyes shut, in a long, earnest prayer for the new roof and praising everyone, the Lord especially, for making it possible. He opened his eyes, beaming. 'Now let's raise that roof – not literally, I hope – with our own special song.' There was lots of laughter.

He handed the mike to a woman with white skin and negroid facial bone structure. Everyone stood. Up and down like a bloody yo-yo, Jacko grumbled privately.

'I'm . . .' A contralto voice, unaccompanied. A pause. '. . . gonna . . .' Another pause, eyes teasing. 'Rock my soul in the bosom of Abraham.' She fair belted it out.

Good God, Jacko thought, excited now. I know this. The Lonnie Donegan version anyway. Everyone was singing around him at the top of their voices. Some raised arms, like a spin bowler appealing for a catch, the girl in front in red among them. Divine bosom, too, Jacko noted to his shame, worrying about locusts and his French beans. Others were clapping their hands as if they were applauding the catch.

By the last line of the first verse, Jacko, inhibitions gone, had been caught up by it all and joined in. 'Oh rock o' my soul.'

The contralto, a solo: 'My soul is weak.'

Everyone, Jacko included: 'Rock o' my soul.'

Solo: 'But thou art strong.'

53

Chorus: 'Rock o' my soul.'

Solo: 'I'm leaning on, I'm leaning on his mighty arm.'

All together now: 'I'm gonna rock my soul in the bosom of Abraham.'

It was sung with such enthusiasm, a musical happening, that Blades called for a one-verse repeat, sung even more joyfully, so he called for an encore and they went through it again from start to finish.

Jacko sat down, flushed, happy, feeling like an innocent child again.

A silver-haired, craggily handsome man in a red tie took up the mike, read a text which half his audience knew (Jacko didn't) and completed with him, singing out the words.

Off he went, raising lots of questions. 'Why pray?'

'Why?' repeated someone on the front.

His condemnation of auto-pilot praying went on and on. 'Prayer has to be filled with spirit.'

'Right,' said someone from the back.

On and on, he went, denouncing foxhole religion, the only sort Jacko practised. 'Blasphemy,' he boomed. 'Yes,' said Dennis next door. Crying children were ushered into a glass-fronted crèche next to a door marked 'Dill's Den'.

On and on. Jacko sent up a prayer of his own, one he hadn't used since his days as a semi-professional soprano at the parish church, blatant foxhole religion. 'Let my people go.'

On and on. The third member of the platform party wiped his eyes with a handkerchief he clutched in his hand, face writhed in agony. Know the feeling, brother, thought Jacko. He yearned for a cigarette. The last thing he wanted, he suddenly decided, was to die and be born again as a Christian and have to sit through all this week in, week out.

On and on for forty minutes. Finally Blades stood, took the mike and mercifully put an end to it. 'Now, brother,' he said very gravely. 'I truly understand the meaning of prayer. And so say us all.' Yeses and Rights rolled around the congregation.

A thirty-strong children's choir, some not yet of school age, filed from their seats to the front. Six men shuffled behind them. Like a conjurer, Blades whipped away lace cloths that covered the trays three were carrying to reveal loaves of bloomer bread. Red wine was decanted into huge silver goblets the other three carried.

54

'Well, now,' sang an angel-faced boy soprano, 'if you want a silver trumpet like mine.'

'Hand me my silver trumpet, Gabriel,' sang the choir. Many of them were less pretty than the soloist and, therefore, far more appealing to Jacko, who had a down on boy sopranos; thought they'd be better off playing conkers or cricket.

The trays and goblets were being handed out at the ends of the rows. Barrington and Jacko got rid of theirs faster than Pass the Parcel but Dennis next door took a large chunk of bread and a short sip of wine.

'Then you'd better learn to play it in plenty of time,' sang the lead boy.

'Hand me down my silver trumpet, Lord,' sang his backing group. They finished to proud applause.

'Tithe time,' Blades announced.

During another hymn, again unknown to Jacko, the six men handed out collecting bags. Dennis wrote out a cheque; £35, Jacko sneakily noted. Surreptitiously, he slipped in a pound coin, making a mental note to reclaim it on exes. Barrington put in a tenner.

Blades wished a woman at the back a happy eighty-first birthday. People around her clapped. He announced the services for the weekend and there seemed to be many of them.

The service ended with a slow, sung version of the Lord's Prayer, substituting 'debts' for 'trespasses'.

It had lasted more than an hour and a half, longer than a soccer match.

'It was fun,' said Barrington, impressed.

'Most of it,' Jacko agreed guardedly.

Only to himself did he admit that he had recaptured just a trickle of that innocent, safe feeling of childhood which he'd lost somewhere along the way. It felt warm and good, Christmassy somehow.

The sermon apart, he was glad he came. He was surprised with himself.

So long did the stragglers linger over their goodbyes beneath the arched doorway that Jacko had time to top up his nicotine level with two Bensons while he waited on the illuminated pathway, feeling the dusk chill.

At last Blades spotted him, speeded up his glad-handing, then beckoned him back inside. 'I take it you're waiting for me.'

'We'd like you to give this tape a little listen.' Jacko patted the square case at his hip.

Crossing the rust-coloured carpet he said Meakin had been charged with one count of murder and was being held in the secure unit up at Tor View Clinic. His eyes went towards the timbered ceiling.

'Best place for him,' said Blades firmly. 'They'll look after him there.'

'Know it?'

'Only by repute. I've not had time for a pastoral visit yet.' He opened the door to Dill's Den.

It was to take some time for Jacko to absorb the details of the office. Right now he only had eyes for her – the oriental girl.

She looked up from counting money as she sat at a table. Was the top covered with a cloth, scrubbed or what? He didn't notice immediately; too occupied studying her.

Her oval face, frail-boned. Her sloe eyes, so big, so brown; such deep brown. Her heart-shaped lips seemed to blow a kiss when they widened into a smile, far, far sexier than Velma Malloy's wink at the start of this long day, or maybe he just imagined it.

'My wife.' Blades sounded justifiably proud.

Lordy, lordy, Jacko thought. Ever since *The African Queen,* he'd always associated missionaries' kinswomen with Katharine Hepburn, inspirational to know, pretty plain to behold. Not this one, though.

He put the machine on a table among neat piles of cheques, five-and ten-pound notes; not many pound coins, even less silver. He rewound, explained when and how the tape was recorded, pressed 'Play'. Meakin's meaningless mumbo-jumbo filled the room.

Mrs Blades stopped counting money, listening intently. There was only one word, a cliché word in the circumstances, to describe her expression – inscrutable.

Her husband's face was rapidly readable – pained puzzlement. He was shaking his head before Jacko switched off. 'It's not dissimilar to what he was saying here.'

'Is it glossolalia?'

56

'None that I recognize. You, dear?'

Mrs Blades shook her head so that her kiss curls danced on both ears. 'I am sorry.' A tiny voice, high-pitched.

'Do you speak in tongues, too?' asked Jacko.

'Runs in the family, so to speak.' Smiling, Blades motioned to his wife. 'This is Jade, by the way.'

'Hallo.' An awkward moment. 'Unusual name.'

'Not her given one.' He gave her given one: Shen-Shen. 'It means spruce but people call her Jade because of that.'

Mrs Blades fingered matt green beads that hung down to her small bosom on a cord round her slender neck. 'Her grand-mother's,' Blades was explaining. 'Not terribly expensive jade but of great sentimental value.'

'Where's home?'

'Shanghai, originally, but we met in Hong Kong.' Blades was over-protectively doing her talking for her. 'On my previous posting.'

'Always wanted to go there.' Jacko put an edge of envy in his voice.

'Not the happiest place right now with worries about the main-land takeover but our own mission was very fulfilling work. Drug rehabilitation, mainly. From among the Walled City, some of them.'

'Been back long?'

'End of June.' Five weeks, Jacko calculated. Long enough to be the Nonconformist minister with charismatic qualities who, ac-cording to Dr Saul, had been the negative influence in sick Simon Meakin's religious life.

'We had a fortnight's leave with my mother in Richmond before coming here.' Blades continued. 'I hadn't seen her for al-most three years. Jade had never met her.' Three weeks. Debby Dawson had gone missing by then. Not long enough, Jacko decided.

'Settling down all right?' This time he made it obvious he was talking to Jade.

She took a little breath. 'Everyone is very nice.'

The cramped room had taken shape now. The pine desk with green phone, the green cabinet, the cream door to the kitchen, the green baize on the table.

'Tell me . . .' Jacko paused to find a gentle lead-in. '. . . but I noticed how cosmopolitan your congregation was . . .'

'Enjoyed the service, I hope?'

'Thank you. Yes.' His pleasant smile. 'You'll remember I told you we had identified only one of Simon Meakin's victims. You may have read the other was of South-east Asian origin, probably oriental, early twenties. You don't happen to have any regular worshipper of that description who's not been seen around for three weeks or so?'

'No.' A mist seemed to lower over Blades' face, then lift. 'Fortunately.'

'You?' Jacko looked at Jade, whose kiss curls waved in time to her headshake.

'And you didn't see Simon Meakin . . .' He described him in detail. '. . . among the congregation in the last three weeks?' Her curls danced another No.

'Just a long shot.' Jacko shrugged. 'No need to get alarmed.'

Blades' face was registering alarm. 'I'll ask around for you, if you wish.'

7

Did I lie? Throughout a long night the question haunted the Rev. Dillon Blades, hardly left him for a waking moment, and was still there next morning when he was alone in his mission.

He was not in prayer before the white-tiled cross. He was sitting in his den, consulting his conscience, weighing his actions in the balance.

No, he finally decided, but you have committed a sin of omission.

He was not pouring out his troubles in tongues which, for him, bypassed limited English and liberated his very soul. He felt no sublime spirit within, no celestial fire; just guilt which overwhelmed him, turning his heart into stone.

It was not, he knew, an appropriate moment for prayer. His subconscious seemed to be warning him that he might not like the guidance he would receive, the dark prophecies he feared.

Of defrocking. Of deportation. Of disgrace. Of doom.

He closed his eyes, in despair, not prayer. He felt frail and lonely.

He must not, he vowed firmly, discuss this with Jade. It was true what she had told the inspector. She was settling down, liking it here. His mother had accepted her. She was one of his personal and his church families, his flock.

The feeling of guilt, of loss, of shame, might make her question her faith, turn her back to old ways. If my fears are unfounded, then, with God's help, she need never know.

Don't panic, he tried telling himself. There were hundreds, thousands about all over the country. He'd been surprised just how many he'd seen in London. Don't think the worst, he comforted himself. Retain your hopes.

But you can't be sure, another voice cautioned him.

He had to know. So he'd keep the promise he'd made, the least he could do. He'd ask around.

Twice in two days he'd been put to the test. He was afraid he'd passed neither. The words of Romans 5 came to him but, such was his inner turmoil, only vaguely – words about suffering producing perseverance, character and hope and, then, most definitely, 'Hope does not shame us.'

Not divine inspiration, he acknowledged, freely and honestly. A mere mortal's interpretation to tell himself what he wanted to hear – to suffer in silence, to persevere patiently to see what happens. It was the best that he could do, all he could manage on his own.

Meantime, he would hold his tongue.

8

'. . . for the prosecution . . .' Charley Chan was already on her feet, a couple of words into her opening spiel when Jacko walked in, only a second or two after ten thirty next morning. '. . . in the two cases on Your Worship's list for this special sitting. Mr Percival Manners is for the defence in both.'

Both? Jacko asked himself, crossly. He was always upset to be late for anything. He hated not being on time, thought the world should wait for him.

The agreement last night was to charge Meakin with one count of murder, so what's developed overnight? he wanted to know. Why wasn't I told? He looked urgently around the day room half-way up the steep corridor at Tor View Clinic.

It was an informal setting for a court of law. A mix of colourful easy chairs, different shapes and sizes, lined a cream wall. Tropical plants sprouted green and healthy in pots on a pink cord carpet. Pictures of hunting scenes hung between half a dozen windows through which he could see patients sitting in the Saturday morning sun at the picnic tables on the grassy plateau.

Small card tables had been neatly arranged, one per person, looking like students sitting an examination.

Charley, in a waist-hugging, pin-striped dark suit, stood at one, back to him. Manners, grey suit less than a perfect fit, sat at another to her right, an empty table between. Both faced the sombrely dressed Barrington who had his clerk to his left, presiding like invigilators.

No Meakin to be seen. Instead a white-coated guard escorted a blinking teenager into the room.

The Stipe must be remanding the arsonist, too, Jacko realized. Feeling foolish at his misreading, he settled into a comfortable chair next to Window Payne. Alongside him were two reporters, notebooks on crossed knees.

The clerk read out three counts of arson. Barrington looked up from his papers. 'Formal evidence of arrest has been deposed, has it not?' he asked courteously.

'By Sergeant Daniel Payne before the lay magistrates when the accused was first remanded last month,' said Charley, crisply. She hinted at more cases to come and even more in his record.

Manners half stood, in a twisted crouch, one hand on the back of his chair, not pushing it back to make room. He announced he had no application for bail.

Barrington ordered a six-day remand in the secure unit for medical reports. It was all over so fast that the prisoner didn't have time to sit at the empty centre table. He was about-turned by two male nurses and walked out again, grinning at everyone who caught his gleaming eye.

Chief Nurse O'Brien pushed Meakin into the room in a cumbersome wheelchair. A thick sage green dressing-gown was draped over lime green pyjamas. His feet were shod in brown leather slippers, no socks. His eyes were shut. His head hung slightly to one side. They had cleaned him up but drugged him up. The liquid cosh, they call it.

Jacko, at ease now, looked around as the charge of murdering Deborah Dawson was read. No Mrs Meakin. Just as well, in her advanced state of pregnancy, that she should be spared this sight of her estranged husband, he concurred.

Barrington anxiously inquired if Meakin understood the charge. Manners neither stood nor sat. 'I have explained his position to him, as best I can.'

Window Payne was called this time and tried to look unconcerned about it. All detectives like to see their names in the paper, though they pretend not to. He walked briskly to a table at right angles to the solicitors, picked up a Bible from it and, still standing, took the oath.

His outline, from the recovery of the body in bits and pieces from the river and the head from the fridge-freezer at the bedsit, to the arrest and charging, took only a couple of minutes.

Barrington looked at Manners who shook his head. No questions, he was saying.

Charley had remained on her feet throughout. 'The prosecution applies for a remand until next Friday, in the custody of the secure unit here, pending further inquiries into a similar serious matter.' She was carrying out Little Velma Malloy's instructions to the letter.

Manners twisted to his feet again, said he had no objections and didn't want reporting restrictions lifted.

'Noted,' said Barrington with a glance towards the pressmen.

'This court stands adjourned,' his clerk added. Everyone stood with Barrington, apart from Meakin, who was wheeled out again.

Charley bent forward to pack her files into a black briefcase. Jacko strolled up behind her. Window Payne overtook him.

She turned, smiling, ignoring Payne, addressing Jacko. 'How did it go last night?'

'Nothing from either Dr Saul or the Rev Blades. A waste of hard-earned drinking time.'

'Ah, well.' Easygoing, no disappointment on her face but then, Jacko was telling himself, she'd made it to the arrest party at the Dolphin.

'What now?' she asked.

'Just had a report in that the wife of a Japanese executive from Nissan hasn't made it home to Tokyo.' Routine, really, and Jacko only mentioned it to explain why he hadn't arrived on time.

She lowered her thick, plucked eyebrows, wanted more details, was told that the missing wife been been holidaying with her hubby who was helping to commission the new car plant near Derby and was overdue on her solo return trip. 'Well worth checking on,' she said, not really enthused.

'We've added her to the list of Chinese waitresses we're still chasing up.'

She turned away and snapped her briefcase shut. 'Percy Manners wants me to see his other client with him to discuss foreshortening the proceedings.'

Cooking up some plea-bargain deal in the arson case, Jacko suspected.

Payne beamed. 'Listened to his taped confession?' She nodded. He looked towards Jacko. 'You should hear it. A real loopy. Every cough and fart. He actually gets a hard-on when he strikes a match.' He laughed briefly.

Jacko realized they were still talking about the fire-raiser, of no interest to him, added nothing. Instead: 'I might as well drop in on Mrs Meakin on my way back.'

'Why?' Charley knitted her eyebrows again. 'We've already got a full statement from her.'

'I want to chase up that loose end you mentioned in the medical report.' She still looked puzzled. 'The fire and brimstone preacher who the doctor reckons had control over Meakin's mind. She could know who he is.'

'Possible, I suppose.' Her mind still seemed to be on the arson job. Jacko understood. The case load in the Crown Prosecution Service is heavier than even the CID. 'I thought that must be Dillon Blades.'

'I've double-checked. He'd never met him before he walked into his mission and confessed. He's only been up here three weeks. Debby Dawson was dead by then.'

'My. My.' Impressed at last. 'You do work hard.' An admiring smile. 'Lunch next week perhaps?' She looked at the deflated Payne. 'A progress report . . .' An explanation of sorts, then back at a surprised Jacko, '. . . give me a ring.'

Without child Mrs Meakin would have been dumpy. In the eighth month of her pregnancy, she was almost as round as she was tall.

In happier times her chubby, homely face would have been pleasant. These days, the worst of her life, it was puffed out from too many tears, too little sleep, like a white balloon, beginning to deflate.

Simon Meakin had deserted a modest but well-kept home for his back-street bedsit hovel, thought Jacko, entering the small, spotless kitchen of a semi-detached on a fifties estate

She gave Jacko an exhausted, unwelcoming look. 'I've had nothing but interruptions.'

'We're sorry to have to bother you again,' WPC Helen Rogers apologized.

'Don't mean you.' A friendlier reception for Helen who had run her home from the station the night before and had helped her break the news of her husband's arrest to relatives and friends who needed to know. 'Bloody reporters. From all over. They just won't go away.'

'What do they want?'

'Photos. They're offering the earth.'

Always the same on any big crime story, Jacko knew. And this was big.

They came up in droves from London and Birmingham. They raced each other round town, promising to empty their wallets to any relative who would empty a family album. When the case finally came to a conclusion and they could write what they liked, all wanted to be able to boast the biggest and best dossier on Dr Death. Or maybe, in view of his job, they'd change the tag to Slaughter on Raymonds Avenue.

'Refer them to his solicitor,' Helen advised. She introduced Jacko. 'He's just come from court.'

'How is he?' Her hostility for him had gone.

'Looking rested.' Mrs Meakin looked disappointed with the truth. He added a lie. 'A bit better, I'd say.'

Sighing, she sat heavily in a straight-backed chair by a grey boiler, two chairs with wooden arms too small to take her. 'I can't understand it.' Her head went down. 'Just can't. I mean . . .' He and Helen sat in the two chairs, backs to yellow wallpaper, diamond-patterned and washable. '. . . he used to be, well, so . . . We were so happy.'

Jacko knew much about Meakin's mental breakdown from the briefing but was happy to let her run through a bit of it again. His devotion for their four-year-old daughter who'd gone off to play at a neighbour's because her mother wanted to keep to routine in the crisis. The hours of overtime he worked at the abattoir to keep up the mortgage payments. No cigarettes, whisky, women, but the occasional small flutter on a big race. His gradual withdrawal from his family about the time the present pregnancy was confirmed. How sometimes she'd found him talking to himself. His religious conversion. His walkout.

'His illness is no one's fault.' Helen was doing her social worker bit. 'You mustn't blame yourself.'

'When he's himself he's so . . . well, normal.' Her puffed-up face made her look too old for her dyed blonde hair that hung in crinkled ringlets. 'He didn't want us any more. He just wanted to go off to his prayer meetings.'

Jacko noted down the names of religious groups he'd belonged to; all for very short spells. 'One was a real freak. Ran a street mission,' she added.

He underlined his name.

'What will happen to him now?' she asked.

'He'll be examined and treated.' Jacko had got what he came for and slipped his notebook into the inside pocket of his grey suit. 'The nursing staff are hopeful of a full recovery in time.'

Mrs Meakin brightened slightly. It seemed to Jacko that she didn't mind a husband in jail for life so long as he was, well, normal. 'Will I be able to see him?'

'I'm sure you will.' Jacko put on an encouraging smile. 'I'd check with Mr Manners or the clinic first, if I were you.'

An idea struck swiftly, a good one. 'And if you do . . .' He stopped, wanting to get the wording right. He nodded at a silent portable radio on a light blue worktop. 'You'll have heard that we have charged him with only one case. That's because we don't yet know the name of the second, the oriental girl. Thus far he's given no explanation to anyone of how they met or who she is or what happened. Maybe he will tell you.'

The glare was back, shocked at being asked to inform on him.

'Believe me.' Jacko hurried on. 'We don't want you to give evidence against him. As his wife, you don't have to.'

The shock subsided into doubt. Helen took over just as quickly. 'That unknown girl is some mother's child.' She was looking at the mound that strained the elastic waistband of her black track-suit bottoms. 'We just want her family to know, that's all. We ought to trace them. They have a right to know, don't you think?'

An understanding nod; no promises made.

Jacko concluded the interview, stirred in his chair, about to get up. 'At least he's in good hands now.'

'That's what the minister said.'

Jacko sat back again, frowning. He retrieved his notebook, planning to circle a name in the list of ministers she had given him. 'Which one?'

'The one who took him to the police station.'

Dillon Blades was not on the list. 'Did you . . .' Jacko was so surprised he stumbled. '. . . yesterday . . . at the station . . . did you speak to Mr Blades there?'

'No. He came here. This morning. Left just before you arrived.'

Jacko tried not to let the shock fill his face. Why? he was asking himself. Why would Dillon Blades pay a pastoral visit here, twenty miles from his mission, to the home of someone who was not a member of his congregation, to talk to the wife of a man he claimed never to have met before? He asked Mrs Meakin a bit at a time.

No, she confirmed, she had never met Blades before and her husband had never talked of him. 'He wanted to explain he had no alternative but to do what he did. He was very anxious that I should understand. I told him it was for the best. He just came to, I suppose . . .' she was faltering, '. . . to offer a few words of comfort.'

Fair enough, thought Jacko, pocketing his book. A kind thing to do, in fact.

Or was it?

He left the question hanging, needing time and solitude to think.

Doldrum days followed. Often the case on a major inquiry, in Jacko's experience.

In fiction, detectives chase around in cars, lights flashing, tyres screaming, from dawn to dusk. In fact, they often work desk-bound office hours.

After the smell of the greasepaint, the showbiz side of the job, centre stage, in the public spotlight, comes what the spectators don't see – the breaking down of the Big Top.

The job done, apart from loose ends, Little Velma Malloy split up the team and closed down the incident room. The circus that was the Major Crime Squad departed to new venues. Only Jacko was left, cleaning up after the show.

He cursed his luck. The job was virtually over. He wanted out, his days off owing, to walk his dog, play back-garden cricket with his young son and, believe it or not, do a spot of gardening.

He'd have hated the boys and girls in the squad to know that, of course. It would have spoilt the image he had so carefully and expensively created as a hard-drinking dick. But the truth was he'd got the gardening bug, loved pottering. He was immensely proud of his night-scented stocks, the first flowers he'd ever grown from seed. And, since those lustful thoughts during that Mission to Adam service, he'd sprayed his French beans as a precaution against locusts.

The DCI and Window Payne got the task of preparing the case for Charley Chan and her Crown Prosecution Service. They went back to desks in the divisional CID office.

Jacko was given a cramped side room, usually used for photo-copying, Helen and the job of putting a name to the oriental girl.

All that happened the following week was that the hide Simon Meakin had built in the wilderness was found by a berry-picker. It was no more than a kid's den hollowed out of bramble bushes close to a footpath alongside the Derwent where it flows fast and clean.

No survivalist was Meakin, thought Jacko, surveying the ashes of a long-dead camp fire; no hunter. His meat had always been delivered to his abattoir dead and skinned, only in need of quartering. He'd caught no fish, no birds. He'd existed on tins, baked beans mainly, bought from the nearest shop whose owner hadn't recognized his ragged customer as the clean-cut freckled-faced man in the wanted photo.

Inside the hide was a mattress of straw and a haversack he'd used for a pillow, stuffed with cheaply printed leaflets on how to get to heaven with a passport stamped by prayer.

Back at the office, Jacko phoned Charley Chan. 'Just a contact call.' An opening line he often used in chat-up calls to women that always led nowhere. 'His prints were all over the cans. No feet or hand from his second victim around, though.'

'Probably still in the river somewhere.' She didn't sound too interested to hear from him. 'What about the Japanese wife?'

'Turned up at home two days late after an unscheduled stop-over in Hong Kong to buy silks. More than half our Chinese catering trade workers have been located, too.'

No response from her, still unimpressed.

'We tracked down that Jesus freak the doc reckoned was the negative influence on him.'

'Nice work.' At last, a pat on the head.

'Not really.' His languid tone. 'He's been in custody for two months, awaiting trial, for buggering his choirboys. Can't have been brainwashing Meakin from prison, can he?'

'Only in spirit.' She laughed lightly, for the first time. 'What now?'

'Well . . .' Uncertain, not having thought that far ahead. 'When we've cleared up the rest of these waitresses, a spin round the higher education colleges, I suppose.'

Another 'Oh' but interested all the same. 'Won't they be on long vac?'

'The admin staffs are back so we'll be able to get at their rolls to see if they have any missing oriental students.' She stayed silent. 'How about that lunch? Friday, perhaps, after Meakin's been up before the Stipe again?'

'Busy all day. The Thursday after looks good.'

But next Thursday, he called it off. Instead he went to Liverpool where he tracked down the last unaccounted-for waitress on his list. He told Helen he had to go personally to double-check, eyeball her for himself, but really it was to boost his mileage in what had been a bad fortnight for exes. A 180-mile round trip was never to be sniffed at.

He spent half a day in the city's Chinatown, once bustling, blighted now, below the red stone cathedral. He traced her to a crumbling terraced row with a Chinese translation on the street name plate. She wasn't much to look at; waif-like thin, slightly cross-eyed and painfully shy, not at all exotic. She'd walked out on her last job because a bullying chef had made her cry. At least she was alive with hands and feet intact.

Coming out of her spotless digs, he saw a distant white building, flag flying, rising above the rooftops at the foot of a long hill. He felt drawn towards it.

After a longish walk, in which it kept vanishing from view, he found the waterfront. He'd never been here before, knew it only from the opening credits of *Brookside*, his wife's favourite TV soap which he never watched himself, preferring to potter and smell the stocks.

Yet, it was a sentimental journey of sorts. Once his father had worked here for a short spell and he'd been told of the great ocean-going liners that landed the rich and the famous, of the trams, Green Goddesses, he'd called them, the overhead railway that ran along the river, of the teeming crowds at Paddy's Market.

But the brown Mersey river was almost empty, just a ferry and a couple of tugs. The rattling trams and trains and the market and the crowds had gone. Many of the docks and warehouses were yuppy apartments now.

The waterfront was breathtaking – stunning, white buildings reflecting the sun, leaded domes and spires, huge clocks, twin towers with their great green birds back to back. 'They flap their wings when a virgin walks by,' he'd said.

Jacko knew, just knew, that his late, still much-missed father would have stood here, and he smiled.

On the way back to his car, he dropped into a barber's. Nothing unisex about this shop, a red and white pole outside.

Last time he regularly used a place like this, in his days on the beat, the assistant would whip off the sheet, look above the mirror to a shelf groaning with Durex, then down into his eyes, wink and ask, 'Something for the weekend, sir?'

And he'd blush and say 'Please,' though the odds were always long on the packet remaining unopened. Must be hundreds, thousands, hidden away somewhere, porous by now.

Christ, he thought, you can buy them in ladies' powder rooms these days with knobs on, all the colours of the rainbow. One of the young stags in the squad reckoned his played 'While we were marching through Georgia'.

'Down to the wood, sir?' asked a chirpy young snipper. 'With a bay rum massage to follow? Keeps the flies away and drives women wild.'

Jacko chuckled. 'Just thin it round the sides.' Spectacle-less, he studied his blurred face in the mirror. 'Can't understand why it's rampant there and so thin on top.'

'Slipped halo, they call it,' said the snipper. 'Comes with age.'

Slipped halo, Jacko repeated to himself, thinking again of the girl in red at Dill Blades' roof-raising service, ashamed of those lustful thoughts at his great age, wondering anxiously if he'd become a dirty old man since he last sat in a place like this. He'd decided against a bay rum massage, not sure who'd be the more thankful – women or flies.

Driving back over moorlands, purple and peaceful, failed to lift his deep depression.

9

'What the hell are you lot playing at?' An angry Percy Manners was on the phone on a very flat Friday.

'And what the hell are you talking about?' Jacko was still depressed, not about to take any crap from anyone, least of all Manners, the kind of lawyer he didn't like.

'Barry Carter.' The name meant nothing and Jacko said so. 'A client of mine, the arsonist up at Tor View,' Manners added.

'Not my case,' Jacko answered, promptly. 'He's a divisional job. You need the DCI. I'll transfer you.'

He was always quick to pass the buck when a weekend off loomed. He dialled an internal number. A cadet told him both the DCI and Sergeant Payne were up at Tor View. He passed on the information to Manners.

'What's going on?' he demanded.

'Don't ask me. I was away all yesterday.'

In a complaining tone, Manners told of a phone call he'd received from Tor View Clinic's Chief Nurse O'Brien who'd informed him that Barry Carter was dispensing with his services.

Got it now, thought Jacko. A fat legal aid fee out of the window.

'Something about a conflict of interest,' Manners grumbled on. 'What conflict?'

'Search me.'

'Is it to do with my other client up there, Meakin?'

'I honestly don't know.' Jacko changed the subject to something that did concern him. 'How is he, by the way?'

'Much better. Back on his own two feet in court this morning after a fortnight looking like a zombie.'

Jacko chanced an arm. 'Will we be able to see him soon about this second girl?'

'You can apply for twenty-four hours with him at the next hearing if you want to.' Manners wasn't exactly volunteering his client for questioning without a court order, but made it sound as if he wasn't objecting, either. 'Is this to do with Meakin?'

'What?'

'Barry Carter sacking me?'

'Why should it be?'

'It's just that after court this morning Carter told me he wanted to see the prosecuting authority. I'd been advising him to cough to more fires. The more, the better his chance of a hospital order instead of prison. I informed the CPS.'

'What did he want with us?'

'I don't know. I was busy talking to Meakin. It's the first time he's begun to make any sort of sense since you arrested him.'

No point in asking what Meakin said, Jacko decided. Defence lawyers tell you nothing.

'Off the record and subject to what counsel say,' Manners went on, 'he'll be putting his hands up to the Debby Dawson case. We'll go for diminished responsibility.'

Jacko could hardly believe what he was hearing and decided to chance both arms. 'What about the other girl?'

'Haven't got round to taking his instructions on that yet. I'll let you know when you see him next week.'

'Thanks a lot.' Jacko hoped he sounded more grateful than surprised. He was both.

'I've always played ball with you . . .' Manners was hardly sounding like a lawyer who deliberately stretched out cases to boost his fee from the taxpayer. '. . . and look what happens.'

Jacko wasn't exactly sure what had happened and said so.

'I think Carter's fixing up a private deal,' said Manners, unhappily.

'I thought the plea-bargaining was already done,' Jacko replied.

'That was before I got his medical report. Carter's dangerous.

The only safe place for him is a secure hospital, and for a long time, too.'

Jacko promised to leave a note for the DCI to ring him. He put down the phone, staring at it for a long time. Why's Manners telling me all of this? What's going on that I don't know?

Without a knock Window Payne burst into the claustrophobic side room, waving a witness statement form. 'Dobbed him,' he said, triumphantly.

His tubby inspector, more circumspect, followed. He was holding the message Jacko had left on his desk.

'He's really dobbed him in it,' Payne repeated, barely able to contain himself.

Dob was a new in-word in the East Midlands Combined Constabulary. Like all new in-words, it was being overworked to tedium. Jacko preferred the older version. 'Who's shopped who?'

'Carter's dobbed Meakin.' Payne placed the statement on the small desk, hiding it under outstretched fingers, beaming proudly. After a teasing, self-satisfied second or so, he lifted his palm. Jacko started to read.

Name: Barry Carter. Aged 19. Current address: c/o Tor View Clinic, Matlock Bath.

I am here awaiting trial on arson charges and undergoing medical examination.

A man I have never seen or met before was admitted to the next room to mine in the secure unit two weeks ago. For several days he never talked and slept most of the time. Gradually he stayed awake longer and opened up a bit.

'What's Manners want?' The inspector spoke, still standing. Jacko ignored him, head down, concentrating, reading on, already knowing what was coming.

Just to pass the time we started chatting through the bars about our families and hobbies and so on. On two occasions both of us appeared before court in the clinic's day room to be remanded. We were not in court at the same time so we didn't know about each other's cases.

71

Yesterday we got talking and, to the best of my recollection, the conversation went like this:

Me: What are you in for, mate?
Him: Murder.
Me: Oh Jesus. That's bad news.
Him: Don't take the Lord's name in vain.
Me: Sorry, mate. No offence.
Him: It was the Lord's work.
Me: What was?
Him: Those two women.
Me: Two? Blimey.
Him: They were harlots.
Me: What?
Him: Prostitutes.
Me: What did you do to them?
Him: Stoned them and put them to death.

He went all strange, spouting odd bits out of the Bible and I changed the subject because, to be honest, I was a bit scared of him.

I couldn't sleep last night, for worry, wondering what to do for the best. This morning I asked to see Chief Nurse O'Brien and I told him what had been said. I agreed with him and Dr Saul that it was my duty to repeat the conversation to the prosecuting authorities.

The statement concluded with the usual pre-emptive denials that he was helping the authorities in return for a lighter sentence.

'What yer think?' Payne stood by his desk, preening like a peacock, the clever boy at school waiting for his homework to be marked A+.

Jacko bought a bit of time, looking up at the inspector to answer his question. 'I think Manners wants to talk to you about this.' He picked up the statement, holding it closer to his face, pretending to read it again.

What do I think? Well, first of all, I don't like remand cell confessions to fellow prisoners. Too many of them turn out to be complete fabrications. Not necessarily as part of any freedom

72

agreement, but the hope has to be for a cushier life inside and an early release.

Sometimes remand-wing grasses manufacture such statements to even a score; sometimes to wangle a day out at court and take centre stage. Too many dobbers like Carter are raving nutters whose testimony isn't worth the paper wasted on it.

And another thing. No country bumpkin like Carter would use a phrase like 'prosecuting authorities'. He'd say the law, the cops, the fuzz, the filth. It has all the hallmarks of being coached.

'Good,' he lied. He tossed the statement back on the desk.

'Good?' Payne looked as though he'd been given a C-. 'It's terrific. Meakin has now admitted Dawson's death to both your preacher man and Carter and the second girl to Carter. We've got him, signed and sealed.'

'Did he give any hint who the second girl might be?' A silly question, regretted immediately.

Payne's face set hard. 'If he had, it would have been in the sodding statement.'

His inspector came in, a softer touch. 'We didn't push for detail. He might have clammed up. We've also got a statement from Chief Nurse O'Brien on what Carter told him. Word for word with what's in there.' A single nod towards the statement. 'Not bad, though, is it?'

Jacko nodded with noticeably more enthusiasm. 'We'll be able to confront Meakin with it personally next week. Manners reckons he'll be fit enough to see us then.'

'Carter's got to be genuine,' said the inspector. 'The stoning explains the oriental woman's stoved-in face.'

True, Jacko acknowledged. The extent of her facial injuries had never been made public.

'With the lab saying both bodies were cut up using the same technique we've enough to charge him with the second count,' the inspector went on.

'Got her ID-ed yet?' asked Payne, a touch scornfully.

Jacko didn't reply. Instead, looking at the inspector: 'Manners is annoyed over being dumped by Barry Carter. What's all that about?'

Payne answered. 'Carter knows that Manners is Meakin's mouthpiece, too. He's worried about his interests probably being in conflict. A brief can hardly have one client on his books stitching up another, can he?'

'No,' said Jacko slowly, thinking: Conflict of interests is another phrase. Sounded fine coming from Manners, part of his legal vocabulary; odd on the lips of a country bumpkin.

What do I think? he was asking himself.

He didn't know what to think.

Thinking time now.

At the end of his seventies estate (smart compared to the back street where he'd been born), by a single-storey primary school (modern by the standard of his old school), Jacko turned off his smile for neighbours working in their front gardens.

He slipped the choke chain over his dog's head and Lucy trotted away from him down a fenced footpath. Letting her loose seemed to set free his mind.

Strange thing, the mind, isn't it? he pondered.

People in jobs like Meakin's (or mine, for that matter) see slaughterhouses full of hearts and brains, but never minds. Impossible to put a shape or size to. They are what you want to make of them.

He saw his own as a large expanse of water. A mill pond when he was calm. An arctic sea when he was anxious. The surface this sunny Saturday afternoon was only slightly ruffled.

Thoughts and ideas would pop up from deep within him and float on that ever-changing surface. Some would sink, almost immediately, without trace. Others would stay afloat, bobbing along, demanding the attention of his mind's eye.

He sorted out lots of things that troubled him on walks with Lucy, a black and tan mongrel, twelve now, a bit too tubby, but dark eyes still alert and full of love for him, stump of a tail wagging as she nosed the bottom of the hedgerow behind the school. Seeking a scent, he thought; like me.

Until this summer his son had come with them on these weekend walks, across the fields; today to the next village to watch the cricket match, a local derby game.

Mark was a big boy now – six – with a friend of his own, a neighbour's daughter, aged seven. Inseparable, they were.

Soon, Jacko knew from experience, they'd drift apart, be sucked into gangs of their own sex. Not until he was a teenager would Mark look at another girl. Not with eyes of friendship then. With lust. It would take him years to discover, as it had his

74

father, that a woman can be a man's greatest friend. If only he could control the lust. The bane of friendships between woman and man is lust.

At first, he'd missed having his son at his side. 'What's that bird/flower/plane called, dad?' Easy to answer, normally. If not, he never made it up. They'd looked it up together when they got home.

Just lately his friend had started taking him to the Sunday school at the local United Reformed Church which her parents attended. 'Is Jesus black or white, dad?'

'Well, he lived in the Middle East where east meets west so a bit of both, I suppose.'

Jacko believed there was a Jesus all right, a carpenter's son, not God's. He accepted that it was medically possible for Mary to have been a virgin, because he'd read in a defended divorce case of a mother whose hymen remained intact. That was evidence. He liked evidence.

'What will my grandads be doing in heaven today?' Mark had asked.

Harder to answer when you don't believe in heaven so he fudged it. (He'd forgotten now how.) In a tight corner he was inclined to fudge. Besides, Mark would eventually make up his own mind, as his father had.

He climbed over a stile into a field from which the barley had been gathered, stubble waiting to be ploughed in. A footpath beside a roughly pruned hawthorn hedge dropped steeply away. From the hilltop he could see the squat tower of a church which overlooked the small crossroads village where he was heading.

Today he was rather pleased his chatterbox son wasn't with him. He'd gone with his friend's family to the church's summer fair. Mrs Jackie Jackson had gone with them.

A puzzle sometimes, his wife. She had no more religion than him but was moved, uplifted even, by the likes of Martin Luther King and Mother Theresa, so she financially supported any church that asked. She saw them as among the final bastions of caring in an uncaring world. 'And, if worship gives people a sense of purpose in life, who are we to knock it?' she said in one debate that lacked its usual heat because it lacked disagreement.

Over a salad lunch, she'd said, 'I suppose you're going to the cricket.' Jackie supposed right, hadn't even bothered to invite him to join them at the summer fair.

Down the hill now, not picking up speed, no longer seeing the church tower or the folds in the fields. A vast expanse of ruffled water stretched out before him. Thinking time now.

A variation of the question that had lain just below the surface for more than a fortnight popped up. What possible connection can the deranged killer of a prostitute have with an oriental virgin?

He could see the link that led Debby Dawson to her death, was one hundred and one per cent sure they'd convict Meakin for it.

But a virgin? Could a virgin be into vice?

Yes, as a matter of fact, she could. Some got up to anything and everything short of full sex; things that made his eyes water just to think about. Charley Chan had been right about that. Sex games are a burgeoning business. Not much romance in them, though; no hugging and holding and kissing.

So, yes, you can be a prostitute and still be a virgin, especially in these Aids-infected days. It was improbable, but it was possible.

But how could they have met? She wasn't a street girl. He didn't have a phone to call her up and out to his place. He didn't drink and couldn't have picked her up in a bar.

Why keep her feet? Difficult to answer. Why keep one hand? Easier. To prevent identity because it was deformed or had a ring on that couldn't be removed there and then. But, surely, Meakin was too sick to think that logically.

Sick. That's what really troubled him, haunted him. Meakin is sick.

Six years before he had locked away a mentally ill young man for a murder he hadn't committed. While he rotted in the State Special, the real murderer killed three more times. A cock-up he'd uncocked in the end, but those three lives weighed on his conscience so heavily that he'd been sick, off work and physically ill, with remorse.

Never again, he'd promised himself. These days he was cautious to the point of nervousness. He knew some younger officers like Window Payne regarded him as a bumbling old fart; didn't matter. He wouldn't be rushed. Never again.

76

Over a wooden bridge across an empty dyke into the next field, Lucy still leading.

The only real proof against Meakin on the oriental girl was Barry Carter's statement. Had Window Payne taken it alone he'd have treated it as suspect. He regarded Payne as flash, a chancer, out to impress people, Charley Chan among them. But the DCI had been at the interview, and he was an honest operator. Yet it had the signs of coaching. Who'd coach him? Why?

OK. There's evidence that Meakin cut up both bodies but that, in itself, doesn't mean he killed both. What can it mean? Let's see.

Take me. Happily married, a good job. I've got a bit on the side, an exotic, thoroughly dirty young lady from the east, who does everything my wife won't. Don't dwell on the details. A private smile, sly.

All turns nasty. Demands for money. Threats of exposure. End of marriage, end of job looms. I have to get rid of her.

Enter Meakin. He comes out of the trance in which he's living, knows he's killed in ghastly circumstances. Who would he turn to? Someone he knows. Someone who's helped him before. Who? Who coached Carter into dobbing Meakin in it? Why?

He turned off his thoughts as he climbed a grass embankment to a little-used railway line, a short cut to the cricket field.

Who? Somebody who wanted rid of the oriental girl. Meakin came up to that somebody and said: 'I need your help. I've killed a prostitute from Derby.'

'You help me and I'll help you.'

'How?'

'Help me to get rid of this other girl.'

A perfect murder. Meakin, in his state, made no sense to anyone. Carter's statement made sure he carried the can for both victims.

Who is this Bad Samaritan? Someone with access to both Meakin and Carter.

Dillon Blades? Odd the way he'd popped in on Mrs Meakin. Was that caring? Or conscience? Coincidence, isn't it, that the victim's oriental and so is his wife? Or is it?

He walked several yards, nothing coming. Soon: But he didn't know Meakin then, let alone Carter. Can't be Blades.

Who did both Meakin and Carter know?

Window Payne. He's questioned them both.

77

Manners. He's defended them both.

Dr Saul and Chief Nurse O'Brien were treating them both.

Both Meakin and Carter appeared before Barrington, the Stipe, who lives down the hill from Tor View and has a taste for coloured women.

Barrington? Barrington! Come on now. You've become a conspiracy theorist, the sort you've loathed for making an industry and a mint out of President Kennedy, Elvis Presley and Marilyn Monroe's deaths.

He scrambled down the bank into the cricket field. Forget it. Enjoy your weekend off. Besides, you'll be talking to Meakin next week. Sort it out then. You think too much.

He watched until just before teatime, his mind mill-pond calm. In ten years' time, he hoped, he'd be watching his own son. He wondered if he'd be a spin bowler like Dill Blades.

'Cup game tomorrow,' said a bearded neighbour who'd had a long lunch in the crossroads pub and had slept through twenty overs. 'Coming?'

'Might.'

What else was there to do on a Sunday? Church? Gardening?

In these last two weeks, ever since he'd been to that service where he'd eyed that shapely girl in red, he'd noticed that the white flowers on his beans had started to drop off before they set. Despite the spraying, the crop would be poor.

Anxiously, a storm blowing up in his mind, he began to wonder why. You don't think, do you, I've really got something like locusts?

Don't think, he snapped to himself, and he calmed himself, concentrating on the cricket.

10

A three-quarter moon hung in a light blue sky directly overhead. The grass was silvered with dew.

No church, no cricket, no gardening now, thought Jacko, gripping the steering wheel, mind buffeted on an arctic storm.

No heavy wagons from John Player, Raleigh, Boots or anywhere else on the almost deserted M1 had slowed his progress.

No local, even national, news was yet on the radio. You know you're in the wrong job when you've been dragged out of bed and have to listen to the World Service, too early even for the fucking farming programme, he decided, switching off.

Mist snaked through the valleys ahead but his eyes failed to find smoke on top of the Heights of Abraham where Control had told him the fire had been.

The cable cars hung still over the empty prom and the greeny-blue river. He turned off at the mission and drove over the pot-holes up the corkscrew hill.

No roast, Yorkshire pud and two veg this Sunday, he was telling himself.

Roasted Carter, though. Down to the size of a blackened log, too full of sap to be completely consumed by the flames.

Not the appetizing smell from a barbecue; more the stench of a garden bonfire on which an old rubber tyre had been thrown.

In the water-logged remains of what had been the secure unit at Tor View Clinic, it seemed to coat his tongue and throat. He knew it would stay there all day, along with a leaden stomach and an aching heart; not a sickness, a wrenched-gut feeling for something going badly wrong; not knowing what, helpless, unable to do anything about it.

In the room next to Carter's, roofless now, with wet, soot-streaked walls of black and grey, a still, naked Meakin was on his bed. He was the colour of smoked haddock, just recognizable.

'This is the seat of the fire,' said a boiler-suited specialist from the fire brigade standing in what had been Carter's room.

'He was in for arson,' said Jacko, very quietly. 'How did he start it?'

The specialist looked down at the soggy debris around Jacko's green wellington boots. 'Give us a break.' He looked up, smiling. 'We'll find it.'

'How about the poor sod next door?' He yanked his head towards Meakin who lay on his side being videoed by a scenes-of-crime cameraman.

'Looks like smoke inhalation. Probably died in his sleep.'

'Hope so,' said Jacko, grimly. And he hoped, too, that his God had stamped his passport to admit him to his heaven.

He turned away, slowly, careful where he put his feet. He'd been among the last to arrive, near the end of a chain of calls from the night orderly to the emergency services, to the CID and Chief Superintendent Malloy.

She was back in charge, wearing a buttercup bright twin set, sitting at a picnic table, surrounded by a group which included the divisional DCI, Window Payne, Helen Rogers and Barrington.

The Stipe looked out of place among police officers in plain-clothes, their Sunday bests today, everyone in suits. He had dressed hurriedly in dark grey creased flannels, darker grey sweat shirt, blue canvas yachting pumps; no socks.

Jacko stepped over fawn canvas-clad fire hoses to reach them. Little Velma was handing out the jobs. She'd stay, she was saying, to supervise the scenes team and take statements from staff.

The DCI and his sergeant would break the news to Carter's parents. She looked at Jacko. 'You and Helen know Mrs Meakin. Perhaps you ought to tell her.' She seldom made any assignment she gave him sound like an order.

He nodded and walked towards his car which he'd left some way down the corkscrew hill, beyond Barrington's house. He glimpsed the sun rising just above the tree line, felt cold in his blue lightweight suit. Morning has broken, he thought. It was odd, eerie almost, how tunes from his childhood kept coming back to him these days on this job.

God, he wished he was back there. Life was so simple then; no responsibilities. He was responsible, was sure of it. You promised yourself it would never happen again and it has.

You knew something was wrong, all the time; knew and did nothing about it. You didn't even discuss it with anyone. But how could I? Who'd have listened to such far-fetched specu-lation?

He looked back over his shoulder to the table where Little Velma still sat, listening to everyone around her.

He saw that Helen was following. He stopped, waiting for her, and saw that Barrington was getting up too. Some of the officers stood at the wooden table, as if he was leaving court.

'Awful business,' Barrington said when he caught up.

Jacko nodded. 'What roused you?'

'The fire bells.' He glanced towards the three red engines on the car-park with hoses running from them across the grass plateau. 'Flames were shooting out the roof when they got here. Nothing anyone could do. Our first fatalities.'

Our? Jacko asked himself. Then, quickly, 'You connected with the clinic then?'

'One of the trustees.' A few steps in silence. 'Any idea how it started?'

'Barry Carter playing with matches is my guess.' A flip answer, unthinking.

A shocked look. 'Surely not. Dr Saul and his staff would never allow that.'

Jacko wore a regretful face. 'They'll soon find out.'

'Such a tragedy.'

'Specially for Meakin. He was getting better, I gather.'

'Nice sort of chap, so they say, when he was . . . well . . . well.'

'So they say,' Jacko repeated, playing for time, asking himself: How would he know? Then find out, he ordered himself. He gave him a side-on look, very questioning.

'He did a spot of gardening for us,' Barrington explained.

'When?'

'When he was first here. On bail after that stone-throwing business.' Barrington looked anxious. 'Before the murders, of course. He wasn't in the secure unit then. He was on bail.'

He'd repeated it, Jacko suspected, to make sure he and Helen had got it. What Jacko had also got was this: No JP should ever adjudicate in a case where he knows the defendant, especially an employee. That was a real conflict of interests. 'How did that come about?' He tried to display only passing interest.

'Dr Saul encourages voluntary patients to do a bit of casual work in the community. The garden's getting a bit too much for us these days. My chap . . . you've met him, of course . . .' Jacko nodded. '. . . engaged him.'

'Did you get to know him?' Still casual, he didn't add: 'personally'.

'Only saw him from the window. Didn't recognize him swaddled in his wheelchair in court or I'd have disqualified myself from sitting.'

Jacko nodded again, briskly this time, trying to make it look as though he was satisfied, thinking: I'm going to have to check him out very carefully.

'They help with the heavy stuff, the logging and so . . .' A thought slowed, almost stopped, Barrington in his step. 'Did Meakin smoke?'

'No.'

A look of total relief.

'Why?' asked Jacko.

'He built a bonfire for us. Just occurred to me that if he was a smoker he might have been the source of Carter's matches.'

'His wife said he didn't.'

'Good.' Pause. 'Just an awful thought.' Barrington turned off at his driveway. 'Goodbye, then.'

'Bye,' said Jacko absently, deep in awful thoughts.

Mrs Meakin was at the window of her semi-detached when they drew up at the kerbside, and had the front door open before they were out of his car.

Her face reminded Jacko of one of those glass balls you shake to start a snow storm – round, white, all confusion. It told him she had already heard the local radio news which they had listened to on the way down the A6, reporting two deaths in the clinic fire. No names, no mention of the secure unit; but she knew. Her face told him she knew.

'It's not . . . oh . . . Please tell me . . .' She shut her watering eyes. 'It's not . . . I can't believe . . .' She swayed on the doorstep.

Helen sprinted forward, surprisingly quickly and lightly for such a heavy woman. She put an arm around her huge waist, turning her, gently pushing her back indoors. 'Oh, no . . .' Into a lounge, as spotless as the kitchen. 'Please . . .' Guiding her to a deep armchair. 'It can't be . . . He was doing so . . .'

Kneeling before her, Helen took Mrs Meakin's hands from the mound that was her stomach, squeezing them. 'I'm sorry, love. I'm so, so sorry.'

Jacko walked into the kitchen, to put on the kettle, hearing her sobs above the water coming to the boil. He took his time, letting the tea brew, almost stew.

He returned with three mugs, one heavily sugared which he handed to Mrs Meakin. 'Someone looking after your daughter?'

She answered a question that hadn't been asked. 'I was going to see him again this afternoon.'

Again, thought Jacko, sitting on a green couch, sipping, letting his original question go, taking his time.

Two mugs for everyone, two cigarettes for Jacko, before the tears were stemmed.

Did he suffer? she wanted to know. Died in his sleep, said Helen. Was it his fault? He was an innocent victim.

She sniffed. 'He was making such good progress.'

'When did you see him?' Jacko began probing gently, not wanting to be the midwife at the premature birth of a child about to be born into a family that overnight had become one-parent.

'Yesterday.' A bleak smile. 'I took your advice. Got the bus up. The clinic said it would do him good to see me. He looked so much better.' Head down. 'He was talking some sense. At last. At times.' She knitted her fingers. 'Not all the time. Most of the time.'

More tears. 'He was very upset about what he'd done.' Sniffing. 'Voices told him to do it, he said. That woman from Normanton, I mean.'

Debby Dawson, she means, Jacko knew.

She looked up, directly at him. 'I asked him what you asked me. He said he didn't know the other woman. He only ever saw her when she was dead. He swore he didn't kill her; swore it.'

I think I believe that, thought Jacko, suddenly sweltering in his blue lightweight suit. Then, very quietly, 'Did he say who did?'

Head down again, shaking. 'I didn't ask. He was going to tell his solicitor ...' Head up, a lost expression. 'What day is it? Tomorrow. He was going to see Mr Manners again tomorrow.'

'Did he say anything else about the other girl?'

No response.

'Anything would help.'

Nothing.

Helen fell back on an old line. 'We have to find out her name so we can inform her family.'

A deep sigh. 'He admitted he, well, you know, di ... di ...'

'Dissecting her?'

A single nod.

'Where?'

'At his bedside.' She shook her head as if to reprimand her wayward tongue. 'Sorry, bedsit.'

'Why?'

'Wouldn't say. Said it was dangerous for me to know.'

'Who asked him to do it? Did he say?'

'Sorry.' Her head came up suddenly. 'He was very frightened. Are you sure it was an accident?'

No, dear, Jacko replied privately. 'We think the man in the next

83

room started it. He was an arsonist.' But who gave him the matches? he was asking himself. 'We'll double-check. Did he explain . . .?' Jacko dried up, began again. 'I'm sorry to ask you this but Simon . . . with the experience of his job, would understand, I think . . . er . . . You see, we can't find the other girl's feet or right hand. Did he happen to explain . . .?'

'Only her feet.' She shuddered, involuntarily.

'What did he say about that?'

'I couldn't understand it.'

'Just tell us in his words.'

'He didn't make sense all the time. He harped on a bit now and then. About the Bible, you know.'

'Try to recall his exact words.' Jacko tried to keep desperation out of his voice.

No response.

'It might help us find her family,' Helen harped on.

'He said it was all to do with the Feast of the Passover.'

Mushroom omelettes for dinner that night, by special request. 'No roasted joint and certainly no barbecue,' Jacko had told his wife Jackie on the phone from the incident room.

An extra place was laid for Velma Malloy, who lived a couple of villages away. She had never been invited round before and had never met Jackie.

No one was very hungry or, to start with, very talkative. Jackie did most of it over the cheap white wine. Small talk like: 'How are you settling down after your move from London? Enjoying it?'

Slowly, Velma began to relax and open up, confirming much of what was already on the HQ grapevine about her, adding lots of new personal detail.

She had a son of her own, twenty, at university, the product of a marriage that came soon after her own university days; a marriage to a fellow officer that had finally failed. She didn't say just when, how or why, but Jacko guessed fighting her way to the top in the macho world of the police service must have put an unbearable strain on any marriage. Any marriage, he corrected himself, where the woman has the ambition.

She loved her own little cottage, had a pensioner who looked after the garden, but did her own housework, including piles of ironing when her son was home for a weekend, she said, rather proudly.

Her social life seemed non-existent – late home, supper for one if she hadn't eaten in the mess, a bit of TV or reading to background music, free weekends catching up with the chores.

'Don't the boys ask you out for a drink?' asked Jackie, wearing a look, part sad, part shocked, which she managed not to direct towards her husband who knew the bollocking would come anyway when they were alone.

'Occasionally.' An understanding smile. 'It's difficult for them, I suppose.'

It's difficult, Jacko was thinking, because if you go drinking with a superior officer you're regarded as a creep, and, if that superior is a woman, you're accused of giving her one, bucking for promotion.

Look at that accident-prone M1 patrolman who got close to a woman traffic inspector called Baddiley. Another constable passed on the gossip to his sergeant. 'Have you heard he's fucking Baddiley?'

'He's not driving very well, either,' said the sergeant.

He decided not to share the story. He changed from an uncomfortable subject to the topic he'd brought his boss into the privacy of his home to discuss.

He began by decanting his thoughts from yesterday's walk and the account of his talk with Mrs Meakin which he had not yet put in writing. 'Helen's still minding her. Both are under strict instructions to say nothing to nobody.'

Velma did not mock him as a conspiracy theorist. Instead: 'Let me understand you. You are saying that someone else killed the Far Eastern girl and asked Meakin to chop her up. Right?'

Jacko nodded.

'Hmmmm,' hmmmmed Velma.

They moved with their coffees from a lace-covered table in front of partially opened patio windows which looked down on a sizeable, reasonably well-tended garden.

The fragrance of night-scented stocks was left behind as they sat side by side on a couch, deep and comfortable with golden fabric. Jacko took a cigarette and a light from Velma, who smoked almost as many as he did.

Jackie went upstairs to fetch the Hamlyn Children's Bible, a present to their son from Jacko's mum who believed in believing in a vague sort of way.

She found the place for them, handed it over. They passed it from knee to knee. 'A lamb was sacrificed for the Last Supper,' said Jacko, feeling slightly silly at the end of a quick read-through.

Velma read more slowly. 'There was a lot of washing of feet, wasn't there?' Pause. 'Foot fetish.' An uncertain shrug. 'If that was your girl's speciality, it would explain why she was a virgin.'

'Mmmm,' said Jacko, in need of thinking time.

He only had one foot fetish story in his store of happy tales. This he did decide to share.

This kerb-crawler, see, winds down the window and says to the street girl: 'How much?'

'Twenty.'

'Double if you do it my way.'

'Piss off, pervo.'

'Won't hurt a bit. Promise,' he pleads.

Well, it had been a wet, slow night, so she hops in and off they go to his place. They strip. She lies on the bed. He stands on the bed. He dibbles in his big toe. Both dress. He gives her forty, plus a tenner for a taxi. That should have been that.

A few days later he hobbles into his GP's surgery. 'I've got this terrible pain in my foot.' He takes off his shoe and sock.

'I'm sorry to have to tell you,' said the doctor gravely, after a brief examination, 'that you've got VD of the big toe.'

'Impossible,' he protests.

'Nothing is impossible in this job,' said the doctor firmly. 'Why, I've just had a woman in here with athlete's fanny.'

Velma laughed politely; Jackie, who had a dirty mind, joyfully.

She was ten years younger than her husband, strikingly handsome (rather than beautiful) with glossy, wavy chestnut hair and a fabulous figure. Annoyingly, despite the money she spent on clothes, she was a casual dresser. Nearly always she wore loose tops; tonight a yellow blouse which hid that figure. He'd discovered, though, that when she laughed her big bosom visibly wobbled, no matter how loose the top. He told her lots of jokes.

He adored her, had never strayed in six years of marriage.

Marriage, however, didn't stop him forming affectionate relationships with women workmates and really fancying one or two. Nothing wrong with fancying, he told himself. Acting on that fancy (and, in one isolated case, fantasy) would be fatal, disaster for everybody, but the moment he stopped fancying was the moment he was ready for the knacker's yard.

He was safe with Velma, though, even if she was quite fanciable with her ice blue eyes, kissable lips and her tight little bum.

'Let's list the possibles,' said Velma, still smiling, not wanting to pull rank but wanting to get back to work.

He began his list in reverse order, like a beauty queen judge.

He started with Dr Saul but added that he was going off him. 'He'd hardly get Carter to set the place on fire, would he? He'd just zap Meakin with drugs.'

'I think we can rule him out,' Velma concurred, 'but not his chief nurse. We found a lighter in what was left of Carter's room. Just a cheapo throwaway. O'Brien reports one of his own missing from the top of his filing cabinet where he keeps them.'

'Saw them there myself,' said Jacko. 'Could have been pinched, I suppose.'

Velma hesitated, then made up her mind. 'Leave him to me. I've got to go up there again tomorrow. I'll suss him out. Who else?'

'Percy Manners,' Jacko went on, 'but only because Meakin had a down on lawyers and classed them with publicans and tax collectors from the Bible.'

'I've fixed to see him, too.'

He dwelt on Dillon Blades for some little time, more or less trying to convince himself, then eliminated him because he hadn't known Meakin long enough and had had no contact with Carter at all.

Velma's face became impatient, and he guessed she had rumbled his technique of keeping the best till last. 'Who else? Who's top of your list?'

'Not necessarily top of the list, but Sergeant Payne. He quizzed them both.'

'What motive?'

'Dunno. Maybe Carter, not Meakin, was the target. Maybe there's something dodgy about his arson confessions.'

Velma fell silent again, taking it in. 'It would give the game away to take him off the inquiry.' She paused. 'So I'll keep him on it but in the dark. Right?' Jacko nodded. Then, quite sharply, 'Who is top of the list?'

He gathered himself for his bombshell. 'Barrington.'

'Why?' Velma's face didn't flicker in shock or rejection and he supposed she'd knocked off bigger legal eagles than a Stipe in her days at Scotland Yard.

He listed his reasons with his fingers. 'His secret taste for coloured women. His access to the clinic – and, therefore, Carter – as a trustee. His previous contact with Meakin who'd worked in his garden. The fact that Meakin told the Rev. Dill Blades: "It was an act of worship" and everyone in court calls him Your Worship.'

Finally, Jacko shrugged. 'Maybe he's our foot fetish man.'

Velma didn't even debate it. Instead, a definite order. 'He's down to you then.'

'But how?' An appealing face.

Jackie, silent for a long time, had the answer. 'Use that sleight of hand you're always droning on about.'

11

'Sorry to bother you, doc, when you're busy.' Jacko had been hammering the phone all morning, a game plan in place. 'But can I pick your brains for a mo?'

'About what?' Dr Saul sounded distant, somewhat harassed, no longer apologetic.

'Well, what's a fetish?'

'You must be well aware . . .' Measured words, on a short fuse. '. . . that I've lost two patients and had my secure unit gutted. This is hardly a convenient time. I've got your colleagues here. The insurance. The fire investigation officers . . .'

'They'll tell you how it started,' said Jacko breezily, 'but they won't tell you why.'

'And you can?'

'Given time.' Pause. 'With your help.' Silence. 'Come on, doc. Five minutes.'

A deep sigh. 'Well, it's obvious, isn't it, so I'm not breaking any confidences, in telling you that Carter had a fetish for starting fires.'

'I've got your report on him in front of me.' Charley Chan had hand-delivered it, by request, on her way to court.

It was in the doctor's usual style, short, snappy and scruffy. His eyes went to sections he had already highlighted in yellow.

HISTORY: Local-born, council care, learning difficulties. Fire-raising from 13 as a source of sexual stimulus.

NEGATIVE INFLUENCE: A scoutmaster, subsequently convicted, involved in group masturbation. (Their bare bums got gypsy burns when they were tossing each other off by the camp fire, Jacko suspected, a diagnosis more cynical than clinical.)

COMPLAINT: Fire fetish, deep-seated.

DIAGNOSIS: Psychopathic personality disorder.

RECOMMENDATION: Aversion therapy under long-term secure conditions.

Jacko's eyes moved sideways to an opened dictionary from which he'd read: 'Fetishism – Abnormal condition in which erotic feelings are excited by a non-sexual object, as a foot, a glove, etc.'

'Exactly.' Dr Saul still sounded unhelpful.

'In Carter's case, I take it . . .'

'I'm not prepared to discuss individual cases.'

'He is dead.'

'Even so.'

Jacko gambled. 'When we first met and I wanted an advance peep at Simon Meakin's report, remember?' Saul grunted, but not curtly. 'I was wrong to ask and you were right to refuse me. I thought we'd kissed and made up last time I was there. I know from that experience that you guard confidences with your life . . .'

'Thank you.' A lower tone, much more receptive.

'. . . so I'm going to share a confidence with you. Someone, we think, wanted Meakin dead and gave Carter that lighter . . .'

'I hope no one thinks that someone was my chief nurse.' The hostility was back. Jacko said nothing. 'Is that why your chief superintendent has taken him away for questioning?'

'She needs to know all there is to know about that lighter.'

'He buys them every time he goes to market. By the handful. Four for a pound. He's always losing them.'

'His white one is missing.'

'I went through all of this with him and your Sergeant Payne last night. He hasn't seen it since Friday.'

The day both Carter and Meakin appeared before Barrington, the Stipe, at his special court session in the day room, Jacko realized. 'He told you that?'

'And I believe him. I trust him implicitly.'

'So do I,' said Jacko soothingly. 'Believe me, my chief's questioning will be routine. Honestly.'

'Mmmmmm.' Finally, he seemed reassured.

Jacko pressed on quickly. 'I wasn't in court that day. What happened after Mr Barrington adjourned?'

'Meakin went back to his room for a consultation with Mr Manners, his solicitor. Carter was put in the waiting-room. The layout of our secure unit being what it is ... was ... meant conversations could be overheard in the next room and Mr Manners understandably wanted to keep the consultation private.'

'Who stayed with Carter in the waiting-room?'

'Not Chief Nurse O'Brien, if that's what you're driving at. He was on a day off.'

'Who then?'

'That other inspector. And eventually Miss Chan from the CPS joined him.'

'Why?'

'As I understand it, Carter wanted to own up to further arson offences in addition to the three he'd been charged with. Surely, your colleagues have told you all of this?'

'And Mr Manners never entered the waiting-room that day?'

'Definitely not. He saw Carter in the day room before court and Meakin in the secure unit after court.'

'Was Sergeant Payne present for the taking of the TICs?'

A pause. 'Never saw him all morning, come to think of it.'

'Anyone else use the waiting-room?'

'Lots of people. They have to walk through it to reach my office. You know that.'

'I mean, immediately before or after the special court.'

'Only Mr Barrington. He often pops in. Just lately especially.'

Jacko held his breath for a second. 'He's a trustee as well as a neighbour, isn't he?'

'Yes, but it was just a social call. For morning coffee. He's been off duty with a bout of malaria.'

Got him, thought Jacko, suppressing an excited feeling. 'Thanks. I'll let you go. For what it's worth, I think Carter pinched the lighter from the waiting-room. I'll tell my boss what you've said. You'll get your chief nurse back as soon as poss.'

'Most helpful.'

'I may have a couple of other questions for you later. In confidence, of course. Could I phone . . .'

'Any time.'

Got him, too, he thought. He was in good form today. Some days he could be. Having people around him who trusted him and his judgement always gave him a lift, made him work well. He was working very well today.

'Go through it one more time.' Jacko was on the phone again, this time to Percival Manners. 'I want to get it absolutely right.' He started making notes.

Friday, Manners repeated, he arrives at Tor View Clinic half an hour before Barrington is due to hold court in the day room. Dr Saul hands him a copy of the report he had prepared on Barry Carter for the Stipe.

One look convinces Manners there isn't a hope of acquittal. He sees Carter in the day room before Barrington arrives. He advises him to put up his hands and ask for any other outstanding offences to be taken into consideration, to clear the books and go for a hospital order and save himself from jail. Carter agrees.

Manners informs both Miss Chan and the divisional DCI that Carter is prepared to make a clean breast of everything.

It's at Manners' own request that the taking of the TICs should be held in the waiting-room immediately after the formal further remand hearings.

Manners himself isn't present and does not set foot in the waiting-room. When the court rises he goes with his other client Meakin to the secure unit to hear his private confession to the killing of Debby Dawson.

Jacko began cross-checking. 'But I'm right, aren't I, that Meakin never got round to telling you about the oriental girl, who she was and how she died?'

'Correct. We were going to go into that today.'

'You've been very patient with me,' said Jacko, gratefully.

A meeting with a dark-suited Charley Chan in the cool, marble foyer of the courthouse, not really by chance. She greeted him with a pleased-to-see-you smile. 'That medical report on Carter any good?'

Jacko gave her his only-sort-of shrug. 'It didn't tell us much we didn't know.'

She eyed him intently. 'Is there something odd about the fire?'

Say nothing, he told himself. Velma had ordered that only them and WPC Helen Rogers should be in the know. 'Only in so far as how Carter got hold of the means to start it.'

'He's robbed us of a certain murder conviction on Meakin, that's for sure.' Charley looked downcast. 'I could have used a bit of success after what's happened this morning.' She tilted her head back towards the doors of the court. 'Barrington's just tossed out one of my best cases. Insufficient evidence, he ruled.'

So, thought Jacko, Barrington's fully recovered from his malaria bout and is back on full-time duty. He pulled a commiserative face. 'Tell me what happened at that last special court.'

'Over lunch, if you like.' An inviting face.

Jacko's fell. 'I have to see my chief.'

She shrugged casually. Your loss, she seemed to be telling him. Well, she began, she got to Tor View Clinic twenty minutes before court. She was handed the prosecution copy of the medical report on Carter. Percy Manners approached her, said Carter would be pleading guilty and wanted more fires taken into consideration. After court she and the DCI saw Carter in the waiting-room.

'With Manners?'

She shook her head. 'He was taking depositions from Meakin in the secure unit. It was routine anyway, or should have been.'

'What went wrong, then?'

A tiny sigh. 'Carter changed his mind again. He said he was denying all the arsons, everything. Even those he'd admitted to Danny Payne. Said he wanted to go to jury trial, fight it all the way. He was potty, as you must have gathered.'

Jacko introduced the next question carefully. 'You know, do you, that Carter asked to see Danny Payne and his DCI in the afternoon?'

A startled look. 'No.'

'Not about the arsons. He made a witness statement implicating Meakin in both river deaths. You know, the old remand cell confession.'

Charley groaned. 'Oh, no.' She tutted. 'We could have got Meakin on a double murder charge.'

So, thought Jacko, she's not dated Window Payne this

weekend or he would have told her about Carter's statement. He gave her a never-mind shrug. 'It will all come out at the inquests.' He went back to an old topic, double-checking. 'At that meeting, there were just the three of you in the waiting-room – you, Carter and the DCI?'

An absent-minded nod.

'No Danny Payne?'

'He wasn't in court that morning.'

'How long where you in there?'

'Half an hour, no more. We tried to get him to change his mind. He wouldn't wear it.'

'Did you see any cigarette lighters on top of the filing cabinet?'

A firm headshake.

'Was Carter free to roam around?'

'We didn't have him chained to a chair or anything, but I don't recall him going walkabout.'

'In that half-hour did Barrington walk through the waiting-room to Dr Saul's office?'

'Not straight through. He stood around for a minute or two and read a magazine. Dr Saul was on the phone. I suppose he didn't want to barge in.'

'Where did he stand?'

'In front of the filing cabinet, flipping through an old mag.'

Jacko sought no more. 'Thanks. Sorry about lunch.'

'Make it soon,' she said.

A short walk in the sun from the police station, away from the river, stood the Dolphin, plaster and beamed outside, overshadowed by the cathedral with its fourteenth-century sandstone tower immaculately restored.

Velma was waiting inside, in one of half a dozen small snugs, pine-panelled with leaded windows and low ceilings. The pub was so old that the approach down a flag stoned passage seemed to tilt at a crazy angle, making Jacko feel as though he'd had a few pints already.

With her was the DCI who, Jacko guessed, had been taken into her confidence. Her decision; not his. He hadn't even been consulted and felt a twinge of annoyance at her.

She ordered white wine and soda, the DCI a pint, Jacko a Coke. He seldom drank at lunchtimes on duty.

'Chief Nurse O'Brien's in the clear,' she announced. 'He was out footslogging through one of the dales with his wife and two neighbours on Friday. He thinks – can't be sure – that he last used his white lighter on Thursday night.

'We've got a nursing sister who helped herself to a light from it first thing on Friday. She put it back on top of the cabinet but it wasn't there when she looked again later on. Thought nothing of it. Apparently O'Brien's always having them nicked. That's why he buys them in bulk.'

As bad as working in a police station, thought Jacko, whose own lighters often vanished.

'Which means,' said the DCI gloomily, 'it could have been taken around the time me and Charley Chan were interviewing Carter in the waiting-room.'

He'd been through it all before for Velma but went through it again for Jacko.

He'd given Charley Chan a lift to Tor View, the DCI began, because she didn't drive. He was the only police officer in court that morning. Percy Manners told them that Carter would be available to him in the waiting-room afterwards. 'He'll co-operate, Manners promised, but the barmy bastard wouldn't cough. I hoped Manners would show up and talk some sense into him, but he didn't. We gave up after half an hour.'

He hadn't seen Barrington personally in that half-hour because he'd been to the canteen. Charley told him the Stipe was in the inner office with Dr Saul when he returned with three coffees.

Shit, thought Jacko. The DCI was only a hearsay witness to Barrington's opportunity to take the lighter which Carter used to start the fatal fire. Still, he comforted himself, Charley Chan was good enough on her own, with Dr Saul as back-up.

That same afternoon, the DCI went on, Chief Nurse O'Brien phoned to say Carter wanted to see him. He took Sergeant Payne with him this time, expecting confessions to more arson cases.

'Instead we got his statement dobbing his next-door neighbour Meakin right in it for the murder of the oriental girl.'

You were conned, Jacko thought, but before he could say so Velma winked and gave her head such a slight shake that her copper hair stayed in place. Clever cow, he thought. This DCI's not fully in on it. He was glad now he'd taken his wife's advice (instruction is more accurate) to invite his boss out for a drink now and then.

'Sorry to bother you again, doc.' In his office, Jacko was back on the phone.

'Any time.' Dr Saul sounded positively friendly. 'Thank you for sending my chief nurse back so promptly.'

'A pleasure,' Jacko purred, softening him up further.

Saul fretted for a moment or two, wondering if body searches on dangerous patients like Carter should have been more thorough. Jacko said his experience was that if cunning people wanted to hide things they'd find a way. 'You can only do your best.'

'How can I help this time?' He had cheered up again.

'Two things. If I push my luck, say so.'

'Don't worry.' There was no menace in his tone.

'I've talked to Mr Manners. He's told me Simon Meakin confessed to him that he murdered Debby Dawson.' Jacko hurried on quickly. 'I'm not asking you to confirm that, by the way. But Mr Manners also tells me that he and Meakin had not yet got round to talking about the second body in the river, the oriental girl . . .'

'And you're asking me if I did?'

'Yes.'

A thoughtful silence. 'Put it this way. If I am called to give evidence at any inquest, I could do no more than confirm all Mr Manners says.'

'In other words, you personally had not discussed the oriental girl with Meakin.'

'I was due to sit in with Mr Manners at his request when he talked to Simon on that very subject this very day.'

Jacko breathed in. 'Thanks.'

'Your second query?'

'We were talking about fetishes this morning,' he reminded him. 'No names, no pack drill, but how do they start?'

A long silence.

Jacko urged him on. 'I mean, leathers and black plastic and so on. I'm talking generally; not about any specific patient.'

'Say . . .' he said slowly, thinking,' . . . your first really stimulating sexual contact was with a girl wearing leather. You might always seek that feel, that smell to recapture that sensation. Macs? How old are you?'

95

'Getting on for fifty.'

'A bit young to recall the great days of Hollywood then.'

'I caught the tail end.'

'Me, too. Right. You're back in your youth, queuing to see your favourite star. It's a bad night. Everyone around you in raincoats, wet and shining. Just thinking of your fantasy arouses you physically.' Gives you the horn, he means, Jacko knew. 'In future you might associate that sight and smell with that feeling and re-enact it so often it's essential to obtain satisfaction. Shall we put it to the test?'

'OK.' Jacko was delighted, prepared.

'What's your particular . . . er . . . thing?'

Jacko knew he meant turn-on. The honest answer was big bosoms, a desire to be safe, warm and comforted, he supposed. 'Black high heels, preferably sling-backs.' Second on his quite long list, so not exactly a dishonest reply.

'And was your Hollywood favourite a tap dancer?'

'Christ.' Genuine admiration. 'Brilliant.'

'Not really.' A short laugh. 'Films can be very influential. I had one private patient who saw something years ago called *Bitter Rice*. It featured a very voluptuous Italian lady wearing black wellington boots, working in a paddy field. He couldn't achieve anything with his wife unless she paraded in the bedroom in black wellington boots.'

'That would never work with my wife.' Jacko put on a gloomy voice. 'She'd object to black welly-bobs. Out of fashion. Green's the in colour.'

A much longer laugh. Jacko knew he'd hooked him now and got down to the real business. 'On the subject of foot fetish . . . after all, it was mentioned in my dictionary . . . let's take a hypothetical case.'

He read from jottings noted down that afternoon from news clips which were far from hypothetical, hoping that Dr Saul would not know Barrington's curriculum vitae.

'Take a man with a sheltered background. An only child. Parents very churchy. Public school, university, the armed services. A posting out east . . .'

Dr Saul got the picture. 'And he loses his virginity by the side of a blue lagoon after a dusky maiden has bathed his feet or something?'

'Something like that.'

'How old was this hypothetical man at the time of this encounter?'

Jacko cross-checked his notes. 'Mid-twenties.'

'I would have expected him to have had that experience, say, ten years earlier, but, given that background, it's possible, I suppose.'

Possible! Jacko felt a charge running through him, a professional thrill, not at all horny. He decided to leave Dr Saul laughing, not wanting him thinking too deeply about their conversation. 'Don't suppose there's much foot fetish about these days.'

'Why so, Inspector?'

'Well, there's not a lot of romance in bovver boots, is there? I mean, not after black sling-backs.'

He left him laughing.

Back to the Dolphin, early evening, just Velma with a spritzer and Jacko on his first pint of the day.

'So it has to be Barrington,' she said. 'We've cleared everyone else.'

Jacko nodded. 'How are we going to prove it, guv?'

Velma told him how. Good God, he thought, driving home down the A52, a hand-job on exes, tossed off at the taxpayers' expense.

That'll teach the missus to order me out drinking with the girls.

12

'How's that feel? Feel good?'

'Mmmmm.' A dreamy, far-off sigh, Jacko just avoiding saying 'Yummy.'

'A bit harder?'

'A bit perhaps.' He closed his spectacle-less eyes.

'How did you hurt it?'

'Prising up a manhole cover.' He nipped his bottom lip between his teeth to bite off a grin.

'Diddums.' She had an elongated local accent, no melody in it.

Odd the way you don't take a lot of notice of women's accents when they're close enough to be whispering, he thought.

'Got no one to . . .' He was going to say 'kiss it better' but stopped, sorry he'd started the sentence. His impetuous sense of humour often made him push his luck too far too early, got him into trouble, especially with his bosses.

Her hands, much more rhythmical than her voice, seemed to take industrial action and went on a go-slow, a work-to-rule, about to down tools. 'How did you hear about us?' There was cold suspicion in her tone.

'A legal pal of mine.'

'Not a policeman, are you?' Her hands went on all-out strike.

'Don't mention those bastards to me. One of them's the reason I've got no one at home to do this.' He spoke bitterly, from the heart, all of it once true; a married sergeant and his first wife, so long ago now that he seldom thought about them. For the first time, he was glad of the memory. Softer: 'Do I look like a policeman?'

He knew the answer to that without opening his eyes. On major inquiries he worried too much and smoked too much to retain any fat. Neither did he have much muscle, those in his visible upper arms were no bigger or harder than in his adolescent days. All but one of his muscles always seemed to stiffen after the mildest form of exercise. In immediate post-war days, he'd have been earmarked for a sanatorium for consumptives.

'What's your job then?' Her hands hovered, undecided.

'Lecturer.'

'Not working today?'

'Hols.'

A show of hands voted to return to work. 'How often do you get these muscle spasms?'

'Half a dozen times a day sometimes.'

'Shall I put something on it?' Not, he hoped, one of those stinging sprays that make you smell like a rugger player fresh off a dressing-room treatment table. 'A little oil?'

Without waiting for his reply, her hands stopped work again. He opened his right eye.

She was taking off the white, shortie cotton gown she'd been wearing when she'd been summoned to the reception desk at the Halcyon Health Club, an inner-city main-street shop, both windows curtained by thick gauze, greyed with dust.

'Your personal masseuse,' the manager had said by way of introduction after he'd listened, only half-interested, to Jacko's pained description of his bad back.

A plump, balding man, he was no advert for the muscle-toning and skin-tanning services on offer on a painted price list behind his tiny desk.

The cover was only skin deep. A pair of dumbbells hanging on a dusty green wall, keep-fit magazines with front covers featuring gleaming girls in bikinis (no male models, though) on a small chipped table.

No point in being over-elaborate, Jacko had acknowledged. Everyone in the local division knew what went on here and took no action. Why drive them on to the streets into the cars of kerb-crawlers? A policy decision, he guessed. A policy he approved of. If Debby Dawson had worked here, she'd still have been alive.

His masseuse had pulled back the yellow curtains to this cubbyhole cubicle but left him to let him undress himself. He'd picked his clothes with care that morning. He'd taken them off with equal care, folding them up far more neatly than he ever did at home where he was inclined to be slobbish.

His dark blue sports jacket hung on the back of a rickety cane chair. Over it, but not quite covering a packet of Bensons stuck in the jacket's top pocket, were blue jeans, then socks and underpants. The pile was covered with a red and white halved shirt, like rugger players wear – or ageing lecturers on their long vac.

Naked, he'd wrapped a white towel round his thinnish waist and climbed on to a hard pillowless single bed where he lay on his stomach, head on one side on a white sheet.

Unrobed, his masseuse, thirtysomething, had a big smooth bosom, less than half-hidden by a high white bra, a size too small for it. She also had a thick waist and thighs on either side of white bikini pants so skimpy that he knew her blonde head of hair was bleached. She looked like an all-in wrestler and he imagined WPC Helen Rogers out of uniform. Good grief, he thought, and he closed his eye again.

He heard liquid slurping out of a bottle and hands being smacked wetly. The rubdown resumed.

She used the thick sweet-smelling oil liberally on the small of his back, rubbing upwards into the valley between his shoulder blades. Suddenly she stopped work.

He gave her another one-eyed glance. She was smearing the surplus from her hands over her shoulders and the bulging tops of her breasts. 'Fancy a tanning?'

An ambiguous invitation, he cautioned himself. 'It's taken years of late-night drinking to get this shape and colour. I don't want to lose it under a sun-lamp.' She gave an uncertain laugh. 'And I'm not ex-public school.' A longer laugh, understanding.

'Want any extras?'

She wasn't, he knew, thinking of the sort of extras – the no-balls and leg-byes – the cricket-playing Rev. Dillon Blades would happily discuss.

He came on all shy. 'It's the first time . . .' He let himself peter out.

'Never done this before?'

'Until she left me it never . . . well.' He looked away.

'Miss her?'

'A bit.'

'Well?' A touch dominant.

'Well.' He tried to sound submissive.

Her fingers slid beneath the towel, just touching his upper buttocks, playing a soundless cadenza on them. 'It's up to you.'

'It's not very private here.'

'We could go upstairs.'

'Would it be you?' An anxious face.

'Why? Like me?' Somehow, with great difficulty, she managed a simper.

'Rather . . . well. Yes. Very much.'

She switched off the simper. 'Depends. On what you want.' He said nothing. 'Hand relief only, me. Twenty extra. Flying Fingers, they call me.' A proud chuckle, professional. 'You want straight, full sex I can fix it for fifty. In advance. Anything specialist, S and M say, by negotiation. It's up to you.'

'Pass me my coat.' He clutched the towel to his waist and, rolling round, began to sit up.

She yanked it off the chair back, scattering the neat pile, his shirt slipping on to the crackled, maroon lino.

Legs dangling over the edge of the bed, he took it from her and laid it across his knee. From an inside pocket he pulled out a black wallet holder.

'No credit cards.'

He showed her his warrant card. 'You're nicked.' A bright smile.

'Jerk.' Her face was a mixture of fright and fury.

'Not today, thank you, madam,' he replied, rather self-righteously.

'Out. Out. *Out*.' The unhealthy manager of the Halcyon Health Club acted a rage after he'd heard a playback on the tape-recorder concealed in the pen pocket packet of Bensons. Not a convincing performance, Jacko thought, but the sweat on his forehead was real enough. 'She's out.'

'No, she's not,' said a fully dressed Jacko.

'I had no idea she was . . .'

'Yes, you did.' Jacko cut in, not at all rudely, speaking quietly, and with great patience. 'Everybody knows.'

'I've had no trouble for years.' The manager slumped down on a chair in a small back office which had a wall shelf as a desk. 'No police visits.'

'We've been turning a blind eye.'

'Then why now?'

Jacko stood over him. 'There's a way out of it.'

His upturned face filled with loathing. 'You putting the bite on me?'

'Only for information.'

'What information?'

Jacko went into a rehearsed explanation, totally fabricated, making it sound vaguely like a confidential inquiry on behalf of the Lord Chancellor's office which hires and fires magistrates, but the summing-up was genuine: 'So you either give me the names of the girls Barrington the Stipe hires or you appear before a different bench of magistrates for running a disorderly house' – a quaint legal name for brothel.

The manager caved. Always did, in Jacko's experience. Vice girls and the men who run them always kiss and tell. To the police, to stay out of more trouble; to the press, for more money. Prostitutes with hearts of gold, bullshit. The only gold they and their pimps want is bankable. That's what they're in business for.

Velma Malloy was waiting for them in the Dolphin when they got back from the addresses of three girls, two blacks, one Asian, the manager gave.

101

Jacko walked in, shaking his head, dispiritedly. 'Nothing.'

Velma turned away from the bar after ordering drinks for him and Helen Rogers. Glasses in hand, they walked towards a quiet corner table. 'Nothing?' she repeated.

'No,' he said as they all sat down. 'The Asian's Barrington's Number One girl. The other two are stand-ins when she's not available.'

All had told virtually the same story and Jacko told Velma. 'Barrington phones on a Saturday morning to confirm. Oddjob, his houseboy, picks them up at six thirty in his master's old Rover from a hotel near the railway station. He drives them the twenty miles to his place.

'Small talk over gin and tonic in the lounge with the view. Into his bedroom. The girl strips to bra and pants. She undresses Barrington on the bed.

'Never full sex. Hand relief only. Nothing kinky. No tannings, no bondage. And certainly no foot washing or massage or toe sucking or dibbling. No foot fetish at all. Another gin afterwards. A solo shower if they want one. Then a lift home.'

'They all adore him,' Helen added. 'Think he's a gent.'

'You're making it sound more boring than *Blind Date*,' said Velma, her face failing to hide her disappointment.

'There'll be more coupling going on after that show than the Stipe's engaged in, that's for sure,' said Jacko moodily.

They sat for some time in a silence which Velma eventually broke. 'We're going about this the wrong way.'

We, Jacko noted. Always the same when a boss has a bum idea. If it had worked it would have been 'my idea'. When it fails it becomes 'our idea'. All the same, bosses. Men or women. All the same. He was in a bad mood. The fun had gone out of his day.

'We're going to have to tackle it from the other direction,' Velma continued. 'ID the girl first and then prove a connection with Barrington.'

By 'we' she means 'me', Jacko told himself. 'How?' he asked. 'We've traced all the AWOL waitresses from Chinese restaurants and that missing Jap wife arrived home safely.'

'How far have you got on colleges?'

'Christ, guv. I've been up to my . . .'

'Sorry.' A swift smile. 'Start on them tomorrow.' She decided to change it from an order to a request. 'If you will.'

Jacko nodded, drinking up, wanting to go, but Helen stood and fetched another round of half-pints. 'Weird, isn't it?' she said, sitting down again. 'The Stipe paying twenty quid a week plus exes for a service like that.'

'Yer.' Jacko studied his drink, biting his bottom lip between his teeth. 'I know a place where you can get what he was getting for 20p.'

Helen didn't bite, seldom did, so he had to go on. 'That's where I'm bound when I've finished this.' He took a long drink. 'Home.'

'You mean,' said Helen, smiling but frowning, 'she charges you?'

'Nope. I charge her.'

Helen gave a flustered giggle and Velma a smile that started out shrewd but, despite her experience of marriage and divorce, seemed to fade into uncertainty.

That's the whole point about sex, see, Jacko thought. No one can be certain. No one is sure what goes on in the privacy of other people's bedrooms because only kissers and tellers talk about it and they make most of it up. So no one really knows.

Velma's smile had gone completely. 'Dirty old git,' she said, only half joking.

'Hear, hear,' Helen hear-heared.

Annoying, aren't they, modern women? Jacko thought. They nag at you for not treating them as one of the boys. Then they get all huffy, come the old sisterly solidarity, when you give them a bit of blokey banter.

Velma's half-reprimand cut deep. He ran a hand down the back of his head, his slipped halo, wondering again with deeper anxiety if he had become a dirty old man. He decided to shut up and drink up.

Velma noticed his sulk and tried to make amends. 'You've had a very tiring day.'

He smiled, but only thinly. The damage had been done.

13

Notices and signs in different languages in half a dozen different colours welcomed Jacko and Helen to a sixth form college in a suburban estate. It was the third they'd called on that morning.

The international touch failed to disguise the sheer Englishness of the buildings. Not olde worlde English like the Dolphin. Stark sixties English; a dire decade for architecture.

The main block was a red-brick cube, four storeys high, with a stairwell visible through the windows on every floor. From it ran single-and double-storey buildings in sections, some of them lime green corrugated metal, some pebble-dashed.

For a place supposed to be on holiday the car-park and cycle shed were surprisingly well filled and so was the echoing foyer where students, not all young, not all white, lounged and chatted.

They discovered why when they finally found the English interpretation of the notices. Outsiders were being directed to summer classes or the library and gym, insiders to pre-term staff meetings.

Even more prominent were the no-smoking signs. They were everywhere. Not so noticeable was the sign for the admin office. With no one on the reception desk, it took time to find it.

No, said the grey-haired woman who came to the counter, they'd had no unaccounted-for scholarship students from the Orient in the last academic year, but they had a Chinese lady lecturer. 'There appears to be some doubt about whether she's coming back.'

'Why?' Jacko got out his notebook.

'She hasn't returned her new contract.'

She went to wall-to-wall cabinets and returned with a thin buff folder, which she obligingly turned on the counter towards him. 'You'd better write it down. We all call her May.'

Li Mei Ling, he wrote. 'What's known about her?'

She took the file back, opening it. 'Started with us in September last year. Part-time. Ten hours a week.'

'Teaching what?'

'Japanese.'

'You said she was Chinese,' Helen pointed out.

She slipped out a form. 'Born Shanghai, it says here. 1-9-67. That's as much as I know. Why not ask the . . .' She said something like 'cough', which, to a CID officer, is slang for a confession, and Jacko blurted, 'Pardon?'

'College of Further Education,' she explained, as if talking to a pupil from the remedial class. '. . . the Cofe head of the languages faculty?'

In a tidy first-floor staff room, the head of the languages faculty broke off from stacking books in neat piles. A couple of Shakespeares, an Austen and a Chaucer. None of which, Jacko realized with deep shame, he'd read.

'You're not worried about her, are you?' he asked after listening to their inquiry.

Jacko didn't know the answer to that yet. 'Are you?'

'It will be most inconvenient if she doesn't show. We've expanded her intake and a replacement will be hard to find at this late stage.'

Jacko flannelled an answer that wouldn't alarm him. 'No more than we're worried about half a dozen waitresses and a Japanese wife we're also trying to trace.'

The faculty head, a tall, thin man in his mid-forties, scratched at his chin beneath a short black beard. 'I'm a little surprised, I must confess.'

'Why?'

Just over a year ago, he said, the college decided to run courses teaching basic Japanese to seventeen-and eighteen-year-olds with hopes of future jobs at the huge Nissan plant or the services that would support it.

May, as everyone called her, applied for the post and he'd interviewed her. Back home, she'd claimed, she'd worked in the tourist trade which had burgeoned until the army's brutal crackdown on pro-democracy demos a year earlier. She was proficient in both English and Japanese which most of the tourists visiting her home town spoke. The perfect candidate.

She was contracted to give eight lessons, one-and-a-quarter hours each lesson, to small groups and earned just over £16 an hour, the rate for part-time lecturers.

'She did so well – excellently, in fact – that we've offered her a new contract for ten lessons at an increased rate of £18-plus. She was supposed to confirm last week but she hasn't been in touch.'

'When did you last see her?'

'July, when we broke up.'

'Where did she live?'

'With Patsy Lloyd, from our English faculty. You'll find her wandering about somewhere.'

They did the wandering about; a lot of it. The library, almost empty, silent. The featureless canteen, red plastic chairs unoccupied. Jacko cursed himself for not asking for a description.

Twice in their wanderings, they passed a black woman, late twenties, sitting languidly on a wooden bench set in a platform of concrete in the middle of big patch of grass, too rough to be called a lawn, shaded from the sun by a barn-like gymnasium.

Her short wavy hair was propped against the back-rest. She wore a clean white T-shirt and shorts. Her muscular bare legs were crossed at the ankles above dirty white pumps. She had a can of diet Coca Cola in one hand and a paperback in the other which she was reading through rimless spectacles perched on the end of her broad nose.

A sporty outsider who'd worked out in the gym, Jacko guessed.

Third time round he asked, 'Do you know Miss Patsy Lloyd, English teacher?'

'Ms. Lecturer,' she corrected him and she wiped her mouth with the back of her hand. 'Me.'

Jacko smiled guiltily. He remembered a police recruiting poster showing an officer holding his helmet in hot pursuit of a black man. 'What's happening here?' A trick question, he'd suspected, so he guessed they were a cop and civvie running to someone's aid. Few got it right. The black was a policeman, too, in plainclothes.

She pulled herself up, placing the can at her feet and the paperback on her knees. On the front cover was a good-looking woman in a yellow hard hat. Jacko and Helen sat down each side of Patsy. 'We're looking for May Lee,' he said, happy the name was so pronounceable after some he'd come across checking on waitresses.

'You, too?' Her deep brown eyes registered concern.

Jacko assumed May's boss had been asking after her, said he'd just spoken to him and repeated more or less what they'd said to each other.

A dark shadow clouded her handsome face. 'You don't think she's one of the women in the river, do you?'

'We've a dozen or so we have to check out,' Helen said soothingly.

'But you are worried about her, aren't you?'

'Are you?'

'Yes.'

'Why?'

Well, she began, May took a room in a grotty bed and breakfast place when she first arrived in Derby a year earlier. She pinned a postcard on the staff noticeboard seeking accommodation. There'd been a £30-a-week room free in a terraced Victorian house Patsy shared with two other girls, not teachers, a short bus ride away. May moved in. 'I got to know her really well.'

Jacko fished out his Bensons. She took one. He was relieved. Smoking meant she wasn't politically correct. To be politically correct, in Jacko's view, was a form of fascism; forcing your opinions on people who had a democratic right to smoke themselves to an early death.

'What's she like?' He was careful to use the present tense.

'Sweet-tempered. Sweet-looking. Jet black hair to here.' She touched her left ear. 'Very quiet.'

May had told Patsy she'd arrived in England from Shanghai by train a couple of weeks before she landed her job.

'By train?' asked Jacko, astonished. 'From the other side of the world?'

'Incredible, isn't it? More than a week, it took. Saved money, I suppose.' An understanding shrug. 'She had to get out in a hurry.'

'Why?'

'Politics. They're a pretty repressive regime.'

'She only works ten hours a week here at Cofe.' Jacko always slipped effortlessly into anyone else's terminology. 'What's she do with the rest of her time?'

'You have to prepare and mark homework.' A defensive reply, nettled by the suggestion that teachers have a cushy number. 'She spends a lot of time at the library. She reads a tremendous amount.'

'Did she go out at all, socially, I mean?'

'Lovers, you're thinking of.' A smile, more teasing than taunting.

Jacko reminded himself that the oriental girl he was trying to ID was a virgin. 'Not necessarily.'

'There was something going on with someone she met at an arts cinema. *The Last Emperor*. Seen it?' Jacko shook his head.

'Me, neither. Set in the Forbidden City, she said. She never talked much about their dates. She was very . . .' She couldn't hit the right word.

'Inscrutable,' Jacko suggested.

'A bit stereotypical, but I'll buy that. She keeps herself to herself.'

'A bit clichéd, said Jacko.

'*Touché.*'

Both laughed, eyes meeting, friendly.

'They went out for a few meals, Chinese naturally. Can't stand it myself.'

'Always hungry an hour afterwards,' said Jacko deadpan.

Patsy turned, grinning broadly, to Helen. 'I like this old boy.'

Jacko regarded that as a great compliment. Far too many cops of his generation, trained in the sixties, disliked (some despised) blacks. Chief constables, short of manpower in those far-off days of full employment, took bobbies off the beat and put them into panda cars to cover more ground, so rookies never pounded the streets and got to know the children of the fifties immigrants, what made them tick, tried to understand them. And what cops don't understand they tend to distrust and the feeling among young blacks became more than mutual. The police service and the public had paid a terrible price for panda cars.

Helen did her mischievous best to spoil a magical moment. 'You don't have to work with him.' He joined their laughter.

'Was this romance . . .'

'Fling.' Patsy was correcting him again, still smiling.

'. . . this fling serious?' Jacko restored his serious face.

'Hard to say. She started wearing a very attractive ring here.' She held up her third finger, right hand. 'A sort of coin.'

A sovereign ring; gold perhaps, thought Jacko, excitedly. A sugar daddy. The reason why her hand's still missing. A breakthrough. At long last. He consciously calmed himself. 'Did you ever see this swain?'

Patsy glanced again at Helen. 'Isn't he lovely? So old-fashioned.' Back to Jacko, shaking her head. 'She comes home by taxi after their dates.'

'Never in an old fern green Rover?' Another headshake disappointed him. 'Have you any clue to identity, age, job?'

'Something in legal circles.'

He covered up his escalating excitement and his tracks with a swift, verbal identity parade. 'Judge? QC? Barrister? Magistrate? Solicitor? Policeman?'

She was shaking her head again, repeatedly. 'That's all she said. Something to do with the law. I made a joke about not wanting any home visits. You know us. All cricket and cannabis.'

A feisty lady, this, Jacko decided, laughing again. He liked feisty ladies.

'This, er, fling, was it a big thing in her life?'

'At first. I think it was good for her. She was dreadfully homesick. But then . . .' She looked down to crush her cigarette on the concrete beneath her right foot. 'Well, she wouldn't talk about it. Like I said, she's a very private person. But I got the impression she wasn't altogether sold on it. Wanted out eventually. She just said that things were happening that were, well, foreign.'

'What things?'

A don't-know shrug.

'Sexual demands?'

'Could be.'

Jacko wore his puzzled frown. 'You see, the girl we're trying to identify is, was sexually inexperienced.'

'A virgin, you mean.'

He nodded.

Her face became grave. 'Still possible, I suppose. May certainly isn't promiscuous. This is not the sixties, you know.' She gave him a look that seemed to accuse him of having had far more sixties sex than had been good for him (or, indeed, had been the case).

She tapped the paperback on her knee. 'Read Lodge?'

Jacko looked at it. 'David Lodge', it said above the yellow hard hat and, below it, 'Nice Work'. He gave his head a shamed shake.

'See it on TV?'

'No.' An appeasing smile. 'But I never missed an episode of *Hill Street Blues*.'

She ignored him, thumbing the pages. It took some time. Jacko asked if it was a set book for her students. No, she replied, more's the pity. She found the place she wanted and began to read.

' "Robyn, who was lying naked, face down on the bed, wriggled over towards the centre of the mattress. Charles, who was also naked, knelt astride her legs and poured aromatic oil from the Body Shop on to her shoulders and down the spine. Then, capping the bottle carefully, he put it aside and began working the oil into Robyn's neck and shoulders with his long, supple, sensitive fingers." '

She was reading fluently, interested and interestingly, the way Jacko's wife read to their son, capturing his full attention. She broke the spell by saying 'Blah, blah' to indicate she was cutting out a sentence or two, then resumed in the same smooth style:

' "It began as a real massage and turned almost imperceptibly into an erotic one. Robyn and Charles were into non-penetrative sex these days, not because of Aids" – blah, blah – "but for reasons both ideological and practical. Feminist theory approved and it solved the problem of contraception." '

She looked up from her reading. 'And so on. In other words, Inspector, there's not necessarily so much actual screwing about in this day and age.'

Jacko nodded. Nor in mine, he conceded honestly but privately. 'You were telling me May wanted to end the relationship.'

'To cool it, anyway.'

'How did she go about it?'

'Put a bit of distance between them. Last month she decided to take off to London. Lots of Chinese down there, a few refugees from Tiananmen Square, apparently. It was a sudden decision. She said she just had to get away. She back-packed and bussed it. She's always careful with money.'

Jacko did some mental maths. £160 a week, less tax, rent and food wouldn't leave a lot. 'Has she sent you a postcard from London?'

'No.'

'Where's the rest of her things?'

'Still in her room. And there's the business about her cheque. It's not like her. She's so organized.'

'What business?'

Part-time staff, she explained, have to claim for the hours they work each month and get paid at the end of the following month. Her cheque for lectures in June had arrived three weeks ago and was sitting on the hall table, along with her unsigned contract. 'You can see why I'm worried.'

Then why didn't she report her pal missing? Jacko was going to ask her, but the time wasn't right for a critical question yet and he had other routine ones to put first.

No, Patsy replied, May had no other close friends. Yes, she did have a couple of photos of her back at home taken at a college barbecue and on an outing to the Peaks. Sure, they could have them.

'Did she get letters from Shanghai?'

'Don't know about that. From Hong Kong, certainly. A sister. But she's over here now. At least I assume she's here.'

'What makes you think that?'

'Because her brother-in-law's been round, asking after May.'

'When?'

She thought. 'A couple of weeks back.' She thought on. 'No, three. Her pay cheque had arrived. I asked him if he wanted to take it, but he said, better not. She hasn't been in touch with her sister either, it seems.' A dreamy sigh. 'A real dreamboat, very fanciable. What a catch for May's sister.'

'Did he give you his name?'

'Dillon Blades from Matlock Bath. A minister, would you believe?'

Jacko immobilized his face to dam the shock. He could think of nothing to say, so he fell back on his unasked question. 'If you're this worried about May, why didn't you come to us?'

'He asked me not to.'

'Who?'

'This preacher man. Who else?'

Shock waves burst over the dam and flooded his face.

14

Two long-haired back-packers, unisex in shorts and heavy boots, fell into each other's arms, hugging, crying, tears of joy. It was as if they had travelled half-way round the world from opposite directions for this one moment. Dill Blades smiled benignly.

A tense bespectacled man demurely kissed the lips, not the cheek, of a wistfully beautiful woman half his age. Their finger-tips brushed. Not a father greeting daughter. Ill-matched lovers stealing an hour, he suspected, about to break a commandment. He averted his disapproving eyes.

Beneath the sage green canopies of the Covent Garden General Store half a dozen other emotional knots were being retied.

His eyes were back on the entrance of the rust-tiled underground station whose lifts disgorged passengers into narrow sun-filled streets as crowded as Nathan Road, which he knew much better.

He'd arrived early on a cheap day return from Derby to keep a midday appointment which HQ's overseas co-ordinator had taken three weeks to arrange with carefully cultivated contacts in émigré organizations. As stipulated, he was wearing his oatmeal-coloured lightweight suit and dog collar. He felt very out of place among the trippers and the tourists.

Not once in his two years' training at the mission's HQ down the Old Kent Road just three or four miles away had he gone 'up west' to stroll round Soho and Chinatown or come here, where half of London seemed to meet.

It was clear to him now that the naïve existence of the novice missionary had been no preparation for the world into which he'd been pitched; those stern lectures that warned of over-involvement with the drug addicts and prostitutes they were dispatched out east to save. Even the door-step evangelism, a cover, really, for fund raising, had been misdirected. Housing estates around New Cross and the Elephant and Castle had little charity to spare.

Here was where the money was, he'd decided, wandering round, an hour to spare, watching wheelie-bins piled high with empty bottles being pushed in convoy out of the bars and the restaurants which seemed to occupy every other property. Here was where he'd make his sales pitch, in the way the Salvation Army sold the *War Cry* round pubs, phlegmatically relying on generous sinners to fund their homeless hostels. That's what he'd do if he made it to a post of power. If. A big If now.

If she didn't come, there'd be no position of power; instead, a stripping of what little he had, to do all too little good. Please God let her come. Not to hug her. Not to kiss her lips or cheek. Not to touch her fingertips. Just to smile upon her.

His eyes were fixed now on the throngs of people that rushed in waves, cross-currents to the traffic, out of the shade of the Tube station over the pedestrian crossing towards him.

'Mr Blades.' A female voice, English at his shoulder.

He swivelled his neck. She had sneaked up on him from the

direction of the white stone police station in Bow Street he had seen on his wanderings. 'Yes.'

She was oriental but had a creamy complexion unbleached by any harsh eastern sun; around his age, thirty, incredibly long-legged in faded jeans and black boots, a sleeveless peachcoloured blouse. Her black hair, so glossy it looked almost greasy, was tight to her skull and tied in a pig-tail at the back. She was stunningly beautiful and he was stunned with disappointment.

She nodded across the street. Only when they had threaded their way through a horde of schoolchildren being head-counted by a teacher did she speak again. 'Sorry for the cloak and dagger.'

Nothing more was said as they walked down a cobbled slope past a grey-bearded tramp rummaging in a rubbish bin opposite a shop with expensively priced books on window display. To their left, a street market, packed with browsers. Ahead, a small funfair, stalls shuttered, cockerels and horses and big wheel silent and still.

Inside a pillared piazza with a glass dome and a flagstone floor she led the way into a coffee shop with three white windows. They queued for their drinks. Most customers took theirs outside to sit at tables beneath colourfully striped umbrellas. They carried their lemonades, warm hands misting the cold glasses, to a quiet corner inside.

She sipped her drink, then ran the tip of her tongue along her lower lip. 'All I know about you is what your colleague told me.'

Blades nodded, holding her dark brown eyes.

'He gave me the name of the woman you seek.' Pause for another sip. 'On behalf of a worried expat member of your congregation, you say?' It was the excuse he'd given his overseas co-ordinator, a part-truth, for initiating the inquiry.

Blades decided on the whole truth. 'My wife's sister, actually.'

'You must understand that some in our community are here illegally.'

'Her, too.' More truth, no holding back now, his future in her hands.

'When did you last see her?'

'I brought her myself from Shanghai twelve months ago and put her on a train from St Pancras to Derby. She wrote to us several times in Hong Kong. We returned home from there in June. In all these weeks she has not made contact and is not at

113

home. According to a lady she works and lives with, she came to London possibly to find old friends. We're desperately worried about her. Something is wrong. I pray not, but I fear so.'

'Have you reported these fears to the police?'

'Not yet. You see, as I said . . .' He looked down guiltily, drying up.

She completed the sentence for him, toning down the criminal truth. 'She is here unofficially.'

He nodded mournfully.

She gave her head a slow sad shake. 'We can find no trace of her here. We have also been in touch with Paris where there is a much bigger community. There, her name was recognized but again no one has seen her. Could she have gone anywhere else?'

Blades shook his head. 'No passport. She came in on my wife's, you see.' He gave her a look of utter desperation. 'She must be here.'

'We will keep on looking, naturally.' A sympathetic smile.

He knew now that they would never find her. She'd been found already. Dead. In the river.

Oh, dear Lord, he thought, his stomach so chilled he could no longer drink his iced lemonade.

Now he would have to confess his sins, and not only to God.

15

As fragile and as delicate as a China doll May Lee looked, standing among two posed groups of college tutors.

Her face had the same oval shape, the same high cheekbones as her married sister Jade's, but her mouth was not so heart-shaped, brown eyes duller, smile more subdued, straight jet black hair trimmed at ear level.

Annoyingly, her hands were out of view, so there was no pictorial evidence of the sovereign ring Jacko so desperately desired to see and had failed to find in a painstaking search of the house she shared with Patsy Lloyd.

In the photo Jacko was holding she wore oven gloves and stood before a charcoal brazier at a charity barbecue on the rough grass behind the college admin block.

He had just taken the photo back from Dillon Blades who was now looking at another picture of May, pinched and cold, like the rest of a winter-clad party walking in the Peaks. In this one all the party wore gloves.

Blades handed it back with a solemn nod.

'Your sister-in-law?' Jacko asked, very quietly.

Another solemn nod.

'And you've been making inquiries about her?'

'Yes.' A low tone accompanied by a doomed look.

'And you told her housemate Patsy Lloyd not to tell us?'

Blades looked up, a bit of fight, not much, in his strained face. 'Only to give me a bit of time to try to find her first.'

'And did you?'

'No.' The doomed look returned, doubled.

'Well, Mr Blades . . .' Very formal; no Dill and Jacko today. '. . . I'd like you tell us all about May.'

Jacko had planned to sit back in an easy chair and let Blades, at the desk in his den at the mission, tell his story uninterrupted apart from occasional questions for clarification, and that was how the interview was to proceed, for a while anyway . . .

The Li (Lee to Jacko) sisters, Shen-Shen (Jade) and Mei Ling (May), were born in Shanghai, he began. Jade, his wife, was twenty-five, her sister two years younger. Father, a Communist intellectual, had been taken away from them when they were young, a victim of the Red Guard purges. He'd died during re-education in a farm camp. Mother had raised them single-handed, not an easy task in a society that didn't prize girls as much as boys and didn't approve of more than one child per family in any case.

Two years back there'd been almost as much unrest on the campuses and in the streets of Shanghai as there had been in Tiananmen Square but, with no star reporter like Kate Adie on the spot, it had never made the same sort of headlines in the west.

Jade, a languages student at the university, had been heavily involved, he continued. In the crackdown that followed she became a fugitive. She escaped by boat down the east coast and arrived in Hong Kong, destitute.

She turned up at Blades' mission, a converted warehouse near

115

the Walled City, where addicts were treated to cold turkey and hot gospel. She got bed and board for her labour.

'And quite slowly over the following year we fell in love,' Blades went on with a slow, loving smile. 'It took me some time to realize she's even more beautiful on the inside than on the surface.'

Get on with it, you romantic fool, thought Jacko impatiently.

They talked of marriage and coming to England when his posting ended but a cloud darkened the horizon to their future happiness – Mei Ling (May).

'She was still in Shanghai, you see, leading a . . .' an uncertain shrug, '. . . a decadent life, you could say, I suppose.'

'In what way?' asked Jacko, breaking in for the first time.

'She was consorting with western tourists.'

'But that's what tour guides have to do.'

For a second he looked alarmed, as though a cricket umpire had just no-balled him and he couldn't understand why. 'More than that. Over here, I suppose, you'd say she was part of an escort agency, if you know what I mean.'

Jacko knew. Call-girls who operate in big hotels. An unlikely occupation for a virgin, but he let it pass, for the time being.

'Not only that, but she was on drugs.' Blades stopped. 'And you know what that means over there?'

Jacko didn't, shook his head, didn't believe him anyway. The post-mortem examination had found no trace of drug-taking of any kind, but he wasn't ready yet to say so.

'They take a very severe view of it,' Blades went on. 'Rightly, too, in my opinion. Destroys the soul. The spirit, too. Traffickers are shot. She'd already been drawn to the attention of the authorities.'

He took a month's leave and told his congregation in Hong Kong they were going to spend their honeymoon in mainland China. They got a visa, took the train to Canton where Jade stayed. Blades journeyed on alone to Shanghai.

He collected May. They travelled to Peking, then caught an express that took them through Siberia and on to Moscow, May posing as Jade.

Jacko held up a hand. 'If you're going to tell me you travelled on to Calais . . .'

'The Hook of Holland . . .'

'. . . and into Britain using the same ruse, then it's my duty to caution you . . .'

'We did.'

Jacko completed the caution. 'I'm arresting you for conspiracy to evade immigration regulations. I must now ask you to come with me to the police station so the rest of this interview might continue on tape.'

'Can I tell Jade?' His wife seemed to be his sole concern.

Jacko nodded to Helen who had sat in a corner seat, silent throughout. 'She'll do that.'

It was the first time, Jacko reflected, walking through the empty church, that he'd ever felt a smuggler by the dog collar.

In church, Jacko had gone without a cigarette for an hour. He lit up immediately he got outside. They drove a mile or so in silence to Matlock, a bustling little town with a busy central business district, to a two-storey stone building, elegant as police stations go, not as elegant as the fine, old, balconied town hall opposite.

To this station Dillon Blades had brought Simon Meakin twenty days earlier; to carry the can for two murders, one of which he hadn't committed and which, Jacko was now convinced, the man who sat beside him had. He was sure that a skilful interrogation, as patient as Job, would prove it. He already had plenty of ammunition.

In the second-floor interview room, Blades declined the services of a solicitor. 'My stipend is very modest.'

'Have one on legal aid,' Jacko said, not urging him.

Blades mumbled something about any state surplus should be going on overseas aid for undeveloped countries in the Third World.

On tape they went through the story so far, Blades altering nothing, and Jacko, very relaxed, said, 'Go on.'

In London, he put May on a train for Derbyshire where he knew he and his bride Jade would be based in twelve months' time. After a night's sleep in a cheap hotel, he went by train, boat and train all the way back to Peking where he changed for Canton. There, after almost three weeks of night and day travelling, he was reunited with Jade. He took a final train with her to Hong Kong.

'Some honeymoon,' said Jacko, feigning admiration.

'My ticket was second class. Hard seat, they call it. I never wanted to ride a train again.'

'Why train?'

'Apart from the cost, security is much tighter on planes. As it was, there were heart-stopping moments both at the Chinese-Russian border and at Harwich but, with a train or boat load of passengers to process, the guards have their hands full.'

'Clever,' said Jacko, softening him up.

'On the Trans-Siberian express I didn't wear my dog collar because preachers are such a rarity there.' A cunning smile. 'But I put it on for the boat train. They barely gave our passport a glance. One oriental looks very much like another to western eyes. In any case, no one questions a minister of the cloth.' He was wearing a bright smile, pleased with himself.

Stick around, sunshine, thought Jacko, smiling thinly.

The sisters, Blades continued, corresponded regularly. 'Mei Ling wrote about her new life and college job.'

Jacko lit up again. 'What does Mei Ling mean?' There was no response to what he accepted was an ambiguous question so he reframed it. 'Your wife Jade's proper first name is...' He'd forgotten it.

'Shen-Shen,' Blades reminded him.

'Which you told me means spruce tree.'

Blade beamed his understanding. 'Beautiful ring.'

Which is what you bought your sister-in-law, thought Jacko, and why you had Meakin cut off her hand so you could retrieve it. More ammo. God, he was working well today. A piece of piss, this. He asked a diversionary question. 'In her letters, did she mention any boyfriend, any dates?'

'No.' A shocked look.

'Why are you so surprised? It would be perfectly natural, wouldn't it?'

'I suppose so.' He spoke as though the idea had never occurred to him before.

'Did she send her sister any photos?'

He nodded at the two on the desk. 'Those and a couple of others.'

'What did her letters say? Do you read Chinese?'

'I can understand Cantonese but they use a different language in Shanghai. Fortunately, they write to each other in English. Practice, I suppose, for a language they'd have to use all the time over here.'

'What did her letters say?'

118

'No mention of a man, if that's what you mean. Mainly about the job, films and the sights she was seeing.' A slight blush. 'The early ones were rather . . . well . . . fulsome in their praise for me.' An embarrassed look. 'For getting her safely here, I mean. You may read them if you wish.'

Blades and Jade had flown home in June. They expected to meet up with May after their stay with his mother down south during which time he'd spent three days at a debriefing and retraining session at the mission's national headquarters just off London's Old Kent Road.

When they finally moved to Matlock Bath to start the new posting no message awaited them from May. 'I went round to her address and her housemate told me she had gone to London during the holiday. I was worried . . . well, more than worried . . .' He couldn't hit the right expression of concern so, '. . . very worried, in fact, about her. By then I knew you were making inquiries about an oriental girl in connection with Simon Meakin's case.'

'So worried that you told her mate not to tell us,' said Jacko, hitting, he gauged, just the right note of sarcasm, warming up a little.

Blades gave him an indulgent smile. 'I can understand you being cross with me. I just needed time to go and look for her. If I could have traced her, there would have been no need to tell you she was here illegally.'

The day before, Blades said, he overcame his aversion for trains and caught one to St Pancras, making contact with a representative of a Chinese expat organization in Covent Garden. 'No sign of her. I was going to come to see you.' Jacko gave him his doubting Thomas look. 'Believe me, I was. If you hadn't come to me, I'd have come to you.'

This preacher man, thought Jacko, more amused than angry, speaks with forked tongue. But he wasn't ready to challenge him yet, to turn him over, tear into him with suspicions growing with every sentence he spoke. 'More inquiries will be necessary and I shall want to see you again. I'm going to give you bail and I want you to hand over your passport.'

'You think it's her, don't you?'

Yes, thought Jacko sadly. 'There's one certain way of finding out.'

*

The samples of blood and hair Mrs Jade Blades gave, with her husband's approval, were DNA-tested against similar exhibits from the dismembered corpse of the oriental girl in the infirmary mortuary. The verdict: Jade and May were sisters. Jacko was not surprised, just relieved he had finally put a name to her.

He broke the news to both Blades at their manse, a rather grand churchy name for a small terraced house up a steep side street. He asked them to say nothing to anyone. They didn't protest that they ought to write to her mother in Shanghai. Odd that, he thought. He left them to their grief; Jade's genuine; her husband's faked, he suspected.

Velma Malloy made the decision not to release the name to the media immediately. The story had gone off the boil. In their reports of the fatal fire at Tor View Clinic some national tabloids had branded Simon Meakin as a double killer, though he'd only been charged with one murder and hadn't been convicted of either.

The press, Jacko had discovered, are always fast and loose with allegations when the target is dead, not so keen (sometimes to the point of cowardice) when the subject is alive and able to issue a libel writ. They operate on a policy that the dead can't sue. Biographers are like that, too.

Anyway, foreigners, especially coloureds, get scant coverage, unless, of course, they've become naturalized and are playing international sport for their adopted country. As for the rest, they aren't newsworthy. The press, in his view, was every bit as much to blame as the police for the gulf that had occurred between the races.

The ID-ing of a Chinese girl in a case already written off as solved wouldn't get much of a show, Velma wisely ruled, and she didn't want nosy reporters making the connection that the second victim was related by marriage to the man who'd turned Simon Meakin in. 'They'll ask too many questions we can't answer yet.'

The two additional photos collected from the manse were portraits of a rather forlorn-looking May, no hands in view, no sovereign ring to examine.

The letters the sisters had written to each other were different in style and content. Jade's to May were recovered with her sister's belongings from the house she shared with Patsy Lloyd; all gossipy, about friends in Hong Kong with Shanghai links.

May's to Jade were handed over by Blades, as promised, and contained word pictures of the Peaks that Jacko, brought up on English, could never match. She wrote so poignantly of her homesickness that it was painful to read. Her references to her brother-in-law were fond but contained no hints of falling for him along the long line from Shanghai to London. (But then she wouldn't tell her sister, would she, Jacko told himself.) There was no mention of a boyfriend or sugar daddy in her new life.

Jade was interviewed in her husband's absence from the manse in a small cosy front room, littered with silk embroidered table and chair covers, wall scrolls, a painting of strange but beautiful black mountains with no foothills, a framed photo of a magnificent waterfront, not unlike Liverpool's.

She fingered her green necklace nervously. In a high-pitched baby doll voice that Jacko found annoying in the end, she stuck by and large to the family history her husband had given him.

The only slight breakthrough came on a day trip Jacko and Helen took to London to the mission's HQ, a crumbling, converted Victorian schoolhouse. Its sparse dormitory with double bunks had a view of floodlit pylons and gasometers; not a charity to squander its donations on swanky buildings, like so many.

They established that Blades had no alibi for any of the three evenings he'd spent there during his debriefing. Given the time the body had been in the water, the pathologist couldn't be sure if May had been alive in those three days, but he didn't rule out the possibility.

Not much, a bit disappointing really, but all Jacko had got, and he'd been trained to accept that a detective has to waltz with whomever he'd taken to the dance. He was as ready now as he'd ever be for the confrontation.

'Now listen to me carefully,' said Jacko an hour into the second interview that had so far only covered old ground. 'We have reason to believe that Simon Meakin may not have killed your sister-in-law.' He had practised this word-perfect. 'We are working on the possibility that someone else did.' Even the pauses were rehearsed. 'Someone who knew Meakin.' Pause. 'Someone to whom Meakin turned for help when he emerged for a brief coherent spell from his illness.' Pause. 'Someone to whom Meakin confided that he had killed Debby Dawson.'

With each pause Blades' facial colour seemed to sink like a pale sun further into the white-rimmed circle that was his dog collar.

'Someone who wanted May dead.' Pause. 'That someone mercilessly manipulated Meakin into killing May and/or disposing of the already dead May in bits into the river.'

A longer pause. 'Was that someone you?'

The sun sprang up, a vivid pink. 'How could you think such a thing?'

'We know there was someone in her life. Someone who gave her a sovereign ring. A beautiful ring.' Jacko tried but failed to put on a smile. 'To match her name. Was that you?'

'Know nothing about any ring. Never seen her wearing one.' Blades suddenly realized he was clipping his sentences and spoke his next slowly. 'I haven't, of course, seen her for a year.'

Jacko looked down at his notes on a table on which twin tape-recorders spooled silently round. 'You stayed three days at your mission's HQ.' He looked up. 'Stayed there. You didn't go home to your mother or wife at nights. Both confirm that.' He looked straight into Blades' eyes. 'On one of those nights did you not come to Derby and meet up with May?'

Blades met his gaze, steady. 'I stayed in on all three nights. To meditate.'

'You have no witnesses to that.'

'Inspector.' Patient. 'You need solitude to meditate.'

'Meditate on this then.' Sharp. 'The St Pancras–Derby trip is four hours return. A local journey in your travelling terms.'

A bewildered headshake. 'But I never made it.'

'I'm putting it to you that you made that trip and, on it, you killed May.'

'Dear Lord.' He closed his eyes as if in earnest prayer. 'No. As God is truly my judge.'

'And on that same trip Meakin approached you – in the street maybe, because of your dog collar. He trusted clergymen . . .'

'Believe me, I never saw him before he walked into my church.'

'. . . and he confessed to you that he had killed Debby Dawson . . .'

'Untrue.' His head was shaking violently.

'. . . and you got him either to kill May or to help you dispose of her body.'

'Please. No more. Please.' He breathed in so deeply that grey-

122

blue smoke hanging over the desk from Jacko's cigarette seemed to be sucked out of the air. 'Why should I do any of this?'

'Because, I suspect, you and May formed an emotional attachment on that long journey.'

'Adultery!' The charge stung him harder than murder. 'I'd never commit adultery.'

'No one's saying you committed adultery. Maybe it was physical in other ways. Maybe it was an affair of the heart. But you formed an emotional attachment.'

'Not so. I loved her.'

Jacko held his breath.

'Spiritually. The way I love Meakin and his poor wife.'

Jacko let his breath go. 'And now you had your wife . . .'

'I love my wife deeply.'

'. . . her sister, with you in this country, that attachment was an embarrassment, a threat to your marriage and career.'

'No. No.' He clapped his hands to his ears, shut his eyes tightly.

'Listen to me,' said Jacko, sharply, not quite a shout. Blades lowered his hands. 'I am not accusing you of adultery.' His eyes opened. There was relief in them. 'Know why?' A dumb look. 'Because May was a virgin.'

'I see.' His expression was wholly unseeing, lost.

'Now explain to me, if you can, what a virgin was doing working as a prostitute in Shanghai?'

'I didn't say she was.'

'You said she worked as an agency escort.'

'She did.'

'You said she was into drugs.'

'She was.'

'Not a trace of any was found in her body.'

'You wouldn't find any. It takes only a month or so to clear the system. That was our experience with addicts in Hong Kong.'

Jacko needed time to check on this and went back to a safer subject. 'You confirm she was an agency escort.' A nod. 'You implied she was a call-girl. Yet she was a virgin. Explain that then?'

A long silence. Then: 'It's not unknown.'

'I'm listening.'

A longer silence. 'I don't know much about these things. Only what I've been told.'

'Then tell me.'

'There's quite a well-documented case which we learned about in training. Of an American beauty queen . . . er . . .' He seemed to be having difficulty dredging up the details. 'Can't recall her name. She had this rather sad obsession for a missionary. Mormon, as I recall. He was posted to England to get away from her.'

'What's this got to do with May?' asked Jacko impatiently.

'I'm trying to explain. She turned to vice in Hollywood. All sorts of things, apart from the full act of intercourse, to raise money to follow him over. You know the sort of things. I forget how it all ended.'

Jacko interrupted. 'I still don't see . . .'

'It's possible, isn't it, she was engaged in similar activities.'

Jacko stopped to think for a second. Possible. He'd conceded that to himself on his walk with his dog. Hand-jobs only, like Flying Fingers at the Halcyon Health Club. Or blow-jobs, Blades was talking about, but he can't bring himself to say so.

Hand-jobs, Jacko repeated, startling himself. Barrington used one Asian girl for such a service. Could he have used two? Was May moonlighting from her college job? Am I grilling the right man here?

A sudden doubt pierced him. He kept his face in neutral, to hide it. 'I don't accept that.' He started shaking his head. 'Everything we know about May indicates a quiet, cultured girl.'

'She is . . . was.' Blades sighed deeply. 'No one, least of all me, is saying she wasn't highly intelligent. It was a way of earning money. They had no father. The family was living in poverty. I don't condone it, couldn't possibly, but I do try to understand it. We should forgive it. The fact that she lived a useful and blameless life since only goes to prove she's redeemed.' His answer ended with his voice on a passionate high.

'What I don't understand is this.' Jacko was opening up a new line. 'There was your bride, safe in Hong Kong. Yet on honeymoon you take her back to China . . .'

'Only as far as Canton.'

'. . . back to a country where she's a wanted woman because of her revolutionary activities. Wasn't that risky?'

'Minimalized by travelling in her married name on our joint British passport.'

'Still risky.'

'It was her decision, her wish. The alternative was to leave May

124

at risk in Shanghai. Jade could not have lived with that.' All fight had left Blades' voice now. 'I doubt whether she would have come with me here, married me even, in those circumstances.'

Jacko pondered this, his confidence ebbing, which allowed Blades to take the initiative. 'Why should I go to London looking for May if I knew she was dead?'

'Who did you see in London?'

'I . . .' He bit off what he was going to say.

'Come on. Who?'

He shook his head sadly. 'I can't tell you, I'm afraid. It would put them in difficulty . . .'

Not half as much as you, mate, thought Jacko. 'Who?'

'Sorry, but I saw someone on the strict understanding that no names would ever be mentioned.'

'So you can't prove you went?'

'You must believe me.'

'Why? You've misled me before.'

'Not about that. You have my word. Why should I go if I knew May was dead?'

'Because not to have gone would be an admission that you knew her fate. Why did you tell her housemate not to report her missing?'

'I've told you. So that if I'd found her I wouldn't have to confess what I've done.'

'Confess it then.' Jacko put on his father confessor's face.

'I've told you I illegally smuggled her in.'

'Have you any other confession to make to me?'

'Many. Many. Too many. But murder and adultery are not among them.'

They went through it for another two hours, a real grilling. Yes, he agreed, it was a risk taking his wanted bride back to mainland China, which is why he left her in Canton, the other end of the country from her home, where she wouldn't be recognized. 'We had to so her sister and I could come out as man and wife.'

'If you handed in her exit papers on the Trans-Siberian train, how did you get your real wife back into Hong Kong from Canton?'

'On false papers,' he admitted, shame-faced. His source, he claimed, was a Hong Kong citizen who'd been treated for drug addiction at his mission. 'He used to sell travel documents for drugs.'

'So, having got him off drugs, you, a man of God, got him back on forgery?' asked Jacko with maximum sarcasm.

The prolonged exchange ended with Blades saying, 'John 8.'

'What the bloody hell's that?' asked Jacko, his temper slipping.

'He that is without sin among you let him cast the first stone.'

Jacko went on remorselessly slinging his verbal stones. None found its target. No confession came.

Temper barely in check now, Jacko renewed Blades' police bail. He wasn't bothered so much that he'd been conned by a minister of the cloth. He'd come not to expect too much from them. But this minister was a cricketer. He hadn't walked when he'd been caught out, and Jacko regarded that as unsporting, not playing the game.

'This isn't over, you know,' he said, threateningly. 'I don't believe you're telling me the whole truth.'

Blades stood and, in a sort of slink, turned away to the door, not denying it, and that, for Jacko, was confirmation enough.

16

A boning session. Velma Malloy wanted a private boning session, to exchange ideas, to discuss scenarios, argue openly and honestly, as they had begun to do, just the two of them, after work in the Dolphin almost every night.

What were the scenarios, Jacko was asking himself as he took a long detour on a footpath behind the police station alongside the River Derwent, fifty yards wide here, on the opposite side of Exeter Bridge to the council-house steps where it had all begun when that angler fished out the first bit of Debby Dawson.

A sunny evening, a touch chilly, a breeze stirring the rushes above the dark, shiny surface of the water. A ruffled surface, he noted. Neither calm nor whipped. Like the surface of his mind.

Several scenarios popped into view. Only four floated; one he didn't like the look of at all. He was ready with them– and with a spritzer for her and a pint for himself – when she joined him at their usual quiet corner table in their favourite snug bar.

'Cheers.' She raised her glass, took a sip. 'Well?'

'Number One. Simon Meakin killed both Debby and May and we're wasting our time.'

She took a longer drink, savouring it. 'Then how did Meakin and May meet? She lived and worked at the opposite end of town, went to libraries, cinemas and restaurants he never set foot in. Helen and I have spent days checking their movements. Their paths never crossed.'

'I don't know how.'

'We've seen Mrs Meakin again. A long chat. She's telling the truth about her hubby's denial over May.'

'Yes, but was he telling her the truth?'

'I've checked on Barry Carter, the fire-raiser, too. Gone right back. He was a Walter Mitty, a liar, easily led. Who put him up to grassing Meakin?'

'Wait a minute. Is Number One out of the window?'

'Yes.' A firm reply, no doubts.

'Right. Number Two. Barrington put Meakin up to it. They met when Meakin was at Tor View Clinic first time on the window-smashing charge and he did some gardening for him. Meakin went to His Worship. Remember that phrase, "It was an act of worship"? He confessed to killing Debby Dawson. Barrington got him to kill or dispose of May, who was becoming a nuisance of some sort.'

'There's no evidence that the Stipe knew May,' Velma replied emphatically. 'All his physical needs are catered for every Saturday evening.'

'Ah.' A salacious smile, risking another reprimand. 'Lots of us are well catered for. That doesn't stop some of us wanting something different away from home.'

She rose to the bait, gave him an extremely fierce look. 'Wanting's one thing. Getting's another. I've checked him, too, very carefully. He eats Chinese, true, now and then. Old habits etc. But he's never been to that arts cinema where May met her man.'

A thoughtful silence, both drinking. 'Next?' she demanded.

'Number Three. Her sugar daddy, whether it's Barrington or not, didn't kill her. Blades did. On a day trip from London. She was making threats or demands. He had to silence her to save his marriage and his mission.'

'Any others?' Velma clearly needed time to think about this.

Jacko gave her his least favourite theory. 'It wasn't Meakin, wasn't Barrington, wasn't Blades. But someone else, someone who hasn't even occurred to us yet.'

Velma didn't like the sound of it either. 'Don't even think about it.'

Nonetheless, they did think about it. They mulled over cigarettes on Percy Manners. May's sugar daddy was in legal circles, after all, according to her housemate, but he lacked the opportunity either before or after that special court hearing at Tor View to brainwash Carter into grassing Meakin or slip him the lighter.

They pulled in smoke, puffed it out and pondered on Dr Saul and Chief Nurse O'Brien. Neither would have given Carter the lighter to burn down their own secure unit, they decided. They'd have killed Meakin another way, they agreed.

They stubbed out and considered Sergeant Window Payne. 'But he wasn't at that Tor View court that morning when someone got to Carter,' Velma said. 'I've examined his file on the haystack fires. It's copper bottom, not dodgy at all. I've taken the DCI word-for-word through Carter's interview where he shopped Meakin. He insists that Payne didn't put a single word in Carter's mouth. Besides, none of them had any connection with May.' Velma had cleared her mental deck. 'Let's rule those four out once and for all.'

'By the same token,' said Jacko, thinking logically, 'you must rule out Barrington. He had no known connections with May either.'

'What's your view?'

'Well.' Jacko hesitated. 'We know he has a thing about this Asian girl from the Halcyon Health Club. If May was doing a bit of freelance hand relief based on her vice trade experiences back home, well . . . Perhaps there is a connection and we just haven't found it yet. We can't rule him out.'

Velma had a drink and a think. 'Motive?'

'Like I say, she was a potential embarrassment if the news leaked to a Sunday tabloid that she was bashing his bishop. OK, he's no wife to worry about. It's not a domestic scandal, but the Lord Chancellor and his diocesan bishop aren't going to be very chuffed, are they?'

'Not quite the done thing for a magistrate and a consistory court official, eh?' said Velma, grinning impishly.

No, Jacko agreed. 'It's a bit like me going to the police ball in aid of the boot fund, bollock naked, apart from a condom on my nose, and when the chief constable asks: "What have you come as?" replying "Fuck nose." '

She laughed so loudly a barmaid looked across at them. 'Definitely not the done thing,' she eventually said. They gave each other warm looks, friends' looks, contented in each other's company. 'Tell me,' she said, 'where do you get all these stories from?'

'Collect 'em from mates. Gonna use 'em when I hand in my badge.' His retirement plan – well, dream really, he admitted – was to write detective novels, roughly based on some of his cases, with a bit of gritty realism and a few sideswipes against the system thrown in.

'What!' An amused exclamation. 'With your typing and spelling? I've seen your reports.'

He shrugged, undeterred. 'I'll get a word processor with a spell check.'

'What will you call this?'

'Depends who did it.'

'If it's the Rev. Blades, how about *Gospel News*?' The mention of his name ended their discursive discussion. 'Was it Blades, do you think?' she asked.

Nine out of ten murders, he was reminding himself, have a domestic background, but why state the obvious? 'Not sure.'

He'd been back on to lecturers at the Mission to Adam HQ in London, he continued. Yes, they confirmed, they did cite the case of the obsessed American beauty queen to trainees as an example to them not to get emotionally involved with souls they were saving.

Her name was Joyce McSomething, circa late seventies, they told him, and Jacko remembered her vaguely. She'd flown over with hired helpers, kidnapped her missionary for whom she had the hellbent hots, held him in chains and had her way with him. 'Not in the missionary position, by all accounts,' Jacko added.

Velma laughed again.

She'd funded the expensive operation from vice in Hollywood; dirty phone calls, dirty pictures, bondage but never the full act. 'She was saving herself for her missionary.'

Velma didn't laugh. 'Maybe May was into something similar.'

Jacko nodded. 'If, say, he slapped it in her hand on that long train trip, that would still be a sin for a married man in Blades' position, wouldn't it?' He looked unsure.

129

Velma looked quite shocked. 'For any married man, I would have thought.'

He ignored it. 'I mean, especially to a preacher whose sister-in-law had kissed whatever and was about to tell.' He fell silent. 'But how are we going to prove it?'

Velma replied promptly. 'Get hold of more letters May wrote. To her dear old mum in Shanghai, perhaps? Maybe there's a photo back home with that ring, too.' She stopped, less positive now. 'We can't do that the routine way, can we?'

The routine way would be via Interpol, an organization often depicted in international thrillers as being staffed by ace cosmopolitan detectives. In reality, it is a paper clearing-house – one man and his fax in every capital city. All that man would do was pass on their request for info to the local police in Shanghai. Sometimes it can take months to get a reply. Not only that, it would reveal to the Chinese authorities the married status, new name and whereabouts of a political refugee, and, perhaps, endanger her family.

'No,' Jacko agreed.

Velma went to the bar and came back with two more drinks. She'd clearly been working on the idea while she was being served. 'Whether it's Blades or Barrington, the answer could be in letters or photos in Shanghai.' She stared into her fresh drink and, more or less thinking aloud, she added, 'I wonder if the chief would let us go incognito?'

Go. Jacko took a long, long swallow to dampen a burning excitement. Go to the Far East. He'd always wanted to go. A trip of a lifetime and on the taxpayer, too. Bound to be a stop-over in Hong Kong. Thirty years after the army denied him a posting there, he would get to travel on the Star Ferry, scale Victoria Peak and see the sun go down in the South China Sea.

Us? he asked himself, suddenly apprehensive. Who's us? Me and who?

Not Helen Rogers. She's a likeable lump of a local lass but she'd tower above those millions of midgets. She's got lady cop written all over her. She doesn't have the guile for an undercover op.

Charley Chan? Useful with her parentage. But would she use him as a substitute for Window Payne who, the gossips had it, was sleeping with her?

For all his talk, faced with half a chance, Jacko always went

cold. He sent up a private prayer. Lead me not into temptation,
O Lord.

Velma. Please, God. Make it Velma. He'd be safe with Velma.
He always felt safe with Velma.

'Never thought we were going to make it,' Jacko said, sitting
down at a small, square wall table with a white paper cloth.

Charley Chan picked up the menu, a single, stiff sheet of lunchtime specials, cheaply priced. 'What's all the excitement about?'

'Excitement?' He put on his cool face and voice.

'On the phone. You sounded excited.' She sounded bored.

'Apprehensive more like.' His modest tone. 'I'm going to
China.'

Head up, all attention. 'When?'

'Tomorrow.' Stiffly, he elbowed up his left arm, which felt as
though it had been pumped full of lead. 'All jabbed up.' She
ignored his blatant plea for sympathy. 'To check on Blades and
Barrington,' he explained.

'Why?'

A waitress hovered, a petite Chinese girl who Jacko had seen
on his tour of restaurants. She didn't recognize him but seemed
to know Charley and gave her a sparkling white smile, a welcome not returned as she ordered a big bottle of Ashbourne
water. Charley hadn't consulted him, but it suited him, not
wanting to mix alcohol with vaccinations.

He waited until the waitress had retreated towards the bar.
'We've identified the second victim as Li Mei Ling, from Shanghai.' He flicked his head in the southerly direction of the sixth
form college. 'She was known as May Lee at Cofe. Worked there
as a part-time lecturer.'

'You've done well,' said Charley, eyes widening a little.

He was about to preen. He liked pats on the head, especially
from women. He paused as the glasses were put before them.
Charley poured and ordered the meal, getting his nodded assent
to her suggestions.

As she and the waitress chatted in Chinese, he took in the
surroundings. It was a long, narrow restaurant, blue on the
outside, a window frieze of red and white flowers. Modern
paintings of mountains and rivers, in stark greys and blacks,
hung on the walls. It was a quiet lunchtime, most of the tables

131

unoccupied, including two large round ones with black turntables.

There was soft piped music – Mantovani-style strings accompanying one of those eastern instruments that plink plonk incessantly, the worst of both musical worlds. It was safe to talk, Jacko decided.

'It gets better,' he said when they were alone again. 'She was Blades' sister-in-law. We think he could be lying about their relationship.'

Charley was dressed for the court session she'd just left on the other side of the market square, sharply and darkly, like a woman out of *LA Law*. Her legal mind spotted the flaw in the case which had always worried him. 'The PM report says she was a virgin.'

'There could still have been an emotional tie-in he didn't want his wife to find out about. He's certainly held back on us and tried to get her housemate to keep stum. He's hiding something.'

'Such as?'

'We know for a fact that Meakin killed Debby Dawson. We're not so sure he killed May Lee. We think his professional carving abilities could have been pressed into service by someone else.'

Her mouth dropped open, sheer disbelief. 'But Meakin admitted killing the second girl to Barry Carter in the secure block at Tor View.'

So, thought Jacko, she's still seeing Window Payne, who's briefed her and boasted to her. No matter, she'd have seen the file soon. 'But Meakin denied it to his wife.'

'That so?' Her dark eyebrows arched. That, at least, was news to her.

'We think Carter's statement was a put-up job,' he said. 'You know as well as I do that remand wing confessions aren't worth a light.'

A trace of concern on her face. 'Should you be telling me this?'

'Why not? You'll be handling the case when it's ready for Crown Prosecution anyway.'

Her turn to preen a little. 'I can see why you're interested in Blades, but why Barrington?'

More difficult to be honest about him, Jacko gauged. He didn't want to confirm the courtroom grapevine about him. The delivery of the sweetcorn soup gave him thinking time and he played safe. 'It was you who put me on to him.'

With some difficulty, he took a spoonful. It was a strange-shaped pot spoon that didn't seem to fit his mouth. When he did manage it, the soup was thick, hot, tasty. He looked across at her, a touch embarrassed. She was looking puzzled.

'First day. Remember?' he said. 'His thing about non-whites from the Halcyon Health Club.'

'Just gossip.' She spooned expertly, swallowed delicately. 'Proved it, have you?'

He gave a sort-of shrug. 'He could have been May's sugar daddy.'

Over lemon chicken and fried rice, Jacko moved on to the real reason for his invitation. 'I need to know a bit about China. I can't come across as the total innocent abroad, can I? People will smell a rat.'

He was travelling alone, he explained. He'd have loved to have taken Charley with him for her knowledge (now it was safe to lie, he did so without conscience) but the tight-arsed chief constable had sanctioned one ticket only and then a last-minute cheapo bucket shop deal for four nights in Peking, two in Shanghai and three in Hong Kong.

'There's twenty or so on the trip on a block visa. I'm travelling incognito. I've told the agency to stick me down as a law lecturer.'

'Why?'

'I've used it as cover before.' He chuckled at a fond memory and shared a bit of it. 'At the Halcyon Health Club.'

'Successful, was it?' She gave him a knowing smile.

He nodded, grinning.

She turned off her smile. 'Dangerous, though. You're getting in under false pretences.'

'I don't want the local militia to know. May was on the run from them.' So's her sister, though for a different reason, he thought, but that secret, he'd keep. 'Might embarrass her family. Don't want to blow the whistle on anyone to the authorities over there, do I? Besides, the official channels can take ages.'

'I still can't see what you hope to find.'

'Letters home from May. Photos, perhaps. Maybe she confided her feelings for Blades to her old mum or named Barrington in a letter to a school chum or somebody.'

She smiled warily. 'What do you want from me?'

Well, he explained, he could busk a believable reason for going

133

to Hong Kong. A spring of youth dream coming true in his autumn years, now he had the money. But China? Who in their right mind would spend a grand going to China?

She chewed on it and her chicken. 'Use the old excuse. Because it's there. You're going to Hong Kong so you might as well have a look-see now it's open to westerners.'

She'd never visited the land of her fathers herself, she said, and had no great desire. But she read news stories in the *Independent* about it with obvious interest.

She ran through the dynasties, the war lords, the opium wars. 'Seen *The Last Emperor*?'

Jacko shook his head. 'Everyone seems to, apart from me.'

'Seen *Empire of the Sun*?'

At last, he thought, and his face filled with pride. 'Read the book.'

Then, she said, he'd know about the international settlement that brought trade to Shanghai and the Japanese invasion.

Some lessons he'd learned at school again filtered back when she moved on to Mao's long march which was followed by his Cultural Revolution.

She ended in the future with the impending handing back of Hong Kong, a sell-out, in her view.

'Only drink this.' She was refilling his glass from the bottle. 'Never tap water. Watch what you eat. They're hot on dogs, slugs, snakes.'

She nodded down at a meal she'd only half eaten. 'This is for western palates.'

She ran rapidly through the sights he'd see in and around Peking, now renamed Beijing, and what he'd miss elsewhere – a life-sized army made from terracotta, the mountains of somewhere that sounded like Qualing and she gestured to a painting on the wall between two red, white and blue glass lamps.

The ice cream arrived with ordinary spoons which he used happily and by coffee time he was well briefed and feeling like an old China hand.

The waitress came to the table with the bill on a plate which she placed before Charley.

'My treat,' said Jacko.

'I'm doing it.'

'It was my invite. You've been very helpful to . . .' His protest tailed away when he saw she had already slipped a credit card from a small wallet from a hip pocket of her striped, black suit on to the plate.

Jacko abandoned the argument. He always granted women economic equality. In that respect, at least, he was New Man. Besides, it was a modest total and whoever settled it would charge it on exes under 'Essential legal consultation'.

They walked across the busy market place and parted on the courthouse steps. 'Bring me something back,' she said.

'Anything.'

'A nice big fan to hang in my bedroom.'

She closed her eyes, tilted her cheek. He kissed it lightly. She turned away, up the steps.

'Thanks,' he called after her.

'Safe journey,' she said, turning, waving briefly.

17

He was journeying in comfort, soft seat. The back of his head rested on a cream lace runner. On the lace-covered table, his hand cupped a mug of cooling green tea beside a crystal jar of mixed anemones and the *China Daily*, an English language newspaper which, in three short paragraphs on an inside page, reported fifty tourists dead in a landslide which buried their hotel. Life was cheap here, he'd already decided, death not very newsy.

The anemones and the antimacassars reminded him of the brothel above the Pigalle bar where he had lost his virginity in his army days, his teenage years. The train had a much steadier rhythm than he'd managed on his début.

His eyes wandered through the window beyond the lace curtains, patterned with bunches of fruit, and ranged over the vast, moving landscape. More of a waterscape, really, so flat the paddy fields, criss-crossed by dykes, grass banks and power lines.

Here and there, widely scattered, were ramshackle whitewashed settlements, not big enough to be called hamlets, where chickens and ducks and pigs roamed free to forage. Peasants in blue loose suits steered clapped-out tractors and less skilled workers in straw coolie hats carried staggering loads on bamboo poles across scrawny shoulders.

The sun was high and harsh and the heat, he knew, was searing but his spacious carriage was air-conditioned and he'd kept on the cream multi-pocketed cotton jacket his wife Jackie had bought him for what she'd called 'his voyage of discovery'.

He was sitting alone. He'd often been left on his own. On the plane, somewhere over the sage green valleys and lime green mountains of Indo-China, an ear infection had developed; not painful, but irritating.

When he was irritated he always became very irritable. At the rain-lashed airport in Beijing, his tour group finally sorted each other out but he'd given short shrift to the introductory pleasantries of his fellow travellers. He saw no point in talking to people if he couldn't hear what they were saying in reply and had to keep on repeating 'Pardon?' like some dunderhead.

As a result, most of the party had written him off as unapproachable, which suited him. A nosy computer operator – most of his group were professional women – had asked him about his job.

He'd replied 'law official' – an ambiguous but technically true description he'd had entered on the visa after Charley Chan's warning produced second thoughts and a last-minute change to be on the safe side. 'Lecturing, mainly,' he'd added. 'Why not say so?' she'd asked. 'Because I give opinions on case files, too,' he'd said, huffily.

Now when people asked him about his work, he reverted to 'law lecturer'.

The natives especially wanted to know about his work, his family, his opinions, everything. He could hardly go to the toilet (and there'd been plenty of such visits) without a local staring hard into his face and demanding, 'Are you English? Can I speak to you?'

They got up before dawn, it seemed, for the English lessons on the radio. They were keen to practise, to learn it, for jobs in the tourist industry and eventually travel to the west; for all the good it did for May Lee, he thought. But he never said so. This was a place where he didn't speak his mind.

Beijing was hours behind him now. What it had lacked – but he'd never shared this thought – was a bit of decadence.

Few cars used its straight, wide boulevards, packed with slow-flowing streams of cycles, thousands upon thousands of them, none with headlamps after dark. A village bobby there would have enough bikes without lights pinches to last ten lifetimes.

136

The tenement blocks were bigger than the bike factory back home. Nothing that town planners did to Britain in the dire sixties could compare with the sheer scale of its ugliness; not enough shops, bars, street stalls, advertising posters to break its monotonous uniformity.

He never said this either to locals, who were hungry to hear how he used his words. All seemed inordinately proud of their country, wanted praise for it, his seal of approval, not his criticisms.

'What do you think of this?' one had asked in Tiananmen Square. He'd thought of it as the world's biggest parade ground, forever bloodstained by the atrocity that happened there. Not wanting to be impolite or provocative all he'd said was 'Impressive.'

'Do you still talk in the west about our great leader?' the local had asked, motioning to a massive, docile queue which westerners were allowed to jump for a view of Mao's embalmed body. 'Oh yes,' he'd said. He didn't add that he regarded him as a tyrant and that he couldn't understand their blind worship of him and why his misdeeds were forgiven by the expedient of blaming everything on his widow and her gang.

The Great Wall with its breathtaking climb and views had held him spellbound but the temples and tombs rolled quickly into one and the Forbidden City of *The Last Emperor* fame was somehow forlorn. Weeds grew out of its sweeping roofs and its high walls were coated with leaded red paint that came off on to his new jacket when he leaned against it for a smoke.

With no 'No Smoking' signs to irk him, he was up to forty a day, but the locals easily outsmoked him. And spit. How they could spit! Every few steps they left their mark on pavements away from the normal tourist tracks where hygiene wardens watched over them. They could out-gob the entire Tottenham Hotspur team, worthy winners, in his view, of the Football Association Spittoon Final at Wembley.

A shadow fell over the lace tablecloth.

'May I sit down?'

Oh Christ, not another, he thought. 'Please.' He gestured, feeling trapped, to the empty seat opposite, sage green, like the long train's outside livery.

137

'How long were you in Beijing?' asked the intruder, twentyish, lithe, not an ounce of excess fat, cream, short-sleeved shirt spotless, grave face with tired eyes behind round specs; the standard student.

'Four days' – and, yes, he hurried on, he'd found it absolutely fascinating.

'What is your job?'

'Law lecturer.'

'What is your wage?' A common question, always asked without embarrassment, not meant to be rude.

'Fifteen thousand pounds.' A stock reply which he'd converted by multiplying by ten into yuan, but he also added the prices in yuan of houses and cars to try to give it some perspective, bumping them up a bit, to assuage the guilt he felt at earnings undreamt of here.

'You are impressed with our trains – yes?'

Well, yes and no. No, because he'd seen the way hard seat passengers were herded into huge waiting-rooms, for hours on end, where they squatted with their pitiful possessions.

Earlier, he'd strayed, accidentally on purpose, into the hard class sleeping quarters. It was like an army billet, Aldershot-on-rails, a sort of troop train, battery hen bunks so packed that passengers travelled all the way lying down; their dozing disturbed by shrill announcements over the tannoy.

No chance of any sort of sexual contact between Dillon Blades and his late sister-in-law here, he'd decided. A knee-trembler standing up in a hammock would have been easier.

Quips, even private ones, amused him, made him smile, and he was reminded of the only train sleeper story he knew.

This bloke on the top bunk, see, was awakened by something poking his arse through the mattress. He pulled back the curtains and looked down into the berth below. On it lay a beautiful blonde, absolutely naked.

'Excusez-moi,' she said in sexy French. 'J'ai froid.' She shivered. 'Donnez-le-moi, s'il vous plaît' – and she languidly gestured towards a spare blanket on an empty couchette across the aisle.

'Would you like me to come down there and we'll pretend to be a married couple – an Englishman travelling with wife?'

'Mais oui,' she simpered.

'In that case,' said the man, 'get the bloody blanket yourself' – and he turned over and went back to sleep.

He'd chuckled, low but out loud, Noel Cowardish, ignoring the eyes on him, some puzzled, some baleful, none recognizing an Englishman who'd been touched by the midday sun.

He didn't share this with his new temporary travelling companion who, like so many, displayed not the slightest sense of humour. But then, he acknowledged, it can't have been much fun over the years living in this place, where one careless word to a neighbour or a workmate could get you life down on the re-education farm. Instead he just gave him the Yes answer. 'Very clean and punctual.'

The young student nodded at his mug of tea. 'You like our national drink?' They'd use any banality, he'd already noted, to keep a limping conversation going.

'It is ours also.' Jacko had got into the habit of talking so precisely that it was close to pidgin.

'Our national dishes are very popular in the west?'

Only when they're westernized, he thought. Cagily he'd eyed the dishes that spun round on a wheel (Lazy Susans, he now knew they were called) at the giant table in the hotel where his party sat. He'd seen no dogs on the streets of Beijing. Men took their caged birds for walks instead, heightening his suspicion that Charley Chan had been right. He longed to see his own dog again, to satisfy himself she was safe. He was eating mostly vegetarian and losing weight his lean, overworked body could ill afford. 'Very much indeed,' he said.

'Have you bought any of our goods?'

Jacko contorted himself to lift his left leg with his right hand to treat his inquisitor to a view of the black flat slippers he had to buy when his rope-soled sandals, another of Jackie's gifts, disintegrated walking on the apron of the airport in a downpour of monsoon intensity that had welcomed them to Beijing.

A shop assistant served him very offhandedly; could afford to be indolent, he supposed, with a state job for life. He'd upset her by refusing scores of pairs so tight his feet felt bound before she found the size 9 broad fitting he needed. 'They will serve you well for a long time,' she said. (This turned out to be true – over two years, until a big toe poked a hole through. Jackie binned them without the authority of Jacko, who treasured his travel souvenirs, and a stand-up row ensued.)

His display of foot fetish attracted the attention of a small chubby boy who wandered up to the table, folded both arms on it, resting his head sideways on them. He listened intently for a while, staring at Jacko with dark saucer eyes. Suddenly, he snatched up the newspaper and ran down the aisle with it, giggling.

'Our children here are always so happy, is that not the case?' said the young man with a paternalistic smile.

'Very happy,' Jacko happily agreed, thinking: Only because the one child per family rule has produced a nation of spoilt brats. Suddenly, he worried about his own son, an only child because Jackie could have no more. He thought about them both often. He'd phoned home twice already.

An awful truth had dawned on this trip. South of Northampton, this international jet-setter became agonizingly homesick.

Another twenty minutes of aimless chitchat and finally he was left in peace. He looked out of the window again. The landscape had changed from paddy fields to rows upon long rows of cabbages and other green vegetables he didn't recognize.

His mind was back on the job. He'd tossed and turned at nights worrying about how to approach May Lee's family and friends, how he'd cope if they didn't speak English. Not that he'd blame them. All any of his party had managed was something that sounded like 'Mehow', a Chinese greeting which they caterwauled to each other each morning.

That tedious conversation and all the others before it gradually became worthwhile, had given him an idea.

Now he needed a way to extricate himself from the river cruise the tour leader, an enthusiastic Englishwoman, had laid on for the next day. That, too, slowly emerged out of that last conversation.

Soon the cabbages were replaced by stack yards and the smoking chimneys of blackened factories and soot-smeared tenement buildings bigger than barrack blocks. Long freight trains slowly drawn by dirty, black engines belched more smoke that fogged out the glaring sun.

He was on the outskirts of Shanghai.

The baked croissants and the rich black coffee looked and smelt mouth-watering, the most appetizing breakfast Jacko had ever been offered east of Paris, but he turned up his nose.

'Beijing belly.' He patted his stomach.

140

'Too much beer last night, you mean,' said a young, cultivated voice at his shoulder. The handsome youth had won a free trip to China with five gold runs on *Blockbuster*, a TV quiz show for teenage children with questions Jacko could seldom answer.

The night before, half a dozen of the tour party had crossed the road to listen to a jazz band in a hotel bar. Jacko, relaxed with his plan in place, had joined them. The audience had been mainly westerners, including a leather-faced American poseur, his grey hair in a pigtail. What few locals there were in the audience were too cultured for pigtails, too sophisticated to stare, apart from a lean, sharp-suited man who kept looking across at their table and whose watchfulness had reminded Jacko of Cajo, Inspector Clouseau's houseboy.

'Nope,' he said. 'Had these rumblings before.' He excused himself and departed with exaggerated speed to his bedroom, a high-ceilinged barn of a place, inhabited by a good few insects he'd surprised when he'd turned on the light after his late night of jazz.

He read the *China Daily* for ten minutes, all it was worth, but not on the loo. He put on a suffering face for his return to the restaurant. 'I shall have to pull out,' he told the tour leader.

She seemed to take it as a personal affront. 'But we're going up to the Yangtse.'

'I'll wave you off then.' A sickly smile. 'But I must stay close to the hotel.'

He joined the ragged procession from the annexe of their hotel. The heat and noise hit him when he stepped into a street so busy that he thought of Wembley Way on Cup Final day.

Orange and cream trolleys were packed to overflowing, passengers hanging from them. Those who had missed their buses packed the pavements. Wardens in Mao jackets concentrated more on pedestrians than traffic. Furiously blowing whistles, they marshalled them across the street towards the hotel's main building, tall and magnificent with oatmeal-coloured stone and a deep rust-coloured roof in the shape of a pyramid.

There were many more cars than on the streets of Beijing, and much more denim. Some women had styled hair. Some men were in smart suits and polo necks; very western, decidedly decadent.

It was just a short walk to the waterfront, the one he'd seen in the picture at the Blades' manse; thrillingly alive now. Lovely, towering buildings, his own hotel among them, sketched squares, semicircles and triangles on the clear blue sky.

Now he could see why his tour guide had called it the Paris of the east but, to him, it was Liverpool in a heatwave in its halcyon days, his father's days there, and that was how he would always remember it.

The Huangpu river was almost as busy as the streets, with lines of sightseeing boats on the long wooden quay, and junks and sampans, and energetic little tugboats towing barges in roped, never-ending convoys. Across and down river grey warships were moored.

The water seemed to give off a steaming yellowy haze, like sweetcorn soup. Hot, certainly, but not sweet or tasty; fetid, in fact.

These sights, so many of them, not of ancient monuments, but buzzing street scenes, threw a silver-haired pensioner in the party into a frenzy of activity with two cameras strung round his neck.

In and around Beijing he'd fired his way through more rolls of film than Jacko had used in a lifetime. His best shots – competition possibles, he called them – were stored in a metal-lined case to protect them from security X-ray cameras. It was already so heavy that he'd tilted when he carried it off the bus from the railway station into the hotel annexe the night before.

Now he was dodging and turning, taking the Bund, the skyline and river faster than a Fleet Street pro. The tour leader had to order him, protesting, on board.

With his idiot-proof camera, Jacko took shots of Blockbuster Boy waving to him and of the OAP Snapper shooting back at him.

Standing alone, he watched the sleek double-decked, white-hulled boat cut through the yellow waters until it was alongside the warships. Then he turned, walking through a park with butterflies flitting, then resting, among weeping willows.

On the gates of the park, the poseur with a pigtail had insisted the night before, he'd find a sign which said: 'No Chinese. No dogs.' – a reminder to locals of the bad old days when snobby white settlers ruled the port. Jacko couldn't locate it and dismissed it as an old travellers' tale.

But there could just as well have been a similar sign where he was heading, he thought. Every sizeable town had a Friendship Store. The one in Shanghai, just a block or two away, had four floors of merchandise and a fifth consisting of restaurants.

Only foreigners could use them. Plus party officials, of course. In this so-called classless society, they were the ones who got the few cars that swept imperiously through the cycling hordes in the broad avenues of Beijing, who jumped the queues at the railway station and arrived at the last minute to take their seats, who took their pick at the Friendship Stores.

The less privileged hung around outside waiting to swap foreign exchange notes, which visitors had to use, for less valuable local currency or to ask for goods to be bought for them as favours.

He stood by a clipped hedge of green shrubs close to the front steps. He knew he would not have to wait long.

The first buttonholer was a spiv in a black leather jerkin who wanted a carton of Marlboroughs. Jacko got rid of him by pretending not to understand English. The second wore a creased safari suit the colour of the Peace Hotel with a black sweatshirt. Mid-thirties, he had a firm body and an eager-to-please face with even, brilliant white teeth, unusual in a nation of smokers.

Again Jacko was reminded of Inspector Clouseau's houseboy. He wanted to say: 'Not now, Cajo' but didn't.

Wait a tick, he ordered himself. OK, the suit's different, but is this the watchful one from the jazz bar last night? Then, again, what had Dill Blades told him – one oriental looks very much like another to western eyes? He dismissed the notion.

Cajo skipped the first few questions that seemed to come with Radio Beijing's crash course on how to pester tourists. 'Where are you from?' normally featured well after job and salary.

'England, Nottingham.' Jacko was ready with his Sherwood Forest and Robin Hood bit with which he pegged his part of the world for strangers to it.

Before he could use it, Cajo asked, 'Is that near to Derby?'

Jacko expressed his surprise at his geographical knowledge.

'Rolls-Royce,' said Cajo. 'Aero-engines.' He was studying aviation engineering, he explained.

Jacko told him he had flown here on a British Airways plane powered by Rolls-Royce engines, which was nearly all he knew about any plane.

'But is Nottingham near Derby?' Cajo repeated, a touch officiously.

'Less than twenty miles,' Jacko replied, caution and anxiety mounting.

For safety's sake he told him he was a law official but gave his usual answer on his pay. The conversation soon dried up and Cajo went away, frowning, leaving Jacko with a sense of guilt and relief, the sort of mixed feelings that came when he'd driven home safely with too much drink inside him to pass any breath test. Well, was he or wasn't he? He couldn't be sure. You should have asked him, he reprimanded himself.

The next went through the whole gamut of job and pay through to food and children. Jacko ended it by excusing himself to go into the Friendship Store where he bought four wooden-spined fans with butterfly designs – for Jackie and his work-mates Velma Malloy, Helen Rogers and Charley Chan.

He stood outside again, idly opening and shutting a yellow one.

A young, very light voice spoke behind him. 'Is it for your wife?'

He looked round into a small serious face with wire-rimmed spectacles on tired bookworm's eyes; another student. 'Yes.'

She wanted to know about his family, not his job, and the books he'd read. She had never heard of Chandler and Dexter.

He fared better with music now that Jackie had introduced him to bits of Mozart and Beethoven.

'You are not a romantic,' she declared with a serious smile. 'You are a classicist.'

Jacko didn't know whether to be pleased or offended. All he did know was that he was enchanted by her, excited by the promise she held (but not in a dirty old man's way).

She was an arts student, not quite twenty, she said. Her hair, in a severe bun, made her look older. Her thin, frail body beneath a fawn waistcoat made her look younger, a fourteen-year-old.

She wanted to know about the Lake District and Stratford, the homes of her literary idols, student life in England, democracy and, yes, Jacko decided, she'll do.

'Will you be kind enough to help me?' He unbuttoned his top pocket and took out a note of the Li family address copied from the statements of the Rev. and Mrs Blades. 'Do you know where this is?'

She studied. 'Really, it is not far.' She stretched out some words like R-e-a-lly. Others came with a short tongued trill.

'Will you show me? You see, I am a law official and I have to go there with some very sad news.' He pointed to the proper version of May Lee's name taken from college records. 'She has died in tragic circumstances in my country and I have to tell her mother.'

Grave-faced, she asked for more details, which Jacko gave judiciously and briefly. 'Will the mother understand you?' she asked.

He gave her his little boy lost look. 'I do not know if she speaks English.'

'It is sensible that I should come with you and we will find out.'

'Thank you.' Feeling pleased with himself, he looked over her thin shoulder towards the teeming street. 'We will find a . . .'

He stopped, shocked, lost for more words, when his eyes fell on Cajo leaning against the knobbly trunk of a spreading tree trying to look as though he wasn't staring at them.

In a temperature already in the mid-eighties he went cold and silent.

He was sure now.

'Is there something wrong?' she asked.

'We will go soon.'

They chatted for a few more minutes, Jacko not concentrating. Then: 'Do not look behind you now . . .' words he thought he'd never say, '. . . but there is a man leaning on a tree observing us.' He described him.

'Many people here look at western people.' In the pause that followed her tired eyes made the trip to the tree and became apprehensive. 'Do you think he could be the police?'

'I think so.' He told her of his chat with Cajo and of seeing him at the jazz the night before. 'If you wish to leave me I will understand.'

'Why should they follow you? Will not the police help you?'

He explained that May's sister Jade was a political refugee.

'I see.' She hesitated. 'Her mother should know.'

'I will find another way. If you think it could cause you trouble, danger . . .'

'No.' Firm, calm. 'We must not give in to them.'

Call it off, the family man within him urged. Go back to the hotel, to bed, lie low. Don't put yourself and this girl at risk. But you can't travel to the other side of the world and go home empty-handed, replied his professional voice. A meditative moment, weighing it up. 'We could shake them, give them the slip.'

145

'How?'

Another thoughtful silence. 'Leave me now. As you would normally. If he follows you, go and buy a *China Daily* and bring it back to me here and we will consider the situation again. If he remains watching me I will lose him. Where can we meet in half an hour?'

She gave him the name of a coffee shop on the Nanjing road and made him repeat it several times. She rose amid profuse thank-yous and goodbyes.

He watched her walk away.

Cajo didn't move from the shade of his tree.

18

For a second, she looked alarmed when he stepped out of the back of a big yellow taxi, Japanese-made, which drew up in front of the coffee shop. 'I did not recognize you,' she said.

'Good.' A parcel under his arm, Jacko was fumbling in his pockets to pay off the sullen driver.

He'd planned to hail another taxi but she began walking. He fell into step, head and shoulders above her. In close-to-pidgin, he told her he had gone into the Friendship Store after she'd left to make another purchase.

Cajo was waiting and watching when he emerged and followed him into the hotel. Jacko collected his room key, took the lift. He changed into a blue shirt and almost white trousers, left his multi-pocketed jacket behind and replaced black slippers with brown slip-ons. In the lift he'd taken off his tinted specs and put on a blue floppy hat. Key in his pocket, he walked straight through the foyer and out. He'd circled the block but Cajo didn't follow.

'Where is he?' she asked in an amused voice.

'Still sitting in the foyer, I hope. I didn't look either left or right. You must not. You must change with great speed. Policemen get facial or dress features fixed in their brains and they are slow to dislodge them.'

He didn't tell her he was talking from the personal and bitter experience of losing track of a madly jealous husband in a conspiracy to murder case who had pulled a similar quick-change.

146

He slowed in his stride to slip the parcel from under his arm.
'Now you must do the same.' He took out a short, black silk coat
with silver braiding bought in the Friendship Store. He'd judged
it a good fit for a fourteen-year-old. 'Wear this.'

'It is beautiful.' Her tired eyes came alive.

'If anyone makes inquiries at the house where we are going
they will not link you with the girl in the park,' he explained. He
helped her on with it as they walked by well-stocked shop
windows. It was a perfect fit and she tugged it across the front of
her waistcoat, very proudly.

'And let down your hair,' he added.

She pulled away pins, smiling, shaking her head, and her dark
hair fell over the braided collar.

'Can you manage without your spectacles?' he asked. She
nodded. 'Then take them off before we enter the house.'

They walked for what seemed a long while. The heat soon
stuck his freshly laundered shirt to the small of his back. They
turned off the main road into side streets and through passages
beneath washing on bamboo poles. Some houses were brown-
stone, some green, and one was timber-framed with overhang-
ing eaves, worth a conservation order, but being allowed to rot.
Most were drab, discoloured grey.

They crossed bridges, some humpbacked, some with steps.
More washing hung in the rigging of lived-in barges which lined
the rivers and canals. One waterway, she said, led to a place –
Sushy or something like it – famous for its beautiful girls.

Her name, she said, was something that sounded like Jenn. She
spelt it for him – Zheng. 'In your language, it means Long March.'

'You are well named,' said Jacko, and they smiled at each other.

She lived on the campus, she went on, because her family
home was overcrowded with two sets of grandparents.

Eventually she nodded ahead of them and took off her specs.
Not a house, but flats, two storeys, grey breeze block, with a dark
courtyard in which yet more washing hung. It was not even up
to the standards of the low-rise flats they built back home in the
sixties and pulled down two decades later as environmental
disasters.

Beyond the washing children played a noisy game alongside
propped-up cycles and rusting black oil drums that served as
refuse bins.

They climbed an open staircase where more cycles were

chained to railings and walked along a covered corridor. They passed windows with steel grilles and he heard the sound of splashing water; the communal shower or laundry block, he guessed. Every door was open and the unmistakable smell of cooking cabbage drifted towards them.

She stopped half-way down, called something and went in. Jacko stayed outside.

Soon she reappeared, an anxious woman at her shoulder. 'This is she and she requests you to enter,' said Jenn, very politely and grammatically.

The woman beside her had a matronly face, hair cropped short and greying. The clefts below her nose and at the point of her chin seemed bottomless.

Jacko stepped into a room which was small and clean; so dim that he didn't notice at first how it was furnished.

'I have told her only that you are an official of the law from England.'

Jacko pulled out his notebook, looked down at it, breathed in and cleared his throat. 'Please tell her this. I am deeply sorry to have to tell her that her daughter Li Mei Ling has died.'

Jenn seemed some way behind in her translation but he couldn't help himself from pressing on. 'I am terribly sorry to bring her this . . .'

Mrs Li was no longer listening. She clutched both her sides, nipping her blue and white striped smock to her waist, and let out a long, low moan.

She seemed to wilt, about to faint. Jenn hooked an arm into hers, walked her two steps to a bench by a table at right angles to a pink, plaster wall and sat her down.

Jacko turned and walked out. He rested his elbows on the edge of the balcony wall, looking down on the dripping washing, not drying in the sheltered shade of the tarmac courtyard.

His eyes followed his ears to the noisy children. He smoked two cigarettes watching them play some form of volley ball over an empty washing line. They kept looking up at him so the rallies didn't last long.

They were stripped to shorts. All had on some form of footwear; protection, he supposed, against picking up skin worms and other infections from the spit and shit in which so many of them had to walk.

Like British detectives, he thought, gloomily.

148

'She wishes to know . . .' Jenn was beckoning him back inside. '. . . what happened to Mei Ling.'

Jacko was directed to a hard chair on the other side of the scrubbed table at which Mrs Li had been chopping vegetables. 'She was found in a river.' He spared her the gory details.

She said something translated by Jenn as 'She was very unhappy.'

'No. No.' Jacko shook his head. 'She did not end her own life.' To make the point clearer, he added, 'She did not kill herself. She was killed . . .' He didn't want to say murdered so,' . . . in a malicious act.' He underscored that, too. 'It was an evil and wicked thing that happened to her and we must catch who did it. That is why I am here.'

Through Jenn, Mrs Li asked, 'Was it political?'

Undefined doubt scratched at his brain. 'No. It was, we believe, the work of someone who befriended her and who betrayed that friendship.' He had a minister in mind, a religious one, not a political one. He looked hard at Jenn. 'Why did she ask if it was political?'

It took some time to get an answer. 'Because of her daughter's activities here.'

Doubt became anxiety. 'What sort of activities?'

'Among the students.'

A cerebral panic now. He took a photo of May out of his shirt pocket. Yes, Mrs Li said via Jenn, that was the daughter Mei Ling they were talking about.

He produced a postcard-sized photo of Jade and Dill Blades, borrowed from the files of a weekly paper which had published it when their appointment to the mission had been announced.

That was her other daughter Li Shen-Shen and her English husband, she confirmed.

'They know, of course, about the tragedy that has befallen Mei Ling and it was from them that I got your address,' Jacko explained, head down, writing in a black plastic-covered notebook he'd carried in his hip pocket. 'They were under orders not to tell you until I arrived.' Pause. 'For reasons of security.'

Gesturing with her holed chin towards him, Mrs Li said something to Jenn which she promptly passed on. 'She says you have come a long way and she thanks you. You are most kind.'

Mind still racing, he pointed back to May's photo which her mother studied with a mixture of sadness and fondness.

149

Slowly, patiently, Jacko double-checked May had been engaged in student politics and had escaped by train to England more than a year earlier.

He directed her back to Jade's photo and asked about her life in Shanghai. It was a long reply, Jenn asking several questions of her own. Then she said, 'She got into trouble and had to get away to Hong Kong.'

Jacko framed his next question carefully. 'Was Mrs Li's other daughter Shen-Shen . . .' he nodded at Jade's photo, '. . . also involved in politics?'

His mind raced on as he awaited the answer. 'No,' it finally came, 'she was involved in the tourist trade, but liked too much of a good time.'

Holy Christ. His brain was bleeding badly now, wounded, sapping his energy. I've travelled half-way round the world at the cost of a grand only to discover that the Rev. Dillon Blades switched sisters on me. Not their names; the personas.

His wife Shen-Shen, aka Spruce Tree aka Jade, was the good-time girl, the prostitute, the junkie.

Lord in heaven. He'd reformed her, married her and wanted to keep her past life secret.

Mei Ling, aka Beautiful Ring aka May, was the political activist and refugee.

That, he knew in a blinding flash, explained why she was a virgin, the quiet life she led in Derby. So frightened of discovery had she been that she'd pinched a line from her sister's CV and claimed to have worked in the tourist trade herself to cover her academic background. But she wasn't and never had been in or on any sort of game apart from politics. Jesus wept.

Jacko put several careful queries and could read the answers in the mother's matronly face for himself – warm at any mention of May, cold for Jade, warm again for Dillon Blades.

Her translated words confirmed she regarded her son-in-law as a good and courageous man who had saved Jade from sin and May from jail.

There was one certain way of proving it, Jacko realized. 'Ask her if she has ever met her son-in-law Dillon.'

'Affirmative,' came the translated reply. 'Just over a year ago when he came here to collect the one you call May and take her to your country.'

'When did she last see her other daughter?'

'Not since she escaped to the safety of . . .' Mrs Li interrupted to add something. '. . . the safety of Hong Hong. Naturally she did not attend the wedding there.'

Life's blood seemed to drain out of him and he knew he had to stem the flow. He asked if the sisters had written home to her. She got up and walked to the sort of plain sideboard he'd seen at his grandma's home just after the war; utility furniture, they called it, cheap, all-purpose.

May's letters spilt from a box with a painted lid. Jade's were held together by an elastic band, no more than half a dozen. She handed all of them to Jenn.

She cleared and cleaned the table with a dry cloth and opened the door to a small kitchen from which steam billowed. He watched the bare plaster walls glisten with condensation. She returned with a flask of tea and three chipped enamel mugs. They drank in silence, the coarse leaves embedding themselves in the gaps in his teeth.

Jenn completed Jade's letters first and summarized them. 'From Hong Kong she writes of her new life and of Dillon and how he has cleansed her and she has found your God. She asks repeatedly about the one you call May and in one letter . . .' she checked the date, '. . . fifteen months ago, she tells of her forthcoming marriage and says that her new husband will be visiting her sister soon to help but she does not say how or why.'

Well, she wouldn't, would she? Jacko thought. Blades and his born-again bride were setting up May's escape to the west and wouldn't want to run the risk of that letter falling into the wrong hands.

'From England she writes once only, quite recently, of her new home and church, says she was looking forward to seeing her sister but the one you call May had gone on holiday to London to see student friends.'

A solemn-faced Mrs Li busied herself in the kitchen, popping in and out, leaving another door open to permit Jacko a glimpse of a tidy, tiny bedroom with a TV set on a stool.

There were many more letters from May, all written on what looked like rice paper with hieroglyphics running horizontally, not vertically. Jenn placed the box at her dainty feet and read extracts out loud as she went through them. It was a slow job.

In early letters from Derby, May told her mother of her big new house and the vast amounts of money she was earning at the

151

college for so little work, but against that, she'd been shocked by the cost of living.

Her homesickness was poignantly described ('I miss you so very much my heart cries'), abated with a wonderful account of her winter's day in the Peaks, but returned after seeing *The Last Emperor*.

Too much of a painful reminder of a country she missed deeply, Jacko supposed. Poor May. Here I am, missing a family I'll see again in a few days. There she was, exiled forever. Friendless. Or was she? He'd find out.

Mrs Li reappeared with food in bowls and pans and one black wok which she laid on the table. She motioned to Jacko to pull up his chair. Using wooden chopsticks, she deftly half filled his white bowl with steaming rice. Then she pointed with her sticks to dishes of vegetables. Not so deftly, he added broad beans, peas in shells and one or two things he wasn't sure about to the rice, but avoided the cabbage.

When she saw that Jacko liked the peas, which were sweet and tender, she pushed that bowl towards him, urging him to help himself to more.

Jenn read as she ate and translated questions and answers between Jacko and the mother at the same time. Yes, she said, May had mentioned somewhere forming a friendship. Yes, she did have photos from England which he could see after the meal.

'Here it is,' said Jenn, not quite a delighted squeal.

She held the letter away from her to focus more clearly. 'She writes of that friend but does not give a name. They met at that film show and had meals together, the cooking not up to the standards of her mother, she says.'

The room went silent again apart from the clicking of the chopsticks. On the whole, Jacko was not really enjoying the meal, preferred the lemon chicken Charley Chan had treated him to. Manfully he ate on.

Jenn was nearing the end of the pile and read directly from the next letter. 'My work goes well but not my social life. My new friend has too much persistence.' She looked at Jacko for guidance. 'Persistence? Is that right?'

He nodded. He was getting too heavy, she means.

The next letter was even more depressed and anxious. 'I am trying to put an end to my outings to concentrate on my work

152

and my reading. The situation is so bad that I lose sleep and I am tired when I should be working.'

She reached the last letter. 'I have been to see a doctor for a pick-me-up but all he gave me was a long talking to.'

Jacko asked for it to be read again and he noted it down. He nodded her on.

'He said there was nothing physically wrong with me, you will be pleased to hear, and that I am in stress and overworked which is only partially true. He suggests a holiday with friends as a cure. I think I have amassed sufficient money to visit London for a few days where I may find college friends. I know all my troubles will be over soon when Shen-Shen and Dillon arrive.'

She was clearly looking forward to seeing him again as much as her sister Jade. Equally clearly, from further extracts, she regarded him as her mother did – as a kind and good man.

Look on the bright side, Jacko was telling himself without much conviction. I have lost one suspect, but have I refound Barrington, the Stipe?

That doctor she consulted sounds more like a shrink than a medicine man. Could it have been Dr Saul at Tor View Clinic? If so, could Barrington have met May there? He was a trustee, always popping in and out. His Chinese Malayan houseboy hired Simon Meakin for a gardening stint. Did he invite a Chinese girl in for a pot of home-brew tea to meet his master, who liked hand-jobs from exotic women?

He reread to himself the phrase he'd noted down: '. . . in stress and overworked which is only partially true.' Ten hours' teaching a week wouldn't overwork anyone. The stress was causing her tiredness and illness. Stress from what? From Barrington making demands for bizarre sexual acts?

It could be on, you know. It's possible. His enthusiasm was returning.

Mrs Li cleared the table again, collected up the letters, went to the sideboard and came back clutching coloured photos which she handed to Jacko.

A couple were of Jade, wearing her jade necklace, taken in Hong Kong by the look of the backgrounds, none from England.

Seven were of May. Four he'd seen. Three were new to him. All had been taken on the bench where he'd interviewed her housemate. They were virtually the same pose. Only the tilt of her head and the sad smile were different.

In all, both her arms stretched out along the back-rest. Her right hand gripped it. On her third finger a ring was visible. Not gold. Silver.

'Is that a coin?' He pointed it out to Jenn but her eyes were so tired now they looked pained and she could not tell.

He asked Mrs Li for permission to take them but she wanted to know why.

'By identifying this ring,' he said urgently but smiling pleasantly, 'we may be able to find the wicked person who ended your brave daughter's life.' If I can tie this ring into Barrington, I've got the bastard, he was thinking. 'I will guard them with my own life and see that they are safely returned to you.'

She nodded consent for him to take the three photos and asked who the wicked man might be.

When he had come into this apartment three hours earlier the honest answer would have been: 'A minister of religion.'

Now he said, 'An official of the law.'

On reaching the bustling Nanjing road, Jenn pointed with her chin away from the direction in which the yellow taxi had brought him. 'I live and work down there. I am late for a lecture at my academy. I must say goodbye.'

Jacko didn't know what to say.

'If you walk on you will find the place of our meeting.' She smiled. 'I have taken much pleasure from that meeting.'

'Me also.'

She began to take off the silk jacket.

He laid a hand on her arm. 'It is for you. Please keep it but do not wear it on your campus for a little while.'

She gave him a quaint, puzzled look. 'Will your wife not require it?'

A smiling shrug. 'It was bought for you. It is to say thank you.'

'Thank you,' she said.

There was pain behind both pairs of eyes as they said goodbye. Jacko did not watch her walk away. He turned, stepping it out.

A billion people in China, he was thinking, and I found the one in that billion.

154

His fellow travellers were disembarking when he reached the waterfront, tired and sticky.

'Better?' asked the nosy computer operator.

'A lot. Good trip?'

'Yellow water wall-to-wall. Pongy, too.' She wrinkled her nose.

'Fancy a Coke?' he asked. Blockbuster Boy had started the rumour among the party in Beijing that Coca Cola was the sure cure for all stomach ailments.

'Later.' First, she said, she was going to the Friendship Store to buy presents, a long job by the sounds of the size of her family. She joined a group that included Blockbuster Boy.

The OAP Snapper staggered down the gangway under his load. 'Must restock with film,' he panted.

'Have a look at this.' Jacko fished out one of May's photos from his shirt pocket. The OAP Snapper lowered his metal-lined case to the ground, took it, fingered his steel-framed spectacles firmly to the bridge of his nose and studied it.

'Will that ring on her finger blow up?' asked Jacko.

'An easy job.'

'You don't travel with a portable enlarger, do you?' Jacko had no photographic knowledge whatsoever.

'Lord, no, but I'm going to a specialist shop in Hong Kong tomorrow. They'll do it. Shall I take it?'

Spread your load, Jacko decided, and he nodded.

The OAP stooped, opened his case and dropped it among the black canisters of used film, shut it again, picking it up as he straightened. 'I'm off to the Store.'

He staggered away, tilting. No point, Jacko knew, in volunteering to carry the case back to the hotel for him. It was rumoured, also by Blockbuster Boy, that he slept with it.

He headed back for the hotel on his own. He felt very lonely and conspicuous among the masses of people all round him in the oven hot streets.

He was that one in a billion now.

19

Whoosh. From the kerbside to his right, the rattling sound of metal wheels on a metal track.

'Hey.' A harsh voice, vaguely transatlantic, from a shop door-way to his left. 'You.'

Jacko flicked his head to his right at a black transit van, still moving, its side door being slid open. Then to his left.

Cajo.

The blow came from his right, unseen. Into the small of the back, contracting his pumping heart, freezing it rock solid. He stumbled towards Cajo, hand out in a strange sort of unsmiling welcome. He just had time to tense his not very firm stomach muscles before a short arm jab exploded just under his rib cage. Molten lead was injected into his stomach.

'Help.' More of a grunt than a shout. Masses of people about, walking round them, looking away.

He felt himself being turned, lifted, feet no longer on the ground. He was pitched through the van's door, forced from behind, face down, on to the metal floor, cold to his right cheek.

Hands grabbed his wrists, pulling them behind. 'Take the money,' he heard himself pleading. 'Take the watch.' Handcuffs nipped skin at his wrists. His tinted spectacles were ripped from his face.

Hands again. Out from the back trouser pocket came his credit cards wallet and a folded roll of yuan, £50 worth, pocket money by western standards, a small fortune here. The notebook at one hip followed; hotel room key, Bensons and lighter from the other. More hands at his chest. Out came the two photos of May and his pen. Four hands close to his eyes dropped them in his upturned floppy hat on the floor above his head.

He spoke to the hands. 'Help yourself. Just let me go.'

Cajo's face appeared, almost horizontal, on his hands and knees, grinning like a devil. 'Foreign devil.' He hissed it. 'We do not wish for your money or your watch.'

'What do you want?' Jacko didn't recognize the strangled sound as his own voice.

'Spy.' He spat it, literally, the phlegm hitting Jacko's left cheek, sliding away down to the floor.

'You've got the wrong man, mate.'
'Academic!' Sneered. 'You are espionage.'
'You're making a terrible mistake.'
'You make the mistake.'

Whoosh. The doors slid back after a jerky journey, all stops and starts, that wracked his body. Shit, shit, you're in the shit, a scrambling brain kept telling him.

He was pulled out of the back by his ankles along the van's floor through Cajo's slaver. His brown slip-ons landed on soft Tarmac. His body doubled. Vice-like fingers at each elbow stopped his fall. He was in a square courtyard, high red buildings on all sides; that was all he could make out as he was lifted by the elbows to a door and down stone steps.

Somehow his floppy hat containing the contents from his pockets had beaten him to a large, cool room where it sat on a large otherwise empty desk. Jacko was placed before it, standing far from upright.

Cajo, at his shoulder, looked much bigger now. 'You are an agent. Confess it.'

Jacko winced round and up. 'I am a holiday-maker, a tourist.'

A brown clenched fist hooked out in front of him, then homed in on him, almost too fast to follow. His stomach became a volcano and erupted.

The lava ran on down inside his legs, melting them. Gasping, retching, he dropped to his knees, forehead crashing down against the desk and he stayed there, mind roaming, hopelessly lost, in steaming yellow fog. His nose was in a spreading green pool of regurgitated peas.

Clunk. The metal door shut in the tiny cell to which he'd been dragged on his knees. Hands unlocked his hands from behind, slipping off his cheap watch at the same time. 'Remove your clothing.' Still on his knees, Jacko rubbed his wrists. '*Now.*' A bark from the rear.

He had to pull back his shoulders to peel off his blue shirt, which was stuck to him. He whimpered slightly in pain. His chin dropped towards his ventilating chest.

'Your trousers.' He stood, unsteady. He removed his shoes first, toe against heel, alternating his weight on his feet. Bending to pull down the once white, now streaked, very damp trousers seemed to ease his pain but only slightly.

'Your pants.' He added them to the untidy pile.

'Give them to me.' He collected them up, passed them over his shoulder, not looking, too frightened really to want to know.

Click. A key turned outside the door. He was naked. He was alone. Catching his breath, he looked round, squinting to focus.

The cell was about three yards by three yards, no more, lit by a bright bulb in the ceiling, no window.

In one corner, a square of cracked porcelain, like the bottom of a shower, a copper tap above; no toilet pedestal. In another corner a grey mattress rolled up on the concrete floor.

Gripe seized his bowels. Nothing phoney about this attack. Not Beijing belly; the Shanghai shits this, the real thing. Arms dangling like an ape, he limped to the corner where he squatted in the wicketkeeper's position for a long time. No paper, so he cleaned himself from the tap, bidet-style.

He turned off the tap tightly, not wanting Chinese water torture. He ape-walked to the mattress and sat on it, to dry himself. For a long, long time, he sat, knees up, forehead resting on them.

The surface of his mind was more than gale-tossed. Inside his head were the innards of a deafening clock, wheels revolving in opposite directions, fears and thoughts pulling against each other. He'd experienced nothing like it before and he couldn't think, just couldn't.

Clunk. At the door, Cajo, waving the black notebook, face jubilant. 'We have you. We have you.' Click.

Clunk. Much later, impossible in this vacuum to say how long. Cajo again, waving May's photo. 'You have been consorting with a counter-revolutionary. Security, you said. Reasons of security, you told her mother. We have got you.' Click.

*

Clunk, much later. 'Who is your accomplice?'

'Please. I'm a tourist.' Jacko used his begging voice with a face to match. Not the time to stand on your dignity, he decided. He had none. Humble pie time. 'You misunderstand.'

'The girl who went with you to the house of Li.'

'What girl?' An incredibly stupid reply, he realized, even as the words came out.

Cajo took a short step forward.

'I don't know.' His brain still refused to function.

'Her name?' Another step.

Jacko snatched at the only name he could remember from the shop signs on the Nanjing road. 'Jinping or something.'

'Her other name?'

'Honestly. I don't know. I just called her Miss Jinping.'

'How did you meet?'

'She stopped me to practise her English. She offered to show me the way.' Better, he was telling himself.

'Where does she live?'

'Somewhere called Sushy or something. That's all I know.' Quite good that, he thought. His confidence rose a little. 'Look, you are making a . . .'

Cajo stepped back out of view. Click.

Clunk. Cajo's fifth or sixth visit. Jacko had lost count.

'The message, Long Nose. What message did you pass?'

'That the daughter of the lady of the house is dead.'

An angry glare. 'What has that got to do with a so-called academic?'

'Look, sir. I'm not a . . .'

'We know.' That devilish smile. 'You are a police officer, a British secret policeman.'

'I'm an ordinary policeman off duty and on holiday.'

'You were on duty at that address. You conducted a velly long interrogation.' Now and then Cajo replaced l's with r's, as if trying to make himself sound like a stereotyped Chinese villain in a Hollywood B-film. 'Explain that.'

'My chief asked me to call while I was here. On holiday. To give her the news rather than write a formal letter. It was a routine interview.'

'Who is this chief?'

'Chief Superintendent Carole Malloy, of the East Midlands Combined Constabulary near Nottingham.'

'A woman?' Without specs, Jacko couldn't read his face but heard the incomprehension in his voice. 'I do not believe you.'

'True. I swear.'

'I do not believe you came for the purpose you state.'

'You have my word for it.'

'Your word has no worth. Your records will show it. You will stay here . . .'

'But I have . . .'

'Here.'

Click.

You, sunshine . . . He had rolled out the filthy wafer-thin mattress and was lying on it, knees up, talking to himself: . . . you must look and you certainly feel and smell like shit and you are deep, deep in it; in deep, dark shit.

No fiction now, that pounding pain in his back. No massage from Flying Fingers at the Halcyon Health Club to soothe it. He rubbed the V below his rib cage, the skin flame pink like his wrists and knees. Chinese burn marks, school bullies used to call them. These bullies have hit you where it won't show.

Think now, he urged himself. Plenty of thinking time here, he added bitterly.

He wondered if they had informed his tour guide, who would have alerted the Consul. He guessed not. Made no difference anyway. They'd just chase the Consul from police station to police station, like we used to do to solicitors and relatives before they changed the law.

There was, he knew, nothing to stop them planting a note among his credit cards to fit him up as a courier for May or heroin in a pocket to frame him as a trafficker for Jade.

Bent cops back home have done things like that, too, and got away with it.

Shame poured through him. They did it. You know some did it. You did nothing about it, turned a blind eye, because you didn't want to blow the whistle. Now it's your turn. Someone has blown the whistle on you. Now you know what it feels like; the fear, the anger of an innocent man in jail. Christ, you're in the shit.

Think, man, think. What are their tactics?

Well, like all bent cops the world over, they're practising isola-
tion in this time warp, humiliation by stripping you naked
and sleep deprivation with these constant visits, and this bright
light.

A bright thought then, the first one.

If only they knew. He sighed. Pain pierced the V of his rib cage.
He waited until it subsided. If only they knew that I am terrified,
truly and totally terrified of the dark, they'd turn it off
and I'd confess to anything, sign everything. Shine on, kindly
light.

A dark thought now. What if they turn it off? His mind went
blank for a moment, then: Won't matter, if I'm asleep. Sleep?
Here? I must try. I need rest to face tomorrow.

Right. Your bowels and bladder are clear. Not half. Don't drink
that water. What about my malaria tablet? I've not missed one.
Will I catch it and have recurring bouts like Barrington thirty
years on? You should be so lucky to be around thirty years on.
Worry about it then. Think. Decide priorities.

Priority Number One is to get through the next few hours. OK,
I don't need a smoke, not with these lungs on fire. What's to stop
me sleeping?

My mind. It's racing away. Slow it down. Think of pleasant
things. Not Jackie, your kid and dog. Will I see them . . . No. No.
Don't ever think like that. You need sleep.

His mind went totally blank.

Should I pray? asked a still inner voice.

A shock ran through him.

Well, should I?

Christ Almighty. An angry rebuke. You can't.

Why not?

You can't go through three-quarters of your life, a disbeliever,
a blasphemer, and suddenly rediscover God when you're in the
shit, for christsake.

Why not? People do.

Yes, and that's what's wrong with religion. You can be the
biggest bastard on earth and a couple of Hail Marys on your
death-bed stamp your passport to heaven. It's hypocritical. It's
not honourable.

Right. A shallow sigh, not hurting so much. Honourable, he
repeated. It was a word that he liked. Right.

Well? Nothing. Well?

161

Remember that Reuters reporter locked up here in China for years. Gray, was it? Or Grey? He kept sane by going through the theory of shorthand in his head. I don't know shorthand but something like that, to occupy your mind?

He went through all the words of every railway song Lonnie Donegan had ever sung until he reached:

> I'm just a weary and a lonesome traveller.
> I'm travelling home.

It made him think of Jackie. He stopped, could go on no further.

Something else. Anything else. He wondered if the gang had gone across to the jazz again at the Peace Hotel. He pictured them, sitting, listening. The computer operator smiling at 'Gettin' Sentimental'. Blockbuster Boy tapping his feet to 'Nobody's Sweetheart'. When the music stopped, he stayed in view.

He saw him on TV in that quiz show where he'd won the travel prize with five gold runs. What FO means go forth and multiply?

Not Foreign Office, he thought angrily. They'll be sitting on their hands, like they did through the Beirut hostage crisis and . . . Fuck Off. He seemed to shout it to himself.

You mustn't think this way, a calmer voice chided him.

In the way his mind always followed a course he'd accidentally charted he saw himself in the *Mastermind* hot seat, eyes of the nation on him. What is your chosen specialist subject?

Can't be books or music so . . . A thoughtful second or two. . . . how about the promotion years of Lincoln City?

Wouldn't the relegation years be better? Are you sure there are two minutes of questions on their promotion years?

He felt himself smiling, actually smiling. How many questions do we need?

From his mine of useless information, he remembered reading that average speech is delivered at three words a second so two minutes is 360 words. He tried a test one.

Name Graham Taylor's championship squad. He reeled off twelve names and counted up the words in both question and answer. Seventeen into 360. A hard one which took time. Twenty-one and a bit. Make it twenty questions.

What was the score against Doncaster Rovers in the champion-ship decider?

So easy that he didn't answer, but he saw himself in the 14,000 crowd, huge by Sincil Bank standards, which launched red and white balloons before that Easter game. Now he was standing in front of the main stand afterwards, feeling childishly proud, as Sam Ellis held up the trophy.

Who scored the goals in that 5-0 win?

Percy Freeman with two headers, Ellis with a penalty, Alan Harding with a cracker and . . .

Christ. Who else? It wouldn't come. He wanted to say 'Pass' but his mind wouldn't move, demanding to be left alone to dwell on that unforgettable day, watching the game again, seeing their goalie's dropkick hitting Percy's arse and looping back towards the net, smiling and, finally, sleeping.

On the high ceiling a huge fan, the size of a light plane's propeller, turned slowly, labouring. Hope that's not going to conk out, Jacko thought. The room was hot enough, stifling. He had to stay cool, keep his wits sharp.

He'd been given back his clothes and his spectacles, offered a watery oatmeal gruel which he'd refused and had been escorted up stone steps into this spacious room by two guards in green uniforms.

He stood before the desk. His legs felt rubbery. His head felt stuffed. His mouth was sewer foul. He smelt rank. But he was calmly alert after his astonishingly deep sleep.

Sitting behind the desk was a small, stern-looking man with grey hair in severe, regulation short back and sides and wearing a grey western-style suit – sharp, well-pressed.

Standing at a big window was Cajo, in yesterday's clothes, his back to flat railed roofs of a round-cornered building across a road from which came the sounds of incessant traffic and wardens' whistles.

The sun was in its mid-morning position, Jacko estimated. It shone through the transparent skin of Cajo's big ears so that they looked as though they were about to burst into flames.

On the desk, next to a stack of files, was Jacko's blue floppy hat into which more possessions from his hotel room had been added, his bottle of malaria tablets among them.

163

On a well-worn flowered carpet stood the two RAF blue hand-grips with which he'd travelled. Beside them the fans, opened, to see, he guessed, if any secret messages had been written down the spines.

The grey man opened Jacko's dark blue passport and slipped out a small, green form, headed Departure Card. It was the carbon copy of the arrival form Jacko had filled in just before he'd touched down on the outward flight.

'You are James Jackson?' asked the grey man.

'Yes, sir.'

He flicked his head towards Cajo. 'You told my officer last night that you are an English policeman.'

'Yes, sir.'

'Here –' he picked up the form – 'you state you are a law official.'

'Yes.'

'Well?' Pause. 'Which is correct?'

'Both. It is the same thing.'

'Why not state you are a policeman?'

'I am a law officer. Same thing.'

'Why not state that?'

'Official. Officer. It means the same thing in my language.'

The grey man exchanged a troubled look with Cajo and Jacko seized on their indecision. 'You, sir, are an official. Correct?' He nodded at Cajo. 'He is one of your officers. Both work for the same service. It is just a question of rank.'

'What is your rank?'

'Inspector.' He decided to drop the Detective prefix.

Cajo smiled glibly. 'You told me you were a law lecturer, an academic.'

Jacko shook his head dumbly. 'Official.'

Cajo went back through their conversation outside the Friendship Store. 'In it, you declared to me that you are a law lecturer.'

Jacko decided not to dispute it, let recognition dawn on his face. 'I do lecture. I'm non-operational on account of my age. I lecture recruits mainly.'

Under lengthy questioning, standing throughout, Jacko stuck to his reasons for being in China and for calling on May's mother.

'The girl who accompanied you there,' said the grey man. 'Who was she?'

164

Jacko nodded to Cajo. 'I have told him. Miss Jingping from Sushy. I stopped her outside a coffee shop and asked for directions. She showed me the way.'

'You know the daughter of the house you visited is wanted by us.'

'I know that now.' An innocent face, easy to maintain. 'I didn't know it then. We thought she was a vice girl, a prostitute.'

He patted a file on his desk. 'That is the other daughter.'

'I gather that now. Her English husband misled . . .' He almost said me, but changed it in time. '. . . us.'

Cajo came in. 'You told the old woman Li that you were security police.'

'No.'

'You did.' His face twisted.

'No. No.' Jacko surprised himself with his calm, even delivery. 'I said we had not released all the details of her daughter's death for security reasons. We wanted to keep certain details secret, so we could catch her killer.'

Cajo's eyebrows came down, puzzled. 'You told the mother that the daughter we seek is dead. We do not believe you. That is a trick.'

Jacko sensed Cajo had stronged up his case to his boss, the way some detectives do. He directed his reply across the desk to the grey man, determined to create doubt in his mind. 'It is true, sir. I would not lie about a thing like that to any mother.'

'When did she die?'

He told him approximately when and how, all the gory details.

A triumphant smile lit the grey man's face, as though at good news, but Jacko had misjudged him. 'It has not been reported in your newspapers.'

They've been on to their embassy in London overnight, thought Jacko, alarmed. What's more, they're right. Velma Malloy hadn't released her identity. 'No.'

'Why not, tell me?'

'I have told you. We have kept her identity a secret from the public and the press in order to catch her murderer.'

The smile disappeared. 'Who is this murderer – the English husband?'

Jacko shook his head. 'An English law official.'

'A senior policeman?'

Too difficult to explain, Jacko decided. 'We think so.' Then:

'That is why my chief has been so secretive about things. That is why she asked me to see her mother. To get some proof to convict this official. We do not tolerate incompetent and corrupt members in our law service any more than you do.'

Not all together true, Jacko conceded privately, in either country.

The room went silent.

The grey man shuffled his papers. 'Have you found such proof?'

Jacko nodded towards his hat. 'Those photos in there might help.'

The grey man extracted them, studying them as Jacko explained about the ring.

'The mother said you took three photos. Where is the other?'

'I posted it to my headquarters.'

'When?'

Right, Cajo, my little yellow friend, I'm dropping you in it. 'At the hotel.' To further questions he added: 'In the post box in the foyer. After I returned from seeing Mrs Li.'

Jacko looked down at the photos. His eyes didn't follow the grey man's towards Cajo. He imagined, hoped, his ears were burning now.

'We must make further phone calls,' said the grey man menacingly, but in Cajo's direction. 'You must wait.'

The apologies, mainly from Jacko, came after a tormentingly long wait in a stuffy side room.

'You see,' said the grey man, no Cajo present, 'your activities were not those of a genuine tourist and our attention was drawn to them.'

'I am so sorry.' Jacko, sitting in a basket chair with peeling brown paint, put on his craven face.

'This is your fault.' He slipped the departure card back inside his passport. 'You should have made your profession much clearer.'

Jacko nodded obediently.

'You displayed great discourtesy not informing us of your presence, entering areas not permitted to tourists without supervision and questioning individual citizens about family matters.'

'I accept that I acted foolishly.'

166

'We would have been honoured to have accompanied you and assisted you to obtain the information you required.'

'Had I thought, I would have come to you with such a request.'

A grey look passed over the grey man's face. 'We informed your guide last night that you were the victim of a street crime perpetrated by hooligans. You, yourself, were under the impression that such was the case at first, is that not so?'

Jacko nodded energetically, thinking: He's about to offer me a deal.

'That being so, it would be a great pity if you complained about what has happened here. We would have to state that the misunderstanding occurred as a direct result of your interference in our internal affairs. We do not wish for a quarrel at a time when our countries are growing closer, do we?'

So enthusiastic was his agreement that Jacko shook the stuffiness out of his head.

'That being so . . .' He dipped into the floppy hat on the desk. '. . . it would be wise to leave this behind.' He held up the roll of money. 'It will pay for your accommodation. The rest will go to good causes.'

'I quite agree.' That won't be going to any widows and orphans fund, you corrupt bastard, he thought, smiling.

Then he held up the two photos of May. 'As for these, should you apply for them through official channels, they will be forwarded to the address you have provided.'

The grey man pushed the hat across the desk. 'Your party have departed for the airport. Transport has been arranged for you to join them to catch your plane. You are free to leave.'

'Thank you, sir.'

Free, he thought, heart spiralling skywards. Free. Freer than some prisoners who have been treated, sometimes worse than this, in police stations back home. Now he'd been on the receiving end, he could understand how they must feel, their freezing fear, their burning sense of injustice. Some of them fought the authorities all the way, never gave up. Not him though. He wanted out and home.

'You have been most kind, sir,' he said, almost grovelling, not in the least disgusted with himself.

20

Bed rest, ordered a doctor summoned to a four-star hotel with a panoramic view of Hong Kong's Causeway Bay and its ocean-going cruisers.

Jacko climbed in after a long and blissful soak in a huge bath and a spaghetti carbonara from room service. In his mining for useless info, he'd read somewhere that cheesy pasta gives marathon runners their stamina. Anything not Chinese would have done, really.

From his bedside phone, he called home first. So long and lovingly did he speak that Jackie asked, 'Have you been up to something naughty? Is this remorse?'

He phoned Velma Malloy. Before he could tell her he'd been Shanghai-ed, she said, 'Have you been causing an international incident?'

Bloody women, he thought. Isn't anyone pleased to hear from me?

She went on, 'I had a late call from the overnight duty officer at the Foreign Office who'd had a very cross Chinaman on from their embassy wanting to know if one of their citizens had died in mysterious circumstances on our patch.'

'What did you tell them?'

'The truth.'

His lips smacked a kiss, his first for any boss, and told her she had sprung him from jail.

She laughed dully. 'I'd have lied if I'd known.'

He explained how and why he'd got into jail and grumbled on, 'Nothing broken but my bruises below the ribs went blue in the bath and my back will need the personal attention, on exes, of course, of Flying Fingers in the Halcyon Health Club. My knees are skinned. I'm covered in mozzy bites so I'll probably get malaria like Barrington, the Stipe, and . . .'

'Talking of whom . . .' Velma cut in callously, uninterested in his aches and pains or his traveller's tales, '. . . how did you make out?'

'It wasn't Blades, that's certain.' Very positive. 'His bride's letters confirm they genuinely believed May was alive in London. May's own letters home make him sound like some guardian angel.'

He gave her a complete rundown. No disappointed expletives, no curses from afar, and he knew then that Velma believed the job of her detectives was to clear the innocent every bit as much as to convict the guilty.

'But if we can establish that homesick May took her stress complaint to Tor View Clinic, we may have the connection with Barrington,' he continued.

'Do you want me to get on to Dr Saul?'

'Why not wait till I get back? He's virtually my very own sex therapist now. Leave him to me. Let's wait to see what this blow-up of May's photo brings.'

'OK,' she said, trustingly.

The OAP Snapper brought the enlargement of the ring on May's finger to Jacko when he was still in bed; sixteen hours, disturbed only by the troublesome teaser over who scored Lincoln City's fifth against Doncaster Rovers.

He could see with one glance that it was a coin all right; Queen Elizabeth's head on a silvery background, but not a coin of the English realm.

'Is it Commonwealth currency?' he asked, thinking of Barrington's long-ago service in Malaya.

'Looks more like Maundy money to me.'

A distant bell rang in Jacko's head. 'Isn't that dosh the Queen doles out to church charity cases?'

The OAP Snapper was equally vague. 'They're . . . well . . . like the Queen's birthday honours but for the Church of England, I think.'

He'd once gone to photograph a cathedral during a royal visit at which specially minted coins were handed to great and small, who'd done their bit for the church and the community.

Maundy? thought Jacko. 'Isn't Maundy Thursday the day before Good Friday?'

The OAP Snapper was unsure about that, too, because while he happily snapped places of worship, east or west, he never prayed inside any of them.

If I remember correctly from that quick read of the Hamlyn Children's Bible back home, Jacko was thinking, that royal ceremony takes place at the start of the Passover, the time of the Last Supper, when Jesus washed his disciples' feet.

He couldn't be sure either. But he knew who would be. Gingerly, he climbed out of bed.

A coat of fresh yellow paint had skinned over the words 'Dill's Den' but their outlines were still visible above a screwed-on name plate with bright barge art flowers round the edges. In the centre it said: 'Rachel's Room'. He knocked.

'Don't knock,' an English voice called from behind the door. 'Just come in.'

He went in. Dill's successor was lying on a bunk. She was around thirty and looked more like an undergrad on a lazy Sunday than a reverend missionary. Flat black slippers, baggy striped cotton trousers in two tones of blue, loose pink blouse.

Her chin was a bit weak, too pointed, but strong cheekbones gave her a confident look. Dark, thick, glossy hair was down to where her dog collar should have been at the back. Her forehead was hidden beneath strands that tumbled down to her brown eyes; warm, welcoming eyes.

'Welcome.' She didn't really have to say it.

He introduced himself as a detective inspector and a friend of Dillon Blades.

'How lovely of you to call.' A lovely smile, a soft, southern voice. 'How are they?'

She gestured him to a cane chair beside a desk littered with papers and medicine and paint bottles; no Bible that he could see. She turned on an elbow on to her side, propping her chin, curling her legs. Her face glistened without make-up or air-conditioning, just a silver electric fan. He guessed he had disturbed her siesta.

'Well, in themselves,' he replied. Both he and Jade liked their new place and their congregation liked them, he went on, and he spoke briefly of the service he had attended. 'But they've had a family tragedy.'

He told her of May's death, his inquiries into it which had taken him to Shanghai, not too many details.

'How dreadful.' Her eyes had saddened.

She told him she'd worked with the Blades here during a month-long hand-over period and was clearly fond of them. She rose slowly, almost seductively from the bed, and walked towards him, hips swaying. 'Jade's a terrific helpmate to him. A wonderful worker. A match made in heaven.' A misty little smile for, Jacko suspected, the Rev. Right she hadn't found yet.

'I'm certain they'll cope with the Lord's help.' She pulled her trim bottom on to the desk, legs swinging. The certainty in her face faded. 'Still, it must be so shattering for them having run such terrible risks to get her sister to safety.' Too late, she seemed to realize that she had said too much and bit her lower lip.

'Yes.' He decided to double-check, to lie, casually but carefully, to make sure Cajo and his boss had not sold him some duff disinformation. 'Dill told me about that. Legally, it was a bit naughty of him.'

'Not in trouble, is he?' Her expression was anxious. Jacko said nothing. 'I would have thought they had trouble enough.'

'I suppose so.'

Rachel's turn for silence.

'Did you meet Jade's sister May?'

She shook her head. 'He collected her in Shanghai and took her home by train from there. They didn't come via Hong Hong. Did you?'

'No.' He spoke very guardedly. 'She was dead, I'm afraid, before we even knew she was in England.'

'Poor soul.'

'What I mean – and I've reprimanded Dill for this – is that it was risky using their honeymoon as a cover to go to China and rescue May.'

'Oh, come on.' A scolding face. 'What alternative did they have? They don't help them through their habit with prayer like we do here. They just throw them in prison.'

'It was a brave thing to do. Jade, too . . .'

'Yes.' An admiring face now, eyes shining.

'. . . with her background in student politics.'

'Know about that, too, do you?'

Jacko nodded.

'Isn't that what real love's about; helping each other?'

Another nod, thinking: Confirmation that Dillon Blades switched the sisters – CVs, not names – here, too. He'd kept the secret of Jade's vice and drugs past from the Rev. Rachel and, no doubt, his headquarters elders, too.

He was happy to let Rachel talk for a while about the work they

171

did. The shelter they gave to drug-and lice-riddled addicts off the streets . . . the beds they provided for them while they took the cure in a top floor here in this old plastics manufacturer's warehouse, breeze block with rounded tiles on the roof that looked from the outside like drainage pipes . . . the jobs they gave them in ground-floor workshops, painting and packing decorations.

On the ground floor, too, was a chapel he'd walked by – oil-stained wooden floor; long, plain wooden benches, an old harmonium, an altar with a cloth of flowered red and gold, barge art, too, high dusty windows, no coloured glass. Simplicity itself.

Every other sentence was drowned by the roar of planes landing and taking off at Kai Tak airport, which Blockbuster Boy had described the night before as being like coming in on an aircraft carrier moored on the Old Kent Road. Jacko had been too ill to notice.

Still stiff and sore, he had taken a taxi through a tunnel to reach the Overseas Mission to Adam in Kowloon, a place no less crowded and garish than Hong Kong island. *En route* he had caught a glimpse down a squalid street of tall tenement slums plastered with printed 'No Trespassing' notices and handwritten 'Remember the Opium War' placards. He asked her about it.

The Walled City, Rachel explained, fronted by noodle stalls and quack dentists' surgeries, lawless seat of Triad power, crawling with rats and open sewers, soon to be pulled down. Thousands had already left. Some, their dope dens gone, were upstairs.

'We give them help and food and work if they want it,' she said without a trace of pride.

'With religion as an optional extra?' asked Jacko, teasingly.

She gave him a serious smile, almost sad, which he returned. He dug the blown-up photo from his jacket. 'I don't have religion so I'm unsure about this. Maybe you can tell me what it is.'

She took it from him, chewing her lower lip again as she looked at it.

'Identifying it may help us find who killed Jade's sister,' he added.

She handed it back. 'A Maundy coin made into a ring.'

172

'So I gather but I don't understand the significance.'

That serious smile again. 'Recall the Last Supper?' He nodded. 'How Jesus washed his disciples' feet?' Another nod. 'And He said, "If I then, your Lord and Master, have washed your feet, you also ought to wash another's feet. For I have given you an example, for you should do as I have done to you." '

No Bible to hand to refer to, she'd just reeled it off from memory, like he remembered successful Lincoln City teams. His nodding stopped.

'What he was saying was that we are all equal,' she explained. 'It was an act of humility, you see, which the leaders of many faiths have followed in some form or other. Back home in England, royals took up the idea but somewhere over the centuries gift-giving replaced the act of feet-washing and kissing.'

To avoid athlete's lips, thought Jacko unpatriotically.

'Now they hand out silver coins. Not necessarily to the poor. Mainly to people who have worked hard for the community. As a thank-you.'

Jacko nodded again, very slowly. 'You see, we think someone had that coin turned into a ring for Jade's sister.'

'In that case, Inspector . . .' That wistful look was back. '. . . it was a great token of love.'

The Star Ferry returned him to the island. He sat on the top deck, oval-shaped and wooden, beneath a white canopy. The sea breeze seemed to relieve his aches and pains as the green and white ferry left the sweltering mainland with a deep-throated groan. It weaved, almost drunkenly, in a heavy swell through gaps in shipping lanes, stern to bow with everything from tiny junks to massive containers. Across the green water, less than a mile away, getting bigger and closer every minute, the island skyline, mile upon mile of skyscrapers, with dark hills behind. Seven minutes was all it took; seven minutes he'd always treasure.

He made another phone call to Velma when he got back to his hotel. 'How about getting hold of a list of all recipients of Maundy coins the Queen doled out when she was last on our patch, a video of *The Last Emperor*, a quick tour of silversmiths and restaurants looking at credit card vouchers?'

'Anything else?'

'Yeah. Can you find out who scored the fifth goal for Lincoln against Doncaster Rovers in that Easter game in their '75/'76 championship year under Graham Taylor?'

'You gone mad?'

'I will do unless I find out.'

'Take a day off.' It was the first time she'd given him a direct order.

A day off in Hong Kong, temperature touching ninety, walking in the shade of packed streets and malls; so many swanky shops and restaurants he wondered where their trade came from; not from the families who lived in squalor outside the tourist traps, that was for certain.

He took the funicular, a thrilling ride 2,000 feet up Victoria Peak, much higher than the Heights of Abraham. He looked down on the outcome of opium, the canyons between the sky-piercing skyscrapers of capitalism.

He looked back over Kowloon and the New Territories towards China. No wonder they hate us, he thought, all we stand for, distrust us still. What a bunch of greedy exploiters we were and some down there still are, with their obscene wealth, money endlessly making money, not a work-worn hand between them.

Given the here and now and what he'd experienced, he decided, his vote would still be for democracy with religion an optional extra, take it or leave it.

In the cool of early evening, he took a sea trip and saw the sun, pink and hazy, go down between two high hills on an outlying island, dwelling in the cleavage, nestling, comforted. He thought of Jackie and home.

Among the non-smokers, he ate, dozed, watched a bit of the film, couldn't get into it, dozed, tried to read, dozed, never really sleeping.

By the time he'd recrossed Indo-China he had replayed the inquiry from Derby to Shanghai back through his mill-pond mind so often that he could remember each and every quote.

He knew now who had killed May.

174

How to prove it nagged and taxed him so much that his mind finally went blank.

Into it came a song, leap-frogging all those years from childhood, and he sang it to himself:

> This little light of mine,
> I'm gonna let it shine.

Somewhere over Russia, nowhere near Damascus, he saw the light.

21

Monday gave me the gift of love.

'Wanna kiss my war wounds better?' he asked, right hand on her bare smooth midriff.

She turned, rolling towards him, an arousing sight.

Gently, slowly, moving her head from side to side, she ran her soothing lips over the bruising between his chest and stomach, then whispered, 'Just here.'

'A bit lower,' he said softly.

'Good Lord,' she said, a little louder, 'you're not *hors de combat* there, too, are you?'

'No, but, with any luck, I'm about to be.'

The kissing stopped while she laughed.

'Sssh,' he ssshed, 'you'll wake Mark and Lucy.'

Tuesday praise came from above.

At police HQ, well away from the division's main office, Velma Malloy had smoked her way through a private viewing of *The Last Emperor*.

'Lot of toe-sucking going on,' she said, as she beamed off the video with the remote control.

'Yes,' said Jacko, not at all aroused. He'd have preferred to have had a cigarette to suck but he had not smoked since Shanghai and was determined not to cave in this time.

175

'We've got the name on the diocesan list of recipients and on the restaurant credit card records. We've got the statement from the silversmith who turned the coin into a ring. Do we need any more?'

'One more thing would clinch it.' Jacko told her his plan.

She didn't enthuse. All she said was: 'How can I help?'

Blue butterflies seemed to float off the golden background of the fan when Charley Chan pulled the outer spines apart. 'How lovely.' A cheeky grin on her tawny face as she wafted it vigorously over her steaming oxtail soup, Jacko's treat, in the station canteen. 'A bit warm for this, isn't it?'

It was a sunny day, windless, but Jacko shivered theatrically. 'I'm bloody freezing.' Over the last couple of days he'd been laying on the theatrics to the point of tedium, boring Jackie, Velma and Helen Rogers with descriptions of Beijing sights he'd hardly second-glanced.

'I thought you'd be showing off your expertise with chop-sticks,' Charley said.

That was one thing he wasn't showing off. Chinese take-outs were now banned at home. He ignored it. Instead: 'Your briefing was sound. Thanks.'

'Success?' She had folded up the fan and started her soup.

'In that we know it wasn't the Rev. Dillon Blades.' He explained why in some detail.

'A bit of a waste then?'

'Not necessarily.'

Soon they had started their roast beef and Yorkshire pudding. He swallowed and started to talk urgently. 'I'll know when I've made a couple of calls up at Matlock Bath.'

She stopped eating, fork under her chin, waiting for more information to digest.

'If what I've got in mind doesn't work, I may have to break the law.'

'How?'

'A bit of burglary.' Pause. 'In which case I'll need your legal advice.'

'That's what we're here for,' she said. 'Anything I can help with now?'

'Not really. It depends on whether Dr Saul will let me have a peek in his files.'

176

'No chance.' She wafted her head like her fan.

He shrugged. They resumed eating and Jacko told her about Beijing. Her eyes didn't freeze over.

Wednesday told me to have more faith.

Dillon Blades' eyes shut tightly as soon as Jacko passed on his mother-in-law's love and Rachel's regards. 'You've been?'

'Yes.'

'So you know?'

'Yes.' Pause. 'Come on, Dill. "The truth will set you free." '

'John 8:32.'

Shit, thought Jacko. He'd gone to the trouble of getting the force's chaplain to find chapter and verse of an appropriate text and he'd still been beaten to the punchline.

Blades slumped round-shouldered on his desk chair in his den at the mission. 'Will I be prosecuted for that, too?'

'I've only told my boss, not Crown Prosecution, and she's not interested in making a case out of it.'

Relief passed over his face. 'Thank you.'

'Why, Dill? Why didn't you tell anyone? May would have got political refugee status; bound to.'

Repentance replaced relief and the truth flowed free. 'I thought Immigration would check up on the family and find out about Jade.' A confused headshake. 'When I was in training, you see, we were specifically warned about forming close liaisons with . . .' He stopped, unable to put a term to his wife's past occupation. '. . . Well, you know, subjects . . . clients. Lecturers were always citing this case I told you about – the missionary and the beauty queen. It would have caused endless embarrassment, could have cost me my job. I panicked, I suppose. Have I wasted your time?'

'It was a well worthwhile trip in the end.'

'I've failed. I know that. I should have taken it to the Lord in prayer.'

Jacko thought he recognized a line from 'What a friend we have in Jesus', but couldn't be sure, and didn't check. 'Have you told your elders at HQ?'

He shook his head mournfully.

'Listen. When the case comes to court, there's bound to be

mention of May's background and how she got into the country. It's part of the evidence. But not your wife's.'

A bleak look. 'Perhaps I should.'

'You should tell them you smuggled May in . . .'

Blades was shaking his head. 'I should own up about Jade, too.'

Jacko started to give him his up-to-you shrug, not really his problem, then decided to put in his two pennies' worth. 'If you do and they don't understand and forgive, you've got to ask yourself this, Dill. Is any church with no room for the likes of you and Jade, after all you've been through together, all you've done for those poor sods back in Hong Kong, tried to do for May, is it really worthy of your membership?'

A sly smile. 'I'll give you a statement, if you like, saying you held nothing back and we couldn't have solved it without your help. I don't mind lying. Do it all the time.'

Blades looked away, shocked. To change a painful subject, he slid something off his desk. 'Coming to this?'

Jacko took it from him. It was an invitation from Dr Saul and his staff to a lamb roast at Tor View Clinic. 'A thank-you to people who helped in our emergency,' it said, meaning, but not mentioning, the fire which killed Simon Meakin and Barry Carter, the arsonist.

So hard did he stare at it (thinking: a gift from heaven, this) that he missed Blades' next question and had to say: 'Pardon?'

'There'll be a court case, you said. Have you solved it?' he repeated. 'Do you know who did it?'

'Oh yes.'

'Who?' Eager.

It was a natural question from any relative, Jacko acknowledged, which he obviously wasn't ready to answer yet, so he applied his thin, fixed smile.

'I see.' Blades smiled sheepishly. ' "There is nothing hidden that shall not be made known." '

'In good time.' Jacko paused. 'Sermon on the Mount?'

'Luke 8:17.' Blades sighed suddenly. 'Oh dear.' A sad shrug. 'It will mean pain for someone and their family.' His face brightened. 'Still, I'm sure the Lord will forgive.' His face became serious again. 'I have sought His forgiveness for my omissions. Will you forgive me, too?'

'Sure.' An easygoing shrug.

'You are an honourable man, Jacko.'

He felt as though he had just been blessed, and blushed. Can't be doing with all this goodness, he grumbled to himself. I'm a detective, for christsake; a detective.

Thursday gave me a little more grace.

Cunningly, he worked his invitation. 'Gonna have a roof-raising service, like the mission down the hill, when you complete your new secure unit, doc?'

Dr Saul laughed. 'Hardly. But we're having a little get-together for neighbours on Saturday about eight. Bring your wife.'

'What colour welly-bobs shall I tell her to wear?' A longer laugh. 'Will Mr Barrington be here?'

'Hope so. Why?'

'I want to see him for a little chat.'

He'd had to wait some time in the gloomy outer office for this ten minutes he'd requested with Dr Saul; time well spent studying the locks on the door to the corridor and to the filing cabinet in the corner. The metal ashtray and lighters had gone from the top of it. His lungs ached for a cigarette. No smoke without fire, he decided.

'Now then . . .' The doctor's face said: to business. '. . . you haven't come all this way for chit-chat. What do you want?'

Jacko told him.

'Out of the question.'

'But why? There'd be no breach of ethics.'

'It's highly irregular.'

'There's no medical confidence to betray. Think about it.'

The doctor thought. 'Go through it again.'

Friday told me to work and pray.

Velma looked down at his handiwork. 'That's the first time your talent for writing fiction and your incompetence at the keyboard have come in useful,' she said, impressed. 'Got the search warrant?'

Jacko patted his pocket.

'Eight tomorrow night then.'

'Right.'

'Fancy a drink?' she said, lifting herself out of her big executive chair.

Drinking, he'd found, was agony without a cigarette but he enjoyed drinking with her, so he said 'Right' again.

Over their first, her treat, she said, 'By the way, someone called Ian Branfoot scored in that game.'

Good Lord, yes, thought Jacko. The right fullback, manager of a first division club now. 'Thought so,' he lied.

'What's that all about?' she asked in her demanding tone.

'It was just one of those daft little things that your memory can't resolve.' Jacko suddenly felt childish. 'It was keeping me awake at night.'

'Sometimes, you know, I don't think you're right in the head.'

Sometimes Jacko thought that himself so he didn't deny it, just laughed.

22

> Saturday told me what to say . . .
> And let my little light shine.

The white cable cars hung in mid-air, still, empty, in the fast-fading light. Coloured bulbs shone brightly among the trees along the lovers' walk across the river. A parade of illuminated boats, led by twin, green Chinese dragons studded with yellow lights, set sail from behind the pavilion with the lead dome.

People lined the river railings, packed the gift shops and pubs. Lots more strolled on the prom, but not as many as on the Bund in Shanghai.

Jacko stepped out of a hotel games room where a juke box played Genesis singing 'Jesus, he knows me', which didn't sound much like a hymn. He handed Charley Chan the white wine she'd ordered. 'Sorry to drag you out.'

'Any time. I told you.'

'It's now or never.' He was desperate for a cigarette, after ten days without, so tense that above the surrounding chatter he could hear himself gulping his Coke, a unique drink for a

Saturday night, needing to keep his head clear and his stomach settled.

They sat down, facing each other, at a table with brown wooden slats, one of the few empty in a flower-decked terrace overlooking the river.

'What's on?' asked Charley, putting down her glass.

'I'm on the brink but can't prove a case without that bit of burglary. I need to know how I stand legally.'

She reached across the table to place a hand on his arm. 'Slow down and explain.'

He blew out fresh air, wishing it was cigarette smoke. 'I don't suppose you've seen that statement we took from May Lee's housemate.'

She gave him an accusing look, as if he'd been holding back. 'It wasn't in the Debby Dawson file.'

'Well, it wouldn't be, would it?' He sounded offended that she'd been offended. 'We got it too late for inclusion, after the fatal fire.'

Charley nodded, accepting his explanation.

'Anyway,' Jacko went on, quieter, calming himself, 'she told us May was dating a person unknown she met at an arts cinema who took her for meals and bought her a ring.

'May was wanting out of the association, too heavy for her. She wrote about it to her mother. No name again, but saying she was trying to put an end to it. "My new friend has too much persistence" were her exact words.'

Jacko repeated them, to make sure she'd followed. 'Much too much persistence; she couldn't get rid. She became so stressed out that she consulted Dr Saul.'

He glanced across the busy A6 and its steady stream of cars, headlights on, lifting his head slightly towards the peak of the Heights of Abraham, gloomy in the twilight.

'Trying to cool it having failed, the doctor advised her that she should go off to London, to put some daylight between them, until Dillon Blades arrived to take brotherly charge of matters. All this is confirmed in letters home, by the way.' 'When May broke the news that it was all over, her swain. . .'

'Who?' Charley interrupted.

Jacko wasn't ready to reply yet. '. . . either killed her . . .'

'Why?'

This he would answer. 'She must have told Doc Saul all about it. In confidence, of course. That was damaging enough. But how many more people was she going to blab to, not in confidence?'

Charley nodded gravely.

Jacko resumed where she had intervened. 'So he either killed her or got Meakin to. Either way, Meakin cut up and dumped the body for him.'

'Clever,' said Charley, grimly.

'He'd have got away with it, too, if Meakin hadn't recovered sufficiently up there to deny May's murder to his missus. To stop further leaks, Carter was given that lighter knowing full well what the outcome would be for Meakin sleeping peacefully next door.'

Charley played the devil's advocate. 'How did he . . . I assume you're not ready to name names yet . . .'

Jacko neither nodded nor shook his head. 'One bit of paper is all I need.'

Charley did nod. '. . . Well, how did he and Meakin meet in the first place?'

'As a result of that window-breaking case. Barrington sent him to Tor View for routine examination. Meakin was released on bail, killed Debby. When the horror of that dawns he seeks help.

'An act of worship, he called his dismemberment of May, remember? Meakin saw it as a sort of religious good deed.'

Charley seemed to savour the theory on her tongue with a sip of wine, working her jaws, ruminating. 'Makes sense apart from the part Carter played.'

'Oh, come on, Charley.' Jacko pulled an irritated face. 'He was coached into giving us that phoney statement claiming Meakin confessed May's murder to him. When Mrs Meakin told us a different story, about to be repeated to his lawyer, Carter was given that lighter to play with. End of witnesses.'

Charley swallowed, seemingly satisfied.

'It all makes sense . . .' Jacko emphasized all. '. . . because it's all true.'

Her face had set. 'We'll never prove it. Not without a confession and, if it's who I suspect it is, with all his legal training, you'll . . .'

Jacko was brooking no arguments, no pessimism. 'Oh, yes, we

182

will. Dr Saul will have that consultation with May on file. Same as those medical reports we read on Meakin and Carter. He always mentions the negative influence on his patient. Not by name, perhaps, but always by profession.'

'He'll never let us see it,' said Charley. 'She'd be a private patient, not sent there by any court. Look at the trouble we had over Meakin's medical report and that case was in the public domain.'

'We don't need permission.' He dangled two keys he pulled from a pocket of his China jacket which he was wearing over a warm grey crew-neck. 'I'm going to help myself.'

'You can't.' Shocked, adamant. 'That is burglary.'

'There'll be no intention to steal, just to look. Is that right? That's what I need to know.'

This she chewed on with another sip, looking into her glass. 'It's trespass then.'

'A civil matter.' A dismissive shrug. 'Not criminal.'

'Makes no difference. It's still illegal. We'd never get a document obtained illegally admitted as an exhibit in court.'

Jacko was shaking his head. 'I don't want to exhibit it. Waving it in front of him will wrong-foot him into a confession.' He set his face far sterner than Charley's.

Silence, then Charley, thinking, 'Hmmmmm.' Pause. 'Still legally dangerous, in my opinion.' Another pause, frowning. 'Why now? Why tonight?'

'Because Dr Saul and all his staff are entertaining neighbours at some barbecue. I'll have a free run to those files in his outer office.'

'What if someone catches you, walks in while you're there?'

'I can say I'm pissed or went for a piss and got lost.'

'You're not even drinking.' She looked at his now empty glass.

'I'll flannel something; some excuse.'

Charley gave him a quiet smile. 'I could get by better.'

He frowned. 'What do you mean?'

'I could go in . . .'

Thought you'd never ask, thought Jacko, but he had to be sure of her commitment. 'I wouldn't dream of . . .'

'I could say I've got the monthly miseries or a splitting headache or something and needed a lie-down on that waiting-room couch.'

'No way.'

183

'It's better cover than yours.'

'Charley, you're not invited.'

'I could be with you. I'm dressed the part for an outdoor party.' Overdressed, in fact, in a tight-fitting chocolate brown jacket with square shoulders, chunky yellow polo-neck, pleated fawn skirt and patent leather shoes with sizeable heels, too smart for a barbecue.

'A legal Bill Sikes?' Jacko wore a lukewarm smile. 'I should caution you that anything you say will be given in evidence.'

She replied with a lacklustre laugh.

He shook his head, reluctantly. 'It's not on, Charley.'

'Why not?' Now she was the one brooking no argument. 'Tell me, why not? Give me one good reason.' Jacko could think of none. 'You keep Saul and his chief nurse talking and Barrington under observation. If you're right, I'll bring the report out to you.'

'How will you get in?'

'Give me time to think.' She thought. Nothing came. 'How were you going to get in?'

A sly smile from Jacko. 'By doing what General Wolfe did. Scale the Heights of Abraham while the enemy's back's turned.'

He gestured towards the motionless cars on their cable high over the river and the road. 'Take that and sneak up behind them.'

'It's shut down for the night.'

'I've arranged a special trip to take me up.'

'When?'

He looked at his watch. 7.50. 'In fifteen minutes. Just after the party starts. They'll all be outside for the fireworks.'

She drained her glass, holding out the other for the keys.

Jacko wore his unconvinced look. 'You sure about this?'

'Come on,' she said, rising.

He retrieved his car from the railway station's packed park. He stopped on double yellow lines after just a short drive, less than 300 yards. He handed over the keys from a pocket and a small, square red torch from the glove compartment. Charley put them in her shoulder bag.

A cloud of midges following, they walked over an iron bridge across the river and under a stone bridge beneath a single track railway line, up a steep footpath, to the steep-roofed funicular station set among trees.

Two attendants waited. Jacko explained the change of passenger to them, adding, 'Give me ten minutes.'

184

He turned to Charley. 'Let me get up there. If Barrington or Saul aren't about, I'll head you off and we'll have to think of something else.'

'Good luck,' she said, smiling.

'You, too.' He turned, grim-faced, and walked briskly back to his car.

Dusty brown slip-ons crunching on crushed stones, Jacko walked from his parked car after driving, engine whining, up the corkscrew hill in first gear, slowly, blanking out everything to concentrate on not running out of road.

Butterflies flitted among his intestines, finding no place to settle.

High above the town, Charley sat alone in the front of three white bubble cars. Her eyes were straight ahead, on the cable lines that ran over wheels at the top of pylons sprouting, one above the other, out of the hillside trees.

Standing on the grass plateau among the picnic tables, glasses in hand, Barrington, the Stipe, and Dillon Blades were in cricketing conversation, Jade only half listening.

Both were dressed in blazers. Barrington looked rather pale, but very relaxed. Not surprising, thought Jacko, after what he gets up to during *Blind Date* every Saturday evening.

His blazer was smooth maroon with a badge and he wore a military-looking tie that didn't match. Dill's blazer was thin blue and white stripes, crumpled, no dog collar or tie.

Jade had dressed down, in a belted, black kimono, not looking at all like a peasant, with those painted heart-shaped lips which pursed in disappointment when Jacko walked straight by, avoiding them.

Charley was walking swiftly on asphalt paths with rustic railings that wound round the Swiss-style pavilions of a hilltop park. Head down, she missed the phantom view of the ruined castle across the fairy-lit gorge.

185

Behind a trestle table, bowed under the weight of bottles, Dr Saul did not look up from the host's task of filling the glasses of guests, thirty or more, sitting or standing around, their chatter creating a hanging pocket of noise in the night air.

Another dozen queued, paper plates in hand, waiting, watching as Chief Nurse O'Brien, dressed in white, like an army cook, carved a golden-brown sweet-smelling lamb on a spit above dull red and grey charcoal in a raised brazier.

Everyone's eyes left him as a silver streak shot heavenwards out of the trees behind the pavilion at the other end of the town to signal the start of the fireworks display. In the almost black sky, it spurted out glinting stars which fell lazily in a large spray. The adults did more oohing and aahing than their children.

Charley stopped on an earth footpath which emerged out of a small copse of young self-set beech, larch and ash.

The bird-song above her had faded with the light, no longer competing with the distant droning of conversation and occasional laughter from the barbecue, out of sight below the single-storey buildings of the clinic.

At the back, only the concrete floor of the secure unit remained, deep trenches cut on three sides for the new footings.

She followed a drought-cracked path downhill through outcrops of stones until it became crushed stone alongside the buildings, stopping again at the front corner. The cantilever entrance was lit, deserted.

She lifted her shoulder bag, nipping it under an arm, took the two keys from it, slipped them carefully into a hip pocket, left the torch where it was.

Four swift paces and she shouldered open one of the twin glass doors. The reception desk inside was empty.

She took off her brown mid-heeled shoes and walked in stockinged feet, soundless, up the steep corridor, smelling of pine from recently cleaned tiles which overpowered the scent of flowers in windowsill troughs.

Bare bricks, roughly cemented, a temporary job, had replaced the fire door at the end of the corridor.

She stooped to put her shoes on the floor. She slipped a Yale key from a pocket at her hip and opened the door. The light from the corridor did not reach far enough over her shoulders to touch the two far corners.

She put the key back in her pocket and bent to collect her shoes. She shut the door and stood with her back to it for a moment or two, steadying her breathing, letting her eyes adjust, until she could make out the glass table in front of the couch and the cabinet in the corner beyond.

She walked to the corner, dropping her shoes and bag on the couch as she passed. She stood before the cabinet.

On top of it was a square metal ashtray. She took a lighter from it. Left-handed she flicked down the wheel. A medium-sized flame shot out, held steady by her thumb.

She took a second key out of her pocket. Moving the lighter across her face, she fitted the key into the lock and turned it. An oval plug shot out. Just a click, but the room seemed to be filled with a deafening sound which made her thumb fly off the lighter.

The room went pitch black.

She took a deep breath, transferred the lighter to her right hand and flicked the wheel again.

Bending, she lowered the yellow flame until it found J–Q on a label on the middle drawer which rumbled noisily on its runners as she pulled it open.

With the first two fingers of her left hand, she flicked to L, then Lee and on to Li.

She removed a green file by its metal tag and laid it on top of the cabinet. The room went dark for the three seconds it took to transfer the lighter back to her left hand. Her face lit up again.

She opened the file with her right hand, held the lighter over it and read:

HISTORY: Shanghai born and educated, arrived illegally in this country just over a year ago. Initial homesickness alleviated by fulfilling academic work and knowledge of sister's impending arrival.

COMPLAINT: Anxiety state arising out of a relationship she viewed as platonic.

RECOMMENDATION: Counselled to discuss with her brother-in-law applying for political asylum to regularize her residence. Meantime, to seek refuge with compatriots in London.

NEGATIVE INFLUENCE: A woman solicitor in Crown Prosecution Service using her knowledge of subject's illegal entry to this country to press unsought and unwanted attentions upon her.

She pulled back her shoulders, held the lighter to the bottom left edge of the report. The flame started slowly, then spread rapidly upwards, casting a shadowy light over the room behind her.

She held up the document between right thumb and forefinger until the flame, blackening and curling the paper in its trail, almost touched them.

Then she dropped it into the ashtray where the flame ate into the last corner of the paper before devouring itself.

The room went dark again.

From behind her, a click and a fresh light.

She looked down for a rekindled flame among the ashes in the tray. The fire was dead.

Cautiously, she craned her head over her left shoulder.

In the opposite corner sat Jacko, lighting his first cigarette since Shanghai.

'Clever,' she said, turning to face him.

Jacko stood. Drawing in deeply, he walked a few steps to a switch on the wall by the inner door to the consulting-room and flicked on the waiting-room light. He saw that Charley had a sour smile glued to her face.

Nothing was said until he sat down again. 'When did you realize?' she asked in a tinny voice.

Not easy to answer, he privately admitted. Should have asked myself why you bad-mouthed a straight legal stick like Percy Manners. Should have rumbled it when I called May's college Cofe and you never queried it because you'd grown used to May calling it that. Should have seen through Meakin's ramblings about 'an act of worship'. In court, you, never Percy Manners, called the Stipe 'Your Worship'.

He stretched out his legs, crossed his feet at the ankles and blew out smoke, feeling light-headed. 'You shopped yourself. Only you could have tipped the cops in Shanghai.'

Jacko knew he was about to sound like J. Carrol Naish, playing Charlie Chan, explaining all to his thick sidekick of a son, and he decided to enjoy it. 'Only you knew I intended to travel as a law lecturer. What you didn't know was that I took your advice and went as a law official. When those goons accused me, of all people, of being an academic, a lecturer . . .' A laugh, more like a cough. '. . . well.'

Her smile sweetened. 'Nothing personal.'

Jacko shrugged his acceptance that she'd had to try to stop him coming home with photos of May wearing that Maundy ring and tracing the coin back to her late church-going mum's royal gift and on to the silversmith who'd turned it into a love gift. 'No real harm done.'

She pulled back her shoulders, resilient. 'It wasn't the way it looks.'

'Never is.' His tired tone.

'I did love her; worshipped her.'

Odd way of showing it, thought Jacko.

'Wrong. I was so wrong. She turned out to be a bitch; a taunting, threatening bitch. She wanted me to get her a British passport or else. I hit her once. That's all.'

That's right, thought Jacko bitterly. Blame it all on the victim. Slander her. She can't answer back, can't sue. Provocation is a shrewd defence, often successful. You can bury 'em, burn 'em, cut 'em up. No matter. The accused's state of mind at the time of the actual killing is all that counts in court. Her quick legal brain was already planning a defence to get the murder charge reduced to manslaughter. 'It doesn't matter now,' he said with a tired shake of his head.

'Not matter?' Her smiles, both sweet and sour, had gone. Her nostrils widened. 'What the hell does matter to you?'

Jacko pulled on his cigarette, thoughtful for a second or two. 'What matters to me is that we've got it right. Meakin killed once, not twice, and, God knows, that's a big enough cross for his widow to bear.'

Contempt filled her face. 'What would you have done? Admit it? He was heaven-sent.'

'Hardly the act of an innocent woman, though, was it, getting a sick bloke to chop her up.'

'It was the act of a woman . . .' angry, unrepentant, '. . . a desperate woman responsible for a tragic accident. No more than that.'

'You could have come to us and explained . . .'

189

'Oh, really. Admit to being lesbian in this macho job?'

'That's not the way Window Payne tells it.'

'You mean . . .' A baffled, betrayed look. 'You've spoken to him? He's told you?'

'My governor has.'

Yep, she was bisexual, Jacko was telling himself; no need to tell her.

She was silent, stunned, her ambisextrous secret out.

He put on his sad voice. 'You didn't have to talk Carter into burning Meakin alive, though.'

'I didn't.' She'd recovered quickly, answered firmly. 'You'll never prove otherwise.' Probably true, Jacko privately conceded. 'You'll prove none of this.'

'My governor's searching your place now. She'll find the ring, photos of you and May together perhaps, won't she?'

She had gone paler than he'd thought possible on oriental skin.

'Tell me,' he said. 'I can understand the hand. You had to recover the ring. Tight, was it? But her feet?' He frowned deeply and disgustedly.

'Meakin. Not me. He took them away to wash the blood away, would you believe?' An exasperated sigh. 'Fool.'

Oh God, Jacko groaned inwardly. It was an act of humility, and she'd missed its significance. He ended up understanding the Bible, or bits of it, better than her. He'd probably given them a decent burial. We'll never find them. Still, he thought . . .

'Still,' he said, 'we'll find the Maundy ring at your place, won't we? You'd never dispose of that, would you?'

A moment's thought, veins standing out at her temple. Then came confirmation. 'Proves association; no more.'

He pointed with his cigarette towards the ash-filled tray on the cabinet. 'That was hardly the act of an innocent person either, was it?'

Her square shoulders sagged a little. 'I could argue that I didn't want it falling into wrong hands.'

'Why?'

'To prevent possible misunderstandings and lengthy explanations if someone like you got hold of it.'

'I've seen it.'

A short laugh, derisive. 'I don't believe you.'

'When I typed it up. Made it up, too.'

All expressions fell from her face. 'You mean, she didn't . . .
you're telling me . . .'

Jacko nodded energetically to tell her that May had never
consulted Dr Saul, not disclosing that he hadn't yet traced the
doctor she really had seen, a loose end in an almost completed
file.

'And I'm also telling you you're being taped.' He flicked his
head towards the door to the doctor's room. 'Helen's in there, so
don't make a run for it. Think of what she did to Meakin.'

'None of this is admissible.' Shoulders back. 'You omitted to
caution me.'

Jacko didn't let his sad expression alter. 'Did. Down in the pub
garden.' He patted a chest pocket in his China jacket. 'Got that
taped, too.'

'Very clever.' A deep sigh, shoulders rounded, defeated.

Not really, thought Jacko. Most cops are cleverer than most
killers, that's all. But that doesn't make 'em clever.

Dillon Blades opened Mrs Meakin's door when they were half-
way down the path. He led them into the lounge. In smiling
ceremony, Mrs Meakin swapped her tiny, sleeping baby for a big
bunch of autumn chrysanthemums which crackled in their cello-
phane as Helen handed them over.

'What are you calling him?' Helen asked, holding him in front
of her for inspection, then shouldering him, like a guardsman in
arms drill.

'Simon.' Mrs Meakin looked at Blades. 'Dill's promised to
dedicate, sort of baptize him when he's a bit older.' She looked
timidly back at Helen. 'And I was wondering if . . . well . . .
you've been so . . . I mean . . . I'd like you to be witness, god-
mother, like.'

No puff of pride from Helen, no glistening of the eyes. Instead,
she directed a pleading look of great guilt towards Blades. 'But
I'm not a church-goer.'

His pastoral beam, comforting. 'Your heart's in the right place.
You live by His message. That's the most important thing.'

He transferred his beam on to Jacko, doing his final tour of
witnesses, about to pull out, the file submitted. 'You'll come, too,
won't you? You enjoyed your last visit, didn't you?'

Yes, he thought, flushing, embarrassed, and look what

happened. Ogling that bird in red with heavenly legs and a
divine bust buggered my beans; I'm sure of it. Worst crop in
years. What if she's there again? What next? A plague of bloody
boils?

Oh, come on. What is it, after all? Just a lust for life, really,
appreciating people around you, enjoying the sights you see; a
bit of fun that makes you work hard and, sometimes, work quite
well. That's got to be worth running the risk of a boil or two,
surely?

'I'll try,' he said, undecided.